Praise ....pper

Seven Minutes to Noon

"Kate Pepper was quite a hit with her debut suspenser *Five Days in Summer* and she keeps up the pace with *Seven Minutes to Noon*. . . . Nail-biting stuff."
                                                    —Mystery Lovers

"In this highly suspenseful domestic mystery, readers are treated to the terrifying aftermath of secure and cozy lives gone chillingly wrong. Likable characters, plenty of suspects, and a relatively shocking ending that stuns and thrills."   —New Mystery Reader

"*Seven Minutes to Noon* starts off running, and never stops until the end. A tightly woven plot keeps the story flowing. . . . You'll startle at every strange sound as you read Kate Pepper's second book. Best not to be alone when turning the pages."   —BookLoons

"Powerful . . . the audience will hold their breath until the last revelation."   —*Midwest Book Review*

"Launches the reader on an emotional roller coaster ride."   —Roundtable Reviews

"A disturbing psychological thriller . . . throat-grabbing, visceral intensity. . . . Kate Pepper knows how to put the pinch on a reader's emotions, and goes in for the kill with slick, controlled cleverness."   —Heartstrings

continued . . .

Five Days in Summer

"Mesmerizing. . . . Your heart will be pounding long after you've turned the final page."
—Lisa Gardner, author of *The Killing Hour*

"Kate Pepper has an amazing eye for detail. . . . Clever and realistic—a gripping, poignant portrait of an innocent family caught in a nightmare of evil."
—Anne Frasier, author of *Hush* and *Play Dead*

"*Five Days* has it all—an attractive female detective, a crusty FBI profiler, and the scariest killer you'll never want to meet." —Leslie Glass, author of *The Killing Gift*

"I put *Five Days in Summer* aside only once . . . to make sure my doors were locked."
—Barbara Parker, author of *Suspicion of Madness*

"[A] tightly plotted debut thriller. . . . Pepper's finely drawn characterizations and taut, clean storytelling make this an enjoyable read." —*Publishers Weekly*

"The pacing is swift, the action scenes leave the audience breathless and the suspense is at a high level. A very frightening book." —*Midwest Book Review*

"Especially hard to put down . . . had this reviewer looking over her shoulder in her quiet apartment. . . . The plot really cooks." —The Mystery Reader

ONE COLD NIGHT

Kate Pepper

AN ONYX BOOK

ONYX
Published by New American Library, a division of
Penguin Group (USA) Inc., 375 Hudson Street,
New York, New York 10014, USA
Penguin Group (Canada), 90 Eglinton Avenue East, Suite 700, Toronto,
Ontario M4P 2Y3, Canada (a division of Pearson Penguin Canada Inc.)
Penguin Books Ltd., 80 Strand, London WC2R 0RL, England
Penguin Ireland, 25 St. Stephen's Green, Dublin 2,
Ireland (a division of Penguin Books Ltd.)
Penguin Group (Australia), 250 Camberwell Road, Camberwell, Victoria 3124,
Australia (a division of Pearson Australia Group Pty. Ltd.)
Penguin Books India Pvt. Ltd., 11 Community Centre, Panchsheel Park,
New Delhi - 110 017, India
Penguin Group (NZ), cnr Airborne and Rosedale Roads, Albany,
Auckland 1310, New Zealand (a division of Pearson New Zealand Ltd.)
Penguin Books (South Africa) (Pty.) Ltd., 24 Sturdee Avenue,
Rosebank, Johannesburg 2196, South Africa

Penguin Books Ltd., Registered Offices:
80 Strand, London WC2R 0RL, England

First published by Onyx, an imprint of New American Library,
a division of Penguin Group (USA) Inc.

First Printing, May 2006
10 9 8 7 6 5 4 3 2 1

Copyright © Kate Pepper, 2006
All rights reserved

 REGISTERED TRADEMARK—MARCA REGISTRADA

Printed in the United States of America

For Oliver, Eli, and Karenna,
my inspirations in everything,
with abiding love.

ACKNOWLEDGMENTS

Another year, another novel, but the list of suspects who have aided and abetted me once again remains mostly the same. Literary agent Matthew Bialer and editor Claire Zion were behind-the-scenes accomplices whose creativity and encouragement kept me moving through mazelike revisions to the reward of a final draft. Thanks to all the talented people at New American Library and Penguin who prodded and polished this novel on its way to publication. I'm also grateful to Detective Robert Burke, Planning Officer Sal Ferrante, and all the guys in the Community Affairs department of Brooklyn's Eighty-fourth Precinct for their warmth, intelligence and willingness to spend time with me answering fictional dilemmas with hard facts. And finally, my deepest gratitude goes to my husband, Oliver Lief, for the razor-sharp editorial eye he brings to reading and rereading rough drafts, and for always holding the torch so high.

Prologue

He watched her as she moved along Water Street, caught perfectly in the crosshairs of his camera's telescopic lens. No part of her was beyond his view now. She walked quickly, as always, her paisley bag slung over one shoulder; she didn't use a backpack like all the other kids. Her long blond hair seemed to float around her, light as cotton candy, and her skin was pale as a doll's. From this distance he could not see her eyes, but his lens had once captured them and they were green. He shifted the camera to follow her as she neared his building. It was the same every morning, on her way to school. She would seem to grow larger as she crossed directly beneath his view, then diminish in size as she walked away.

Today she gave him an unexpected gift: She stopped walking, dropped her bag on a patch of cobblestones where asphalt had worn away, and stepped into the middle of the street. A single car passed by and then she was alone again . . . or so she thought. Without hesitation, she did a jazzy kind of pirouette, landing with arms outstretched and bowing just slightly in thanks for imaginary applause. He took her picture and felt a flush of excitement: He could do it now, right now, without being seen. But then a man in a suit and tie walked by, smiled, clapped a little, and she took another bow. She didn't seem embarrassed and he loved that about her. She picked up her bag and kept walking, exhilarated, smiling. Then, like every other morning, she moved beyond the scope of his lens and he was overcome with sadness.

He twisted the lens off his camera and set it down on a shelf of plants next to the tripod. He didn't know why, but this morning felt worse than usual. Hopeless. He had been waiting three months without the right opportunity.

Surveying the collage that covered one whole wall, his attention landed on an old four-frame photostrip. He picked up a pair of scissors from the floor, carefully cut off the fourth frame and slipped it into his pocket. A moment captured on film: an innocent kiss. Proof that he was more than just the monster they would all say he was, when this was through.

Chapter 1

Tuesday, 6:33 a.m.

Perched on a kitchen stool in her yellow chenille robe, Susan Bailey-Strauss listened as a loud creak announced the opening of Lisa's bedroom door. Her little sister took seriously her new status as a ninth grader at the city's top performing-arts high school and had been waking up even earlier than she needed to. Susan looked at the round clock that hung on the wall beside the fridge; a quick calculation told her that Lisa would probably be half an hour early to her first class if the subways weren't delayed. Her footsteps receded into the hallway bathroom and the door banged shut.

Dave, Susan's husband, sat beside her at the loft's black-granite kitchen counter, preoccupied by something in the morning paper and oblivious to the peal of noise. Normally she enjoyed Dave's gentle morning silences, the long arc to full awakening he required before he could begin his day. But today she felt a low hum of nervousness beneath the comfortable surface of their routines. She had something difficult to say and didn't know where to begin. She wanted him to look at her, to pull his mind out of world events and talk about the bedroom door whose hinges he had neglected to oil as promised, to compare their schedules for the day, to thank him again for the beautiful birthday gifts he had given her last night: the teardrop diamond necklace and fist-sized bloodred roses and orchestra seats to the Broadway show it was impossible to get tickets to. She wanted the distractions of meandering chatter so she could find the exact right moment to tell him—"Dave, I want a baby"—and to experience with him the relief of his happiness, as he had practically begged her for children since they were married a year and a half ago. The problem was, she had something else to tell him first.

She had a confession to make. To Lisa, in private. Then to Dave.

But early morning on a workday and school day was the wrong time to begin any important discussion; she knew that, and as she thought it through— for the hundredth time—she reminded herself that it would be best to get them alone, separately, preferably when the other was out of the house. *One thing at a time,* the little voice in the back of her mind restrained her impatience; *it's only fair for Lisa to know first.* Susan was just so anxious for Dave to know that he would soon get his wish!

She took a sip of her orange juice, then thumbed her BlackBerry to see if any new e-mails had come in since she'd last checked five minutes ago. Nothing. It wasn't unusual, though, for her electronic lifeline to bleep alive this early. The first shift of workers arrived at her small factory at six to begin making the basic daily chocolates and accept early deliveries. The intimate chocolaterie she started three years ago had grown faster than she had ever imagined, and now Water Street Chocolates was supplying fancy treats to some of the best restaurants in New York. Since Lisa had come to live with them last year, Susan had started the nerve-racking habit of letting her most trusted apprentice—like Susan, a graduate of the French Culinary Institute—open her business without her so she could stay home until Lisa left for school. Passing on a measure of control was the natural progression, and she shouldn't have worried, having come up the same ladder of apprenticeship to a somewhat startling early success when she'd branched out on her own, but worrying was in her nature. She checked her e-mail again; again, nothing.

Dave peered over a folded-down corner of the paper—finally—and a smile flourished on his handsome, unshaven face. "Anything now? How about now? Better check again. Watch out! I think I feel an e-mail on its way in!" He mock-rubbed the side of one arm. "I think that one grazed me. Got a Band-Aid, sweetie?"

"Ha, ha, Dave." She kicked his foot with her fluffy pink slipper. "I have to make up for you *never* checking your e-mail."

The corners of his dark brown eyes crinkled up. "In the cosmic balance, you mean?"

"Yup."

"Yin to your yang."

He leaned through the space separating their breakfast stools and kissed her. They had made love in the predawn darkness and his salty lips lingered now. She ran a hand down the back of his soft black T-shirt and slipped two fingers through a belt loop at the back of his jeans. The taste of his mouth reminded her of the moment they had first met, three years ago, during a work shift at the Park Slope Food Coop. "Taste," he had told her, offering one of the garlic-stuffed green olives they were bagging for sale. It was that moment, the tangy taste, she still recalled as a life-altering talisman. They kissed each other again, pulling away at the sound of the bathroom door opening and Lisa's footsteps padding up the hall.

She appeared, barefoot on the wooden floor, and went straight to the refrigerator. She had already put on some makeup and brushed her long hair, which made a pale blaze down her back. The outfit today was borderline: tight low-rise jeans and a cropped tie-dyed camisole exposing a rhinestone belly-button stud. Susan knew that if she were a teenager now, she would have body piercings, too. But she wasn't a teenager anymore; she was the adult entrusted with Lisa's care.

"I realize it's a style," Susan said as soberly as she could, "but you're only fourteen and I'm not sure it's a good idea for you to dress so . . . provocatively. Especially in the city."

"Thanks for the tip, Suzie. Did Dave mention you looked pretty hot in those hip-huggers you had on yesterday?" Lisa swung open the fridge door and gazed inside.

Dave was staring at the newspaper again, but Susan heard his gentle snort and saw the right side of his mouth pucker.

" 'Mama never told me . . .' " Lisa's honeyed voice trailed into a hum. Another nascent song. She grabbed a plastic bottle of drinkable peach yogurt and shut the fridge door. "I hate to say it, Suzie, but . . ." She shrugged, uncapped the yogurt and shot the blue plastic coin across the narrow kitchen into the garbage can. "Score!"

Were all teenagers masters of the half-finished sentence? The loaded opener, the unspoken refrain? Generally set to music? Susan could hear the rest of the lyric: *But you're not my mother.* Lisa took a long swig of the yogurt drink, leaving behind a pale ghost that hovered above her upper lip. Susan held herself back from reaching over with a napkin and wiping clean Lisa's awkward but achingly lovely face.

"You know what I just remembered?" Lisa took another drink of yogurt. "When you were eighteen and I was around two?"

"Three," Susan corrected her, then sealed her lips, not saying what she was thinking: that no one could remember that far back.

"I remembered how you used to fight with Mommy about your clothes. I thought you got to sass her because you weren't adopted, and since I was, I had a whole other set of rules."

"I never knew you thought that."

Just last weekend Lisa had announced that she was considering a search for her birth parents. It worried Susan. The triangular relationship between Lisa, Susan and their mother, Carole, had always suggested faults. Carole had worked hard to conceal them, and Susan had followed suit, but Lisa wasn't the type to conform. What she wanted, she sought.

This past year had given Susan a glimpse of their mother's sacrifices and frustrations; that, and so much else. Lately Susan had begun assessing her past with an almost narcissistic abandon, like a teenager herself, peeling back the layers of her finely constructed

adulthood, recalling her early youth and with crys-
talline precision remaking old decisions. Their
mother, she now suspected, had sent Lisa to her for
this very reason.

"What does your day look like?" Susan asked
Dave.

His dark eyes, set slightly too close together, veered
up from the newspaper. "I thought I'd go to the gym,
then head over to the library later this morning." If she
checked e-mail enough for both of them, then he did
all their reading; a diagnosed-too-late dyslexic who
never read for pleasure, Susan had been startled at
first by how keenly Dave consumed books, magazines
and newspapers. "I don't have to be at the precinct
until four."

She hated when he rotated into the late shift in the
detective squad. Her workdays started early in the
morning and she was zonked by evening. When he
worked late, they hardly saw each other.

"Any chance you could squeeze in an hour to paint
the yellow line?" Susan had been asking him for
months now. "Yesterday someone double-parked me
in, and Jackson was two hours late with a delivery to
Manhattan. It was the second time. I nearly lost the
account."

"I'll try to do it today, my darling." He folded the
newspaper, stood up and leaned over to kiss her. "I
promise."

" 'Promises, promises!' " Lisa's voice rose in what
she called her "Broadway boom." She was learning all
kinds of voice techniques at her specialized public
high school and didn't hesitate to share the riches at
home. Susan mostly liked it, but sometimes the sheer

volume of Lisa's prodigious vocalizations took her by surprise.

Dave laughed and walked down the hall toward their bedroom. When the door shut, Susan lowered her voice; she had often found this worked best when she wanted Lisa's attention.

"Any chance we can talk later today?"

"How about now?" Lisa came around the counter and slid onto the stool Dave had just abandoned.

"Can't now, actually. I have to get to the factory—we're making a thousand chocolate truffles for a benefit at the Metropolitan Museum of Art tomorrow night. How about after dinner?"

"I've got rehearsal at seven. After?"

"I'll be here whenever you're ready."

"Cool." Lisa scanned the front page of the newspaper but found nothing of interest. "I'll be home by ten, definitely. Hey! While you wait for me, you could start the puzzle I gave you."

Beneath the riotously colorful birthday wrapping, the puzzle's box was plain white. There were five hundred pieces and no clue to what picture they would construct.

"I will," Susan said. "And then when you get home, we'll talk."

The clock on the stone mantel read 10:02. Susan sat at the collapsible card table between the living room's two large windows, facing west and the river—she kept the table set up for the puzzles and games the family always had going—and worked on the plain blue edge of Lisa's gift. The TV was on across the room. The news announcer had just run down the night's headlines—war, floods, a simmering volcano—earthly disasters that should have trumped anyone's petty concerns. At the first sound of the front door locks snapping open, Susan crossed the room and picked up the remote control from the coffee table, clicking off the *Nightly News.*

Lisa dropped her canvas bag, with its purple-and-pink paisley design, by the front door. She sloughed off her denim jacket, kicked off her sneakers and walked into the living area, where Susan had curled herself into a corner of the sofa. Lisa draped herself over the back of an overstuffed armchair.

"Don't stop watching on my account."

"It's just more of the usual," Susan said. "Death and destruction, murder and mayhem. I don't want to watch it."

"Hasn't Dave rid the world of crime yet?" Lisa's smile pulled smooth her dimpled chin.

"Not yet. How was rehearsal?"

"Good." Lisa's small, lithe body found its way onto the chair's seat cushion. She laid her head against the back and stared up at the high ceiling. "Long."

"Lisa, honey?"

Lisa lifted her head to look at Susan. The tendons in her neck braced, making her appear more fragile than she was. "You don't have to say it," Lisa said, "because I've already made up my mind, and it's final."

"No, Lisa, listen to me."

Lisa shook her head. "I'm going to tell Mommy before I do it, but I really don't think it'll hurt her if I look for my birth parents. Mommy *knows* I love her. She *knows* she'll always be my real mother."

"It isn't that."

"I need to know who I am, who I really am."

"You're unique, Lisa. There's no one like you."

"So true." Lisa grinned, then scowled. "But that's not the point."

"I understand—"

"No. You don't. You can't. No one can who isn't adopted."

"I'm not going to ask you if you've felt safe and loved," Susan said, "because I know you have."

"That isn't the *point*."

"I understand that you want . . . that you need to find your birth parents."

Silence. Lisa was listening.

"I want you to be happy. I want you to find them. I would never stand in your way."

Lisa's pale eyes seemed to darken. "What did you want to talk to me about, Suzie? Something else?"

"No, this."

"So you agree it's a good idea?"

"I agree it's inevitable," Susan said. "I agree it's important."

"So?"

"So . . . I want to help you."

"Cool! I've already been on the Internet. I found the best site to start with. And I thought maybe Dave, being a detective and all, could help out with official records and stuff."

Lisa had popped forward onto the edge of the armchair; her eagerness broke Susan's heart.

"We don't need any help," Susan said carefully.

"But—"

"I know who they are."

Lisa's face appeared to freeze in that moment, like an instant caught in photograph. Everything about her seemed visible on the surface: the brilliant promise of her future, the anomalies of her past.

"You *know* them? Have you *always* known them?"

Susan nodded. "Brace yourself, honey."

"Just *tell* me!"

Susan sat forward and clasped her hands over her knees. Today she had deliberately worn baggy pants, red cargo capris, though it was getting cold out for bare ankles.

"I'm your birth mother." Had she really said it after all these years? "I never gave you away; we kept you with us. You see? You were always wanted."

Lisa's jaw had gone slack and her mouth hung open with an abandonment uncharacteristic for a girl who was always sharply right on the moment. Her eyes glazed, then snapped into focus.

"You?"

Susan nodded.

"But you're my sister."

"I gave birth to you," Susan said, "when I was fifteen."

The salient fact hung between them like a weapon, spiky and ready to swing in any direction.

"Does Dave know?"

"Not yet, but he will."

"He'll leave you."

So that was how it would be; the punishment would begin in heaps.

"We'll see."

"You could have kept it a secret," Lisa said. "Kept on lying." Her eyes darted around the large room before settling back on Susan with precision. "Lying to me, and to Dave, and to yourself."

Lisa sprang up. The curves of her young woman's body seemed to melt and there she stood, the little wisp of a girl Susan had always openly adored.

"I love you so much," Susan said. She rose from the

couch, crossed the space between them and reached out to touch Lisa. Her daughter. There: It was a *fact*.

Lisa pulled away, her arms dangling.

"We were trying to do what seemed like the best thing, Lisa."

"Best for who?"

"For *you*."

"Mommy and Daddy, they lied to me, too."

"We all agreed it was best."

"What about my father? Who was he? Or don't you know?"

"That's cruel."

"Oh, *I'm* cruel? That's a good one!"

Susan inched closer, her whole body pleading, but Lisa recoiled. She ran to the front door, jammed on her sneakers and banged her way out. Susan felt a chill at the thought of how cold Lisa would be outside, alone, at this hour of the night.

Chapter 2

It was dark out, and cold. Lisa ran along Washington Street, where patches of asphalt had worn away to reveal hand-laid cobblestones. When she got to the old rail tracks—twin seams of metal emerging from the lumpy stone—her bright blue suede sneakers immediately landed on one of them. She walked the years-polished track heel-to-toe like a tightrope, arms flung out for balance.

I am your birth mother.

It couldn't be true; this had never remotely been one of Lisa's daydreams. She had pictured her birth mother as valiant, brilliant, alone; an outsider with a dissident's inability to practice the language and habits of the mundane world. A woman whose soul would die from the stench of a dirty diaper; a woman whose essence was nonetheless transformed by the act of birth; a woman who was unable to seek Lisa out, for the sheer practical effort of it, but who had spent fourteen years waiting to be found.

Her mother was a rebel; her mother was a genius,

someone living far above the workaday crowd. And she had inherited her mother's genius, the inextinguishable light.

She used to think her mother was Joni Mitchell, and Lisa was Little Green, that memory of a lost springtime. But that dream evaporated when Joni's birth daughter tracked her down and there they were, reunited in the public eye: two grown women, lookalikes. Lisa had known the dates were all wrong, anyway; wrong dates, right idea. Joni's voice and her spirit evolved into Lisa's next conviction: that there was a mother for every girl, a father for every boy. Out there, answers waited.

Like her, her mother had a fantastic gift and was certain of her right to possess it.

Her mother was not an insecure college dropout who made fancy chocolates in Brooklyn.

Like her, her mother was small and blond and radiated an inner beauty; her mother was loaded with talents; her mother was her long-lost twin.

Her mother was not a strong-limbed woman with short, dark, practical hair. Her mother did not wear a white coat and a porkpie hat and shape truffles until her hands ached.

Her true mother would never question her clothes or her hours or her friends. Her true mother would intuitively understand everything about her. Her true mother could not possibly have changed her diaper, been that close to her dark smells, or tasted her salty, inconsolable cries as a baby. Her true mother had never suffered her, and so was untainted by her faults. Her true mother would thrill at the chance to know her.

She had imagined her birth mother so many ways: a queen locked in the tower of her own brilliance; an abused mother of seven who couldn't feed another mouth; a Monte Carlo con woman. Her mother was at the epicenter of a drama. She was a magic trick who knew herself in and out and had made the only possible choice in giving up her baby.

Not Susan. Her sister. A woman who had it both ways, patched together with a lie.

Lisa walked the old track, heel-to-toe, heel-to-toe. She could hear the undulating water just beyond the swell of green lawn and curved stone paths of the Empire-Fulton Ferry State Park. The ship-themed playground, dubbed the Brooklyn Bridge Park, hadn't been there when she was a little girl—how she would have loved a designated place to play when she first visited at the age of five. Back then, the only things this neighborhood offered up were left to the imagination. She remembered tightroping these same tracks but with much smaller feet, visiting her big sister in her big loft in the big city. Such a far cry from their hometown of Carthage, Texas.

Back then Susan's loft was like a palace, with its big windows drinking in the glittering Manhattan view; back then Lisa had no interest in the loft's lack of hot water or even, in winter, heat. Susan was a princess living a fairy-tale life far away from home. The streets were empty way back then, when it was an urban backwater here in Dumbo—Down Under the Manhattan Bridge Overpass—a derelict neighborhood of abandoned warehouses beneath two roaring bridge ramps. Now every ghostly, echoing warehouse was a renovation project, a fixed-up blight, mixing the overhead bridge noise with the grind of nonstop construction. By day, the neighborhood was deafening, overcome by its own sudden growth. But by night, when the workers left and the galleries and patisseries gated their gleaming windows, Dumbo became as strange and impossible and thrilling as it used to be: a flying elephant, magical thinking, an undisclosed secret.

Lisa remembered their parents' faces when they had first walked into Susan's loft: unabashed shock and dismay. She remembered Susan's twenty-year-old eyes flickering down to catch her little sister's expression of enchantment, and the confidence that ignited in Susan's face as she remet the astonished gazes of their parents.

Much as Lisa now appreciated the luxuries of Susan and Dave's rehabbed condo, she could still sense the raw discomforts of the original loft under all the polished wood and granite. The loft seemed a little bit sad now, for all its strident effort—like an overdressed maiden aunt, pulling out all the stops at the last minute—but the smell of it, the decades-old perfume, was still the same. If you closed your eyes and sat quietly in the middle of the posh living room, you were flung back a decade; it was chilly and exciting in the rough-hewn space; you were Spiderwoman, Cinderella and Little Green all rolled into one.

Lisa hopped off the track at the entrance to the park. It was a peaceful time of night, with just a few people wandering by the waterfront: a couple with a dog off its leash, and a balding blond man, a loner. Susan and Dave never let her walk out alone at night unless she was returning from somewhere, and then every minute had to be accounted for; she had to show up at home exactly on time or her cell phone would start ringing. She was glad she had left her purse with her phone in it back at the loft. She walked into the park and took a deep breath. It was so easy to forget that New York City was an island, and such a happiness whenever Lisa remembered; back in northeast Texas, where they lived, you were landlocked in every direction.

She sat on a bench and drew her arms across her chest, scant protection from the chilly air. The East River was calm, barely moving now; all the boats were moored for the night. The sky was clear and velvet black, pierced with tiny white stars. *Star light, star bright, first star I see tonight, I wish I may I wish I might, have the wish I wish tonight.* She began to cry; suddenly she wasn't a child anymore, because she knew something that was simply true.

Susan was her mother.

Susan was her mother.

Susan was her mother.

The dog, an auburn terrier, bolted past her; the couple trailed casually behind. They didn't look at her and she didn't look at them. She stared at the water lapping gently against the stony beach. Big rotted beams of timber were stacked off to the side. A *pling* sound caught her attention: It was the loner guy, trying to skip stones into the river. Finally, one skipped twice before sinking. He tried again and this time it skipped three times, *pling pling pling* across the charcoal gleam. Lisa couldn't help a smile; she would have called out to him—"Congratulations!" she would have said—if he hadn't been a stranger.

She wondered if that was how love happened, a *pling* in the night that made you look. She wondered if that was how Susan had made her: a few *plings,* and a sinking stone.

Lisa realized she must have looked crazy, sitting

there crying and half laughing on a bench in a park at the rock-crusty edge of a river. Alone in a city, late at night. Crazy. So she got up and started walking, following the curved path out of the park and onto Main Street.

The lobby restaurant at One Main was still busy and the street was well lit. The front of the building was encased in scaffolding and she didn't like to walk under it—she was convinced that if she did, it would fall—so she followed the rails that made a seam up the middle of the street. Heel-to-toe, heel-to-toe. Past the Main Performance Space—a little church of a building with a lime-green roll-up garage door—and around the corner onto Water Street.

All up the right side of Water Street were little brick town houses, the restored ones right next to the dilapidated ones, until you reached the old Empire Stores warehouse: a huge brick monster of a building that was stone-cold empty, for now. Needless to say, a splashy renovation was planned. Across the street were a theater, a gallery, a café closed for the night, and Water Street Chocolates—Susan's shop.

Lisa stood in front of the pretty European-style chocolaterie that her sister—no, her mother . . . that Susan had opened three years ago. The big plate-glass window was framed in dark wood and decorated for autumn with toasty leaves and berried branches. Pressing her face against the glass, Lisa could see that the wooden shelving to the right of the door was starting to fill with dark-chocolate apples and milk-chocolate pumpkins and white-chocolate ghosts. Frosty orange ribbons closed the cellophane packages. Lisa felt a pang; she missed this, and she wasn't even gone.

All last summer she had worked here with Susan, helping out in the front of the shop or in the adjoining factory. The whole staff had treated her so nicely, taking the time to teach her the littlest things. She would sing for them sometimes, just to make sure they understood she would not be spending her life working in a store. But the truth was, deep down, she really liked it there. She liked the people who worked for Susan, and she liked the cozy feel of the shop, and she liked the factory's cold steel tables and huge porcelain machinery and neatly stacked molds. And she had come to love the smell, that burned espresso smell of good chocolate. She was addicted to it now. She could almost smell it right here, standing outside the shop.

If Susan was fifteen when she gave birth, then she was only a year older than Lisa was now. Lisa knew she had been awful to insinuate that Susan hadn't known her baby's father. Lisa's father. Knowing Susan, it would have been a case of true love. Or maybe it was someone Mommy and Daddy didn't like. Or maybe both. Lisa began to wonder about the story there. Maybe Susan was the very mother Lisa had always imagined, just a different version of her; maybe she *had* been at the epicenter of a drama. It occurred to Lisa that Susan might have aborted her; that was what all Lisa's friends vowed they would do if it ever happened to them. Which it wouldn't, because they were virgins, but still. There was a big difference between fourteen and fifteen years old, fifteen and sixteen, sixteen and thirty. Anything could happen.

Maybe what Susan had been, way back then, was very brave.

Maybe Mommy and Daddy had been brave, too.

Maybe the thing to do was to give them all a chance to explain.

Maybe Susan's being her birth mother was a stroke of brilliant good luck. Because it meant that never, ever in Lisa's lifetime had she been unwanted. Not for a single moment.

Lisa sat on the curb in front of the shop, hugging her bent legs against her chest, drying her eyes on the knees of her jeans. She had always loved Susan, *loved* her.

So, it was Susan. Susan.

Did that mean Lisa would no longer need Mommy and Daddy's permission for things in advance? Did it mean she could consult Susan as the last word on . . . well, whatever? A little thrill zipped through Lisa at the thought of the tattoo she'd been wanting to get at the base of her spine: a tiny starburst. She'd have a better chance with Susan, she realized, than with Mommy and Daddy. But it was confusing; weren't they still her parents? Or would they now be expected to turn over the controls to their own daughter? To Susan? After all they had done for her and Lisa?

Lisa pressed the heels of her hands into her eyes and tried to shake her head free of the questions she couldn't answer. Footsteps clopped along the cobblestones: A group of five women came laughing up Main Street and turned left onto Water, in the opposite direction, toward the subway. Then Lisa was alone again. It was creepy out here on the street, all by herself. She stood up and thought that maybe it was time to go home and face Susan, who had probably left a dozen messages on Lisa's voice mail by now.

Then, just as Lisa thought she'd head back, she noticed something: the curb in front of Susan's parking garage was the same motley gray it had been all year. Dave had not kept his promise. He had not painted the yellow line.

Lisa found the store key on her key ring, which she kept in her pocket. She rolled up the gate, then let herself in, turning off the alarm system with the code she had memorized last summer. She flicked on the lights and saw a huge smiling chocolate pumpkin on an ornate metal stand. It was a masterpiece, with all the lumpy texture of a real pumpkin, jaunty stem and all. His eyes were stars and his nose was a fancy triangle. His mouth was an ecstatic curlicue smile. A white paper tag showed a hefty price, and Lisa wondered who would get Susan's first grand Halloween creation of the year. She wished she could be that lucky child. Maybe she already was. She bent down and, nearly touching her nose to the cellophane, stole some of the smell off the air.

The swinging doors to the factory were propped open. She kept the lights off when she passed through. The door leading into the garage was locked with a simple bolt, which she lifted and slid.

The old-fashioned pickup truck, painted cream with WATER STREET CHOCOLATES in brown script on both doors, was parked in the small garage. In the far corner was a heavy-duty plastic cabinet containing tools, odds and ends, and the small can of yellow paint Susan had long ago bought for Dave to paint the line that would warn cars against parking in front of the garage. A brand new paintbrush, still in its plastic sheath, sat on top of the can.

Over the summer, Lisa had offered to paint the line

herself. Susan had hesitated, almost accepting, but changed her mind.

"Dave said he'd do it."

Lisa wondered why Susan didn't just let someone else paint that line; she had no lack of employees. She was probably trying to give Dave a chance to keep his promise. Well, the summer had passed and it was autumn now, colorful and chilly, and he still hadn't done it.

Lisa would do it herself, right now; she would paint the yellow line not to keep a promise, but to make one. She would promise Susan her love.

It seemed like a bad idea to open the garage door, putting Susan's truck on display so late at night, with the interior factory door gaping. So she took the can of paint, a screwdriver to pry open the top, a stick to stir the paint and the brush to paint the line, and crossed back through the factory and the shop. She shut the front door behind her but didn't lock it. Besides the distant buzz of bridge traffic, her footsteps were the only sounds, echoing a little as she set herself up in front of the shallow naked curb that would soon be a bright, warning yellow.

The oil-based paint went on thick and syrupy, oozing into cracks and pockmarks in the curb. Lisa liked the sour smell and the heavy feel of dragging the yellow paint along the old, worn stone. The line was two-thirds finished when the clip-clop of someone walking materialized in a lull of the traffic drone. The footsteps were slow, casual. She looked up: It was the loner guy from before, the stone skipper. She saw now that he was wearing the kind of tan canvas jacket you ordered from the outdoorsy catalogs that were always piling up in the magazine rack at home in Texas.

Daddy had one of those jackets in blue. Loner Man walked along the middle of the street, tossing a rock larger than a skipping stone from one hand to the other. He wasn't exactly looking at her, but somehow, she felt, he saw her. Watching him keenly, she lifted the dripping paintbrush off the curb.

Chapter 3

Susan leaned out the open window through which she had caught her last glimpse of Lisa entering the park on their corner. It was where Lisa went to read or sometimes play her guitar when she wanted to be alone. It was now fifteen minutes since Susan had seen her beloved daughter—her daughter!—navigate the old iron tracks heel-to-toe just like when she was a little girl. Seeing her tightrope the same curved lines had brought hope to Susan's heart, reminding her that only labels had changed tonight, not facts. *Mother* would substitute for *sister,* and when Lisa realized that, when she understood that nothing had really changed, things would begin to fall into place for both of them.

Fifteen minutes, a small piece of an hour, yet time felt slow as a dream, when a minute could take a year, a year a minute, or time ceased to move altogether. Lisa had stepped off the rail track and walked into the park, rounding the asphalt path until she was beyond Susan's view.

Now, leaning out the broad window into the cold night, Susan couldn't see Lisa anywhere. Across the street, the empty windows of a gutted warehouse held shadows abraded by dusty filaments of moonlight. The street was quiet and a few people walked casually in the park.

From Audrey McInnis, the mother of Lisa's Brooklyn best friend, Glory McInnis, Susan had learned that eleven o'clock was the witching hour, when parents were allowed to worry. Until the strike of eleven, you were required to grind back all concerns about your errant teenager. There had been so much for Susan to learn since Lisa came to live with them last year. Raising a teenager, you were supposed to strike a perfect balance between caution and release. Susan had discovered that it was easier said than done.

Lisa was mostly polite and well behaved, but when her forceful personality reared up, you learned to step back and give her space. With negotiation, shifting limits on clothes and rules had inevitably righted themselves. There had been a stream of friendship dramas and unrequited crushes to assuage, but those were easy compared with power-related conflicts. "You're not my parents!" had been a favorite refrain. And a true one, as far as Lisa knew, until tonight. The decision to tell Lisa the truth had been Susan's struggle for years; countless times she had had to resist the temptation just to blurt it out. Concluding that it was time to tell Lisa had been an important, careful, even inevitable decision. One she was beginning to regret, deeply, as the clock ticked toward eleven.

The wait was brutal but she had to give Lisa her allotted space. Then she began to wonder if the eleven o'clock rule applied to e-mail.

If she had gone to Glory's, they were probably huddled together over her computer, IMing their eighth-grade friends who had scattered to different high schools. Susan picked up her BlackBerry from where she'd left it on the coffee table and opened a new e-mail to Glory's address, which she had saved the last time Lisa had sent a message from her friend's house. *Lisa are you there? If you're reading this please just zap me back to tell me you're okay. There's so much to talk about but we don't have to say it all now. I just love you so much. And I'm so so so sorry. And I want to know you're okay.*

She sent the e-mail and plunked backward into the soft cushions of the couch, reminding herself that this was not the first time Lisa had been out past her curfew. There was the time she had stayed late at Glory's, when they were new friends, testing the rules Susan and Dave had outlined upon Lisa's arrival in their home. Then there was the time the girls and three other friends had gone to an agreed-upon movie, only to slip into the multiplex's neighboring theater to catch another show for free. Their cell phones had all been turned off, and it was eleven thirty before any of the frantic parents heard from them. And then there was last June, the night of Lisa's middle school graduation.

After a day of ceremony and celebration, Lisa had gone out with friends and overlooked her ten-o'clock curfew by two hours. The ten-to-eleven buffer hour, as Susan thought of it, had passed slowly. The worry hour before midnight had been sheer hell. Even Dave had showed signs of concern, though in his work he was used to parents thinking their teens had gone missing when actually they were just ignoring the

rules. They had phoned everyone Lisa knew from
school, and then some. Carole and Bill Bailey—Susan
and Lisa's parents; now, Lisa's grandparents—who
had come to town for the graduation, had been roused
from sleep at their hotel and were about to call a car
service to bring them to the loft. Within one hour, the
particles of a full-fledged vigil had begun to gather
shape—and then, like Cinderella resuming normality
at the stroke of midnight, in walked Lisa, indignant at
all the fuss.

As Susan recalled those nights of worry, she began
to relax a little bit. They had fought and Lisa was
upset; she had every right to her strong reaction; she
would be back any minute. It was now a matter of en-
during the torturous passage of those minutes—one
and then another and another still. Susan willed herself to wait until exactly eleven o'clock before she
picked up the phone.

She got up, walked over to the puzzle table and
picked up a piece at random. But she quickly realized
she was too restless to sit and concentrate, so instead
went into the kitchen and emptied the dishwasher. She
wiped the counters, though they were already clean.
With window cleaner and paper towels she cleaned
and polished the stainless-steel cooktop, oven door
and cabinet handles. She worked slowly and carefully,
feeling the minutes move through her. She checked
her watch; it still wasn't time. So she picked up the
phone and speed-dialed Dave's cell, knowing he
would give her the courage to hold tight and wait. His
voice mail answered and she left a message to call her.

She walked through the loft and turned on all the
lights. She didn't like this, any of it: Lisa gone and
Dave unreachable late at night. Ever since last Octo-

ber, fully a year ago now, when with a stroke of remarkable bad timing Dave's phone battery had run out
on the worst night of his career, Susan's automatic response to his inaccessibility had gone from mild un-
ease to unalloyed worry. He had finally called home
fourteen hours late with news of a missing person that
would soon galvanize the city with fear. Thinking of
that missing girl now, Susan's worry jelled into hard
anxiety.

Her name was Becky Rothka. Becky's mother had
called the Seventy-eighth Precinct, the call was routed
to the Detectives Unit, and by chance Dave caught the
call—and in this arbitrary way the case became his.
Becky, thirteen years old, had left her middle school
one afternoon and was never seen again. Lisa had
come to live with them just before Becky vanished,
and with no good schools in Dumbo she had briefly
attended the same grade in the same Park Slope middle school as Becky; though with ten classes per
grade, they had never met. Dave had once remarked
how much Becky and Lisa resembled each other:
same age, both slight and fair-skinned with longish
blond hair and green eyes; in appearance, they might
have been sisters. But by then he had failed to find
Becky and everything seemed to remind him of her.
Susan still caught Dave gazing at Lisa sometimes and
suspected he was thinking about Becky, the girl who
got away, the one big case he had failed to close. She
knew it haunted him, though he rarely spoke about it
anymore.

Thinking of Becky, Susan's resolve melted completely. It was now ten fifty-four, only six minutes to
go until eleven o'clock, but she couldn't wait. Setting
down the bottle of window cleaner and handful of

soiled paper towels, she picked up the phone and speed-dialed Lisa's cell number.

Gradually Susan became aware of the repeating crescendo of Lisa's phone ringing somewhere in the apartment. She put the kitchen phone on the counter, letting the call ring and ring so the sound would lead her to its source. It was loudest in the living room, where Susan saw that Lisa had left her paisley bag on the floor. Digging through a pile of crumpled papers, pens and lipsticks at the bottom of the bag, she found the phone. She held it in the palm of her hand and watched it ring before finally flipping it open, then answering and ending her own call. Without the electronic tether of her cell phone, Lisa's vulnerability exploded in Susan's imagination.

She returned to the kitchen and called Glory McInnis. Her mother, Audrey, answered, and Susan quickly explained that they had argued (leaving out why they had argued) and that Lisa still wasn't home. Through her end of the phone, Susan could hear footsteps as Audrey went to find Glory in her room, a door opening, voices. Glory herself came on the line, saying, "I haven't talked to Lisa since she was on her way home from rehearsal, and that was, like, almost ten o'clock." Susan felt a plunge of disappointment, but also a sense of relief that Glory had not yet been filled in on Susan's confession, which had taken place after ten o'clock. The truth still felt too raw to become news; she and Lisa had to finish their conversation before it could be broken into socially digestible bits.

One by one, Susan called Lisa's friends; and one by one, each said they had not spoken with her that night. No one knew where she was. Susan hung up the phone and thought about what to do.

She could search the neighborhood, but it was late and she was alone and what good would that do anyway? What would be the point of running around the neighborhood in a city where Lisa could be anywhere at all? She had a Metrocard, she was smart and adventurous and she knew her way around. Still, she was only fourteen and had been in the city only a year. Wandering the streets alone at night, in a state of emotional upheaval, could not possibly be a good idea.

She tried Dave's cell again, and again his voice mail answered. This time she wouldn't give up so easily. She called the precinct's landline and was told he had left on a call a while ago. She imagined him in a tunnel or a basement or any solid structure that eluded penetration by satellite signals; or maybe he had forgotten to charge his cell phone, a bad habit he had worked on, though not altogether successfully. She waited less than a minute and tried his cell again. On the sixth try, she finally got through to him.

"Sweetie!" he answered.

"Can you talk?" When he was working, she always asked before plunging in.

"It's fine. I'm with Morgan Schnall on a drunk-and-disorderly in Prospect Park."

In the background, Susan heard Officer Schnall objecting noisily to Dave's remark. He didn't usually team up with a street cop on routine calls, but occasionally at the end of a slow shift he'd go along on his way home.

"Schnall wants me to tell you that he is not the drunk and disorderly individual of which I speak." Dave said it in his cop voice, dipping into the earthy rhythms of Brooklyn cop talk and shedding his Ivy

League polish; he had once told her that he feared his education alienated him from his colleagues. "He's not drunk—yet—just disorderly, and that he cannot help."

"Dave"—she felt too nervous to kid around with him—"I'm worried."

"What's going on?" His tone grew quieter.

"Lisa's not home." She explained the essentials, once again leaving out the reason for her argument with Lisa; that was something she would have to explain to him carefully, at the right time. "Her cell phone's here and I can't reach her, and none of her friends have heard from her. I don't know what to do."

"Let's give her till midnight. She's never stayed out later than that."

"But, Dave, I'm really worried."

"Sweetie, listen to me. You've got to keep in mind that Lisa's a teenager, and teenagers are masters of the disappearing act."

"Right. But do you think I should go out and look around for her anyway?"

"I think we should give her until midnight; she's stayed out that late before. Just hang in there and wait for me, okay? I've got another hour on my shift, then I'll be home."

How could he have such a casual attitude about this? She guessed this was what people meant by *hardened cop.* But the Dave she knew was anything but hardened; he was quiet and intense, hard when he needed to be, but mostly, with Susan, soft. Dave was hands down the most loving and reliable man she had ever known, and the truth was she had trouble thinking of him as a cop. He was the lover in her bed, the friend at her ear, the guy who grocery-shopped when she didn't have time. "Midnight," he had said, "wait until midnight." How could she? But she had to trust his judgment; she didn't have any better ideas.

She sat on the couch, tried and failed to calm down, then got up and paced the floor. How could she wait a whole hour when each minute was now broken into small eternities? *One hour.* Standing at the card table between the windows, she was able to place two puzzle pieces in the growing blue edge, but patience failed her and she continued to pace. Finally she went to the bedroom she shared with Dave. The green chenille bedspread was still pulled flat from the morning. She picked up a few spare coins and receipts from her nightstand and put them away; folded her nightgown over the back of the chair by the window; hung Dave's navy-blue robe on the closet's inside hook. That was three minutes. One *hour?*

Plucking a tissue from the box on her bedside table, she dusted the frames hanging on the wall by her dresser, stopping at one: a newspaper article about Dave Strauss, the Harvard graduate who had made the inscrutable decision to become a New York City cop. (Not so inscrutable to anyone who knew him; he had simply followed in his father's and *his* father's footsteps.) The Rothka case, which had so vividly captured the city's attention, had briefly made Dave a minor celebrity. In one of the piece's two photographs, Dave was a young man wearing "the bag", the blue uniform of the street cop; in the other, he was shown in his current evolution as a detective, relaxing between Susan and Lisa on the living room couch. It had been published last November, and looking at the picture now, Susan felt moved by the happy triad of their newly minted family. She dusted the black frame and polished the glass protecting the newsprint, then turned to her dresser.

She ran a clean tissue over her collection of perfume bottles, thinking she should go to the kitchen for her real cleaning supplies but not bothering to,-because that really wasn't the point. She was passing time, keeping busy. She arranged some stray papers in a pile behind her jewelry box, then dusted the box itself, then opened it. On the top tier were all her earrings, arranged by size in numerous compartments. Below, in a larger section, were necklaces and bracelets. Her attention landed on the little chain coiled in one corner; nestled into the curl of gold was the small crucifix she had received for her first Communion. Back in her hometown of Vernon, Texas, she hadn't had a single girlfriend who didn't go through that rite of passage. She wondered what those girls were doing now; she hadn't seen most of them since she was fifteen, pregnant but not yet visibly so, and the Bailey family had moved away.

She reached in and took out the necklace, dangling it long and then recoiling it in the palm of her hand, remembering how she used to wear it every day, how special it had been to her as a young girl. When she looked at her childhood necklace now she felt a strange pang of remorse, realizing that the last time she had taken it out and held it had been the one time she'd shown it to Dave. Dave, who openly called himself "a devout atheist," had chuckled at the sight of the crucifix, and she had kept it hidden from him ever since. Religion was the one thing they couldn't agree on. But she had been lapsed in her religious devotion for so long that she wasn't really offended, just a little bit bewildered about her relationship to God, though she couldn't begin to explain that feeling. Holding the necklace now, Susan decided she would give it to Lisa, and wondered why she had never thought of it before. She carefully replaced the necklace in the bottom of the jewelry box and looked at the clock: six more minutes had passed.

In the bathroom she brushed her teeth and then her hair. She splashed cold water on her face, patted herself dry and returned to the living room to continue the wait. On the way past the kitchen she picked up the phone and sat on the couch with it cradled in her lap. She had already talked to all Lisa's friends. Whom else could she call now? For all the people Susan knew, it struck her that she had no really close friends of her own to rely on; she had acquaintances, neighbors and employees, but had never made the time for a best girlfriend who would forgive her such undisciplined worry.

She thought of her parents; she could call *them.* But shouldn't she wait? Her mother, Carole, would quickly become distraught, and her father, Bill—well, she didn't know how he would react. Since he'd stopped drinking twenty years ago he'd become the kind of dry drunk who needed to control everyone around him in order to keep hold of himself; the top-ranking salesman in his office; the devout Christian; the neighbor with a perfect lawn. His reaction to a call about Lisa being out late could land anywhere in a range from concerned to outraged. She fingered the phone's rubber buttons and thought about it but didn't dial. She would wait, she decided, before she said anything to them, because probably Dave was right: Lisa would waltz in any minute now and Susan's worry would dissolve. She would have her sister/daughter back and they would have their chance to really talk it out. Then she would prepare herself to make the same confession to Dave.

She set the phone down on the coffee table and walked over to the open window. Leaning out, she felt the night chill on her face. Goose pimples formed on her uncovered arms. She looked toward the right, in the direction of the park, then toward the left, in the direction of Water Street. It was quiet out, and cold. Lisa was nowhere in sight.

At the card table, she snapped three more puzzle pieces into place, increasing the length of blue. It seemed like some kind of background, but there was still no indication of what, if any, image would emerge after all the pieces had been assembled.

She picked up her BlackBerry and thumbed another message, this time directly to Lisa's e-mail address. *When I was your age I was in love. At least I believed I was. Madly madly in love. His name was Peter and my dear sweet darling the truth is that you look like him. You look like your father. The boy-man who gave us all the gift of you. I have so much to tell you.*

Chapter 4

Riding upward in the mirrored elevator, Dave closed his eyes and took a deep breath, feeling the exhaustion of a long day seep into him. He hoped Lisa was home by now. Susan's call had alarmed him more than he had let on; he knew the statistics, and Lisa was a ripe age for the creeps who loved girls so much they didn't care how badly they hurt them. A little overripe, actually, the peak age being closer to eleven. He hated thinking this way about his own family, but after a shift at the precinct it was hard not to see criminals everywhere or to think of your loved ones as potential victims. It was a bitter, skewed view of life you constantly fought and never quite overcame. He took another deep breath, and opened his eyes to the mirrored kaleidoscope of himself.

This elevator had always made him uneasy; someone's bad idea to make a small space feel larger by installing mirrors everywhere, instead trapped you with the nagging crone of your own self-doubts. Faced with his multitudinous reflections, he was reminded of how his good looks were fading as he neared forty. If a mirror didn't lie, these mirrors were a funhouse of stark physical truth. His leanness was threatening to turn his face gaunt, and his eyes were becoming permanently underscored by dark shadows. In the bathroom mirror, he had dozens of gray hairs salting his short hair; here, hundreds. Like it or not, time was on the move. Forty years old, almost. How had he gotten to this moment on the clock of his life, this tipping point between youth and middle age, energy and fatigue, idealism and resignation? Lately, he had been thinking a lot about that, looking backward at the decisions that had set him on the road to the here and now.

Just tonight, in the slow hours of an uncharacteristically calm city—after putting away his files on Becky Rothka, which he had combed for the umpteenth time with no fresh revelations—he had finished rereading Vladimir Nabokov's *Lolita.* He had read it first in high school, then had chosen it as the subject of his senior thesis in college, and recently had decided it was time to read it again to see if he understood it differently now. *Lolita,* after all, was ultimately the reason he had become a cop. Though he had been born into a family of cops, college had broken most of his assumptions about his future; he had felt pulled to become a cop like his father and grandfather before him, and at the same time pulled *not* to become a cop so he could follow his more intellectual leanings. He had thought, for a while, that he might teach or even write or possibly both. But then *Lolita* clarified everything for him. Lo. Lola. Dolly. Plain Dolores. A girl charmed and manipulated and finally kidnapped, raped and held hostage for two years by her handsome stepfather-monster Humbert Humbert (avowedly hiding behind that ironic pseudonym), Lolita was transformed by a cunning mix of authorial brilliance and morally ambivalent cultural interpretation into a "nymphet" at the center of a profound if indecent love story. "The great love story of our century," touted a magazine quote plastered on the front cover of Dave's copy. When he'd finished reading tonight, he'd flipped to the cover to see if the quote really called it a *love* story. Three reads in, he was still sure that was not what Nabokov had meant. In his thesis, Dave had reconstructed Lolita into, simply, a victim, received a middling grade and been told he had missed the point. *Simplistic,* his thesis adviser had noted. *Remember that on page xx* she *seduces* him. As if a child's seductiveness could ever bear responsibility in the context of adult sexuality, particularly that of a pedophile. Frustrated and appalled, Dave had finished college with misgivings about the usefulness of literary interpretation, and became determined to stop the Humbert Humberts of the world, deciding it was more valuable to save little girls from the blind, narcissistic misogyny of a half-baked culture than interpret them into its fabric.

Most people didn't know that his college career had ended bitterly for him (good grades, bad attitude), and his Harvard degree certainly hadn't hurt his ability to climb the ranks of the NYPD. He had worked the streets, made detective, gloried in heroics—and yes, he had managed to save some little girls and also little boys and women and men. Seventeen years into it and he was a bona fide old hand; it was a gratifying job when it went well and a genuine torment when it didn't. Failing to close the Rothka case had sealed that sense of torment into him; he studied her files at least twice weekly, and she was never, not for a single hour, far from his thoughts.

He had tried to find her; how he had tried. One year ago, in the chilly days of October, he had searched his heart out for the thirteen-year-old girl. It was a case that went from bad to worse. The first taunting phone call from the bad guy came to Becky's mother, Marie, the morning after the abduction. That afternoon the family received a letter in handwriting forged to resemble a child's; it was signed in Becky's name but had obviously not been written by her. This was the one piece of evidence that had been withheld from the public and press; even Susan didn't know about it. Dave would never forget the faint script asking for a closed-casket funeral and the instant nausea that had forced him to swallow an upsurge of bile. He would never forget Marie Rothka's shaking hands as she read that letter. The next morning, traces of Becky's blood were identified in a Dumpster in the Bronx. Dave's entire squad had pitched in and searched. Becky's Brooklyn neighborhood had rallied, and so had the area around the Bronx Dumpster. Everyone had wanted to find Becky. But to this day, she was still officially missing.

Becky Rothka was the one case Dave had failed completely, which her abductor—they had dubbed him "the groom" for his phoned-in promise to marry Becky before he killed her—liked to remind them all of in his smarmy voice. Over the past year the groom had called Marie Rothka numerous times just for the pleasure of taunting her. He never told her whether Becky was dead or alive, just showered her with splin-

ters of unforgettable details, like how easily the buttons had popped off her shirt or that she had seven
beauty marks on her back. Marie always reported the
calls, and Dave always had them traced. Each time,
the trail ended in midair. It had been six months since
they had heard from the groom.

Dave often wondered if Becky was alive somewhere today. Hurt and scooped out, but alive. Lolita
had survived *her* ordeal. Sometimes when Dave was
feeling particularly grim he wasn't sure what scared
him most: finding Becky alive or dead. If she *was*
alive, the thought of what she might have suffered and
how the groom monster may have bent her to his will
made Dave wonder if life was always preferable to
death. But he couldn't wish death on poor Becky, at
any price. Sweet, lost Becky who floated through his
consciousness at every moment of every day. Sometimes he couldn't take his eyes off Lisa, the two girls
looked so much alike.

Now, riding up in the elevator, he felt the pinch of
something brand-new: He saw what they meant when
they said that the hardest thing for a cop was the feeling that you couldn't really protect your own family.

He glanced at the round silver face of his watch,
which flashed in the mirrors as he raised his wrist. It
was eleven past twelve. He stepped out of the elevator
and turned right into their branch of the hallway.
Susan was waiting for him in the open door.

"She's *still* not home!" Susan's short hair was di-
sheveled around her pale, oval face, and her eyes were
bright with worry.

Dave leaned in to kiss her. "What exactly happened
between you two?" Stepping into the loft, he noticed
cleaning supplies on the counter by the fridge, which

meant Susan had been cleaning at night, which meant she was really upset.

"She came home after rehearsal, about ten o'clock, when she said she would."

"And then?"

"Then we had the argument—"

An argument with a teenager. A teenager like Lisa: a good girl, but headstrong.

"—and she took off," Dave finished Susan's sentence.

He had three older sisters and recalled the heady drama of an average day growing up in his childhood home; one minute the girls were fighting and the next minute they were best friends. Their father, a storied beat cop who had worked the streets of the South Bronx, mediating corner drug wars and ingratiating himself with everyone from pimps to grannies, had declared himself "out of his league" when his daughters' antipathies flared. Their mother, as Dave recalled, knew to step out of the way until the storm had passed. And it always did.

"What was the argument about?" he asked in his calmest "Dave voice," as Susan called it. He knew she relied on his equanimity; her moods tended to be quick and hot, whereas his boil was reliably slow and steady. It was their dynamic, their marriage dance, and so far it had served their happiness. And they *were* happy. Susan, without question, was the love of his life.

"I've called everyone I can think of and she's *nowhere*."

"Sweetie, she has to be *somewhere*."

"Shouldn't we look for her? I saw her go over to the park."

She had avoided his question about the argument, yet it seemed key; they had argued, Lisa had fled and she'd be back soon licking her wounds. He settled his hands on her shoulders and looked into her brown eyes, which up close were flecked with black and green and bright specks of light. Large and slightly almond shaped, her eyes had transfixed him from the very beginning.

"What happened between you two?" he tried again.

"I'm so worried about her I can't even think," she answered, or nonanswered, in a hoarse whisper.

As she stared at him with those eyes, he felt her anxiety transfer into him through a tunnel of air as tight as connective tissue. This was *Lisa* they were talking about, Susan's beloved little sister. She was still a *child.* His next thought, *Becky Rothka,* cinched his inability to follow protocol and wait until morning before ringing alarm bells.

"All right," he said. "Let's go."

Susan crossed the room to get her purse from the coffee table, picking up her BlackBerry and zipping it into the purse's outside pouch. He could just see her fretfully cleaning and e-mailing into the night as she'd waited.

Everything at this late hour seemed conspicuously noisy: their footsteps down the rose-carpeted hall, the door to the elevator sliding open, its five-floor descent to the marble-and-chandelier lobby. On their way out, Dave stopped to ask Dexter—the night doorman, sitting behind the high faux-marble counter—to tell Lisa they'd be right back if she got home first.

Dave held the front door open for Susan. Neither of them had thought to bring a jacket and it was cold out now, colder than just a few minutes ago when he had

come home from work. Unless it was the contrast between home, its warmth, and now this. Susan hugged
herself, and Dave pulled her close against him as they
walked in synch in the direction of the park.

Bridge traffic at this time of night was growing thin
enough to tease out the sounds of individual vehicles.
Vans and cars had different tenors, trucks were a low
rumble, motorcycles a high whiz. Dave was used to
the soloist meanderings of night, and was reminded by
the intentness of Susan's listening that she was not.
She was accustomed to—and a direct part of—the
neighborhood's boisterous resurgence. She was noise,
energy, progress, day. He inspected and chased the
night. She shivered against him and he ran his hand up
and down her bare, goose-pimply arm.

Moonlight and the bright haze of Manhattan across
the river drenched everything in the park—lawn, path,
bench, shore—in a tarnished silver glow. This park
that would wake with color in the morning was now a
kind of sepia recollection. Dave scanned for signs of
Lisa. And then, as he realized that he was looking for
signs of her—that he wasn't really expecting to find
her lolling on a bench, staring at the river—he felt the
lurch of his mode switching from home to work, the
pit of his stomach sinking.

They walked the curved stone path to the Main
Street entrance, their shoes tapping softly on the cobblestones as they crossed over to the sidewalk. Dave's
eyes searched; he listened and he smelled. The night
air was crisp and acrid with the hours-rotted garbage
waiting for Sanitation's morning pickup.

"I don't like this," Susan said.

Dave wanted to answer, *Neither do I,* but he stayed
quiet. He wanted to keep Susan as calm as possible,

because probably this was nothing; probably Lisa was already home, lying on her bed with her iPod whirring out a song. He unclipped his cell phone from his belt loop and speed-dialed home. There was no answer until voice mail picked up after five rings.

"Doesn't she have keys to the store?" he asked.

"Good idea," Susan said. "Maybe she went there."

As they neared the corner of Water Street they were met by a breeze that must have hooked through the yawning, eyeless Empire Stores warehouse to their right. And on that breeze Dave smelled a trace of paint. He remembered the yellow line: He had forgotten to paint it today. He wondered if the paint he thought he smelled was real or a nagging guilt at having neglected his promise; he hated to disappoint Susan.

He glanced at her profile as they walked quickly together. Marriage, or at least marriage to her, was nothing like he had expected; when their initial passion had somewhat cooled, the deep friendship that blossomed had saturated him with contentment. She was a full decade younger than him, and a sweetness still clung to her face, a shine to her glorious eyes, but tonight there was something new. She had turned twenty-nine just yesterday, and now her face had the sober look of a woman about to cross thirty, heading forward in life, understanding the inevitability of . . . what? Something had changed.

They crossed the street to the sidewalk and turned right toward Water Street Chocolates. The smell of paint grew stronger. Across the street, a new café was being built; in fact, its opening was just days away, and the smell might have emanated from any one of its freshly painted elements.

"What's that?" Susan pointed to a splotch of color in front of the factory side of her double storefront.

The patch of yellow moved through Dave's mind with the evolution of a Rorschach image gathering a certain shape. It looked like part of a footprint. Nearby, an unfinished, freshly painted yellow line edged the sidewalk's curb. The line was steady and careful, completely filled in with color until it abruptly stopped in a smear of drips. The paintbrush lay in the middle of the street at the end of a long yellow dribble, as if it had been thrown. The garage door was scrolled down and the shop's front door was closed but the store lights were on.

"Come on," Dave said, heading toward the shop.

He untucked his T-shirt and used the bottom edge to cover the brass knob as he turned it. Susan looked disturbed by his action but didn't ask why he was doing it: protecting the last fingerprints to touch the knob. Dave was too aware of how botched evidence could wreck a case to destroy any himself, even though he hated thinking of this as a case or the surfaces of Susan's shop as possibly bearing evidence of anything other than the blessedly mundane business of making and selling chocolate. He mentally noted that the door was unlocked and the alarm system was off.

Everything looked as usual: the pretty shop with its built-in polished walnut shelving filling up with Halloween treats; cellophane twinkling under soft, clear lighting; three small round tables by the window; the cash register, quiet, on a raised section of counter.

"Lisa?" Susan called. "Lisa!"

They moved through the swung-open doors leading into the gleaming factory. Using his shirt over his hand again, Dave turned on the light in Susan's small, organized office. So far, other than the store being unlocked and the lights on, there was no sign that Lisa had been here; but *someone* had.

"The inside door to the garage is open," Susan said, heading in that direction. Dave followed her.

In the far corner of the garage, past the cream-painted delivery truck, the plastic storage closet hung open. Susan stood in front of it, studying its neatly organized contents.

"Nothing else is missing, just the paint and the brush," she said. "But she was here, Dave."

"Maybe."

"Maybe?"

They had no proof, Dave thought, and assumptions were dangerous.

"We don't know if it was Lisa who painted the line," he said. "The footprint out there is bigger than her shoe. Someone else might have come here, one of your workers."

"In the middle of the night? After Lisa and I argued? Who would come here to paint this line in the middle of the night when I didn't ask anyone to?"

Dave ground his jaw. "I'm sorry I forgot again."

"No, Dave. I'm not angry at you about not getting around to painting the line. I *know* how busy you are. I'm upset that she came out here in the dark and did it herself, that's what I'm upset about, and now she . . . she . . . ." Susan raised both her hands to her face.

Why was she weeping? What had Susan and Lisa argued about to predicate this much drama? He put his arms around his wife and tried to calm her down. "Sweetie, we don't know who did this," he tried. But how could he convince Susan that Lisa might not have been here tonight, or that anyone else in the world might have thought to paint the yellow line, right here, right now, in the emotional space between Dave's failure to do it himself and Lisa's determination to have the last word in some mysterious argument?

"Dave," Susan sobbed, "you *know* Lisa, you *know* how she makes impulsive decisions. I don't understand how you can look at this and not see that it was her."

"I see exactly what you see here." He struggled to keep his voice calm. "All right, Susan, since it's Lisa . . . well, I agree with you that it's a good idea to think the worst."

"A *good* idea?"

"No," he said. "The only idea, at the moment."

He unhooked his phone from his belt loop and dialed 911, since he didn't know the number for the local precinct.

"I need to report a missing child," Dave said. Without prompting, he gave his name and the location of the factory. He knew this would draw out a first responding officer from the Eight-four—the Eighty-fourth Precinct, covering downtown Brooklyn, Boerum Hill, the Heights and the waterfront. And he knew what would happen next; there was too much eye-level evidence to deny that something unexpected, at the very least, had happened here.

After the call they walked back through the garage, the factory and the store, into a cold night that seemed to have grown darker. Susan went to the footprint and knelt in front of it. Dave crouched down beside her. The partial print was definitely too large to have come from Lisa's small sneaker. He could see by its shine that it was sticky, still wet. Susan reached down to feel the paint.

"Better not touch it," he said.

She pulled back her hand, rubbed her yellowed fingertips together and lifted them to smell the paint. Her body then uncoiled as she stood up suddenly and ran down the middle of the street, shouting, "Lisa! *Lisa!*"

Her voice echoed, then seemed to dissolve into pockets of silence. For a moment, Dave thought he heard Lisa answer, but realized it was just wind looping through the abandoned warehouse across the street. He went to its nearest window. Leaning in, he saw a vast, broken space of darkness cut into haphazard diamonds by whatever little light filtered in from the street, the sky and the river.

"Lisa!" His voice sped through the space and boomeranged back to him. "Lisa, are you there?" But she couldn't be. Could she? He could see no floors, just a crosshatch of beams through open space. "Lisa, answer if you hear me!"

Susan, meanwhile, was calling Lisa's name up and down Water Street. When he turned around, he saw her trying doors, darting in and out of side streets, shouting. He cringed at the trail of fingerprints she was leaving on door handles—but so be it. He couldn't and wouldn't stop her from doing this, because she *had* to, just as he had to call Lisa's name into the gutted warehouse, if only for the strange comfort of hearing his own voice return to him.

It was one thirty in the morning now. He noticed that all the buildings with windowpanes, the ones where people lived or worked, were dark—except one, on the third floor of a brick house in the middle of the block. The harsh fluorescent light in that single window caught Dave's attention. It looked like a full-spectrum plant light; beneath it was a shelf of greenery soaking it in. He thought he saw a face materialize briefly in the blinding light before moving back out of the window's frame, but he wasn't sure.

He reminded himself that he was not a detective in this precinct and that as a family member his involvement would be accepted warily. He had to be careful about taking initiative in what might become some other cop's case. What he could do now was watch the brick building's front door. When the precinct cops arrived, he would inform them that someone may have been watching from upstairs; but the more he thought about that vaporous face, the less certain he became.

The wait for the police seemed very long. Susan sat on the curb, hugging her knees for warmth. Dave stood alone in the street, arms dropped at his sides, becoming calmer as Susan's agitation simmered. And then it started to happen: the sixth sense stoked by years of training and practice that brought a scene alive. The cobblestone street, the splashes of yellow paint, the ingresses and egresses of the surrounding buildings—all window eyes and blind spots—webbed together by glowing strands of possibility. Connected.

In his gut he believed that Susan was right, that Lisa had been here. Someone had been with her. A man with yellow paint now on his shoe.

Susan was shivering. He sat beside her and put his arm over her shoulders. Right away he felt her skin and muscles softening and warming.

"What are you thinking?" Her voice was scratchy, exhausted.

"Can you tell me now," he asked, "what you two argued about?"

Her eyes seemed to open to him, dilating in search of any available light in the darkness. "Oh, Dave—" she began, when a police car came rolling along Water Street and pulled to a stop in front of them. He felt a twist of frustration as she abruptly withdrew the explanation.

The first responding officer was a rookie from the Eight-four, a young, clean-cut black man with creased slacks and a polite attitude. His badge read, P.O. ZEB JOHNSON.

Dave introduced himself to Officer Johnson as an MOS—Member of Service—by showing his gold shield. Johnson seemed nervous at first about running a detective first-class down the initial response checklist for any missing-child call: Where was she last seen, when, what was she wearing, how was her mood? Dave noticed with approval that Johnson swallowed his nervousness quickly, pulling a small notepad and ballpoint pen out of his jacket pocket and continuing with his questions: Could she be with a friend, where did she live, where did she go to school, any custody issues? Dave answered calmly and carefully—he knew a report would have to be filed—but he had already satisfied an internal checklist and was ready for the next level. A girl was unaccounted for. A girl with a loving family and good friends. A girl who liked school. A girl too levelheaded and well aware of her special gifts to squander them on extreme recklessness. Johnson continued: Had she run away before?

"Lisa didn't run away," Susan said.

"I apologize, ma'am," Johnson said, "but nine

times out of ten with kids this age, they've run away. Sometimes they don't even realize how worried everyone is until they see their own face on a poster."

Susan's squeamish expression made Dave wish Johnson hadn't said that. They both knew the police didn't distribute posters unless an amber alert was issued—then they'd tap the National Center for Missing & Exploited Children's LOCATOR system and broadcast posters via e-mail and fax at lightning speed. Without an amber alert, it was a case-by-case decision.

"We had an argument." Susan's tone was firm.

"Mind if I ask what about?"

Susan kept her eyes fixed on Officer Johnson. "About her birth parents. She wants to find them."

Johnson jotted a note. "Are you her adoptive mother?"

"I'm her sister. Our parents live in Texas. Lisa moved in with me and Dave about a year ago."

"Why's that?"

Dave watched a million thoughts pass through Susan's mind before she answered the question. *Because Texas was too small for Lisa. Because she had outgrown the Baileys. Because she was too brilliant and insufferable for the church community of their small country town. Because she was a diva destined for the city's stages, magnetized toward them, and Brooklyn was to be her launching pad.*

"Because she wanted to attend a certain school here in the city and she needed residency to qualify."

A good, simple, true answer. Yet Dave's mind reeled; he sensed there was more. What had they really argued about so fiercely that Lisa would leave?

Why had she wanted to paint the yellow line herself? Why now?

"That's LaGuardia, you said before."

"Yes," Susan answered.

LaGuardia High School of Music and Art and Performing Arts, the renowned public school where every year a few hundred freshmen were culled from thousands of applicants. Lisa had come to New York for a chance at her dream and she had been chosen.

"She's hoping to go to Juilliard eventually," Susan said. "She sings."

Dave stood still and quietly next to Susan but inside he burned with impatience: They needed to move this forward. A flash of thought returned him to Lolita, for whom no one had known it was necessary to look as she and her abductor zigzagged their way across the country, living in hotels, motels and cabins where every layer of her innocence was stripped away.

"Don't mean to rush you, Zeb." Dave smiled. "But let's bend it a little tonight, what do you say? Let's call the detective squad and get someone down here."

Johnson looked steadily at Dave before answering, and Dave knew the young man was weighing the request. It would mean raising a red flag himself, without getting the paperwork in first and letting the precinct detectives make up their own minds.

"The paint," Dave said, which was all it took to remind Zeb Johnson that there was enough here to suggest the real possibility that Lisa had not run away; nor was she out late with her friends, all of whom had already been contacted and none of whom had heard from her. There was the paint, its jarring termination, the angry splash of yellow, the thrown paintbrush, the footprint.

"Well, since you're an MOS, maybe we can throw protocol to the wind, just this once," Johnson said.

To the wind. As Dave's mind spun over and into and against that wind, he reached for Susan's hand. He thought again of Lolita and he thought of Becky Rothka and he thought of Lisa, and into all his senses the yellow paint kept spilling. He held on to Susan's hand, which had grown warm and was sweating now, and watched the hour split open like a burst metal can.

Chapter 5

When Detective Lupe Ramos saw the white couple standing on Water Street, shivering, she figured they were either very cold or very scared. They had good reason to be cold—it was the time of year the temperature started to drop at night. They might also have had good reason to be afraid—though they couldn't possibly have known that yet.

Last week, Lupe had responded to a call about a suspicious person lurking around the Water Street area. Supposedly some guy had been seen around the neighborhood on street corners, keeping a little too still, staying a little too long. The officer who took the message hadn't been able to get the caller's name. He couldn't even say for sure if the caller was a man or a woman; it was either a man with a high voice or a woman with a low voice. Translation: Some jerk was probably pulling their chain.

But the cops were always on the lookout for child molesters and such, and as a policy they took these calls seriously. There was a methadone clinic in that neighborhood, a psychiatric halfway house and up the hill was the world headquarters for the Latter-day Saints; all manner of wackos roamed the waterfront alongside the artists and lawyers and bankers who were buying up apartments like hotcakes. So Lupe had grabbed her partner, Alexei Bruno, and gone to check it out.

The person who'd called in the complaint wasn't waiting when they got there, like s/he'd promised, and the information s/he'd given the officer on the phone wasn't much to go on: white guy, blond hair, not tall, not short, not even good-looking. *Plain,* the message said. Right; thanks. *And oh, yeah, by the way, the guy's got a fleshy pink scar under one of his eyes.* Now *that* was something to work with. They walked around for two hours and nothing. No scar-faced loners were loitering in any dark doorways wearing placards reading, STALKER. Not a one. Most of those guys had some kind of radar that told them when to get lost, so it had been a long shot to begin with. Ramos and Bruno had filed their report and that was that, until tonight.

Bruno had been nearly out the door on a sandwich run when she'd reeled him back in, saying, "Not so fast, Bozo." She put down the phone and told him, "Missing girl over on the waterfront, general location of our stalker the other day, family member's an MOS. Let's hit the road."

He punched his big fist into his big hand. "*Shit.* My stomach he is volcano of hunger." She was used to his heavy Russian accent and had long ago stopped treating him like someone with a brain defect, though she wouldn't swear on a Bible that he didn't have one. Sooner or later, every detective's brain got warped.

"Yeah, and my stomach she is hurricane. Come on,

this is New York City; you got a deli open twenty-four-seven on practically every block."

"In my dreams."

"That's right, baby, in your dreams."

He picked up his leather cap from the corner of his desk, put it on and followed her out of the detectives' squad room.

"Don't think about that corned beef on rye," she razzed him as they walked along the buffed linoleum to the staircase leading down into the lobby of the Eighty-fourth Precinct. "Don't think about that hot coffee and cream. *Do not think about that piece of coconut cake.*"

"Loopy, you are going to kill me one of those days."

Man, she loved this guy, just loved him, the way he mashed up the American language.

In the little bitty police parking lot right out front, they got into the gold sedan that was their specially designated unmarked car. She let him drive, figuring all guys liked the ego boost. Personally, she didn't need the wheel in her hands to know who was boss.

At twenty-eight, Lupe Ramos understood herself. She was young enough to call herself a girl and old enough to know better. She knew when people looked at her they labeled her in a thousand ways—girl, woman, girlfriend, cop, partner, bitch, fashion diva, life of the party, single mother, irritant—the list went on and on. She didn't much care. In her relatively short life she'd been through it all, on the streets and off; these days, when she sipped her coffee, she paused to taste it. She paused because your thoughts were clearest when you took the time. And she tasted it because she knew that in her line of work every sip could be your last one.

Mother at fifteen from dating some kid who was dead before their baby was born. Hector; okay, she'd loved him. Cop at twenty while working on her college degree. Detective at twenty-four while getting her master's in criminal justice. Couldn't have done it without her own mother, a "premature grandmother" she called herself, like all the other grannies on the bench watching their grandkids while their own kids finished growing up. Lupe hoped she wouldn't be a grandmother at thirty, but if she was, so be it. She'd learn to knit and make the booties herself.

She checked her watch: It was a little after two a.m. Most of the other detectives hated working the eight-to-four night shift, but she had requested it; it was a crazy schedule but it worked for her life. At home in the wee hours, she'd catch up on her e-mails and surf the Internet or do her nails or read a magazine to unwind, then have breakfast with her mother, Chiquita, and son, Orlando, before he went off to school. She'd sleep until about four, hang out with Orlando if he came straight home from school, then shower, pretty up, and eat her mother's dinner before hitting the road for another night of Chase the Criminals. Wednesdays and Sundays were her days off, and today she and Orlando had a date to work on his social studies project after school. Ancient Mesopotamia, trade on the Tigris and Euphrates rivers, early family life—the works. She'd looked forward to skipping her primping routine, throwing on some sweatpants and hitting the books with her son; and still did, if there was any chance of this call wrapping itself up neatly.

She hoped the missing girl turned up soon, but as she was a family member of an MOS it could easily get complicated. Well, Lupe thought, there was hope and there was hope. First of all she hoped the girl was safe; it was always a strange, angry kind of relief when the teenager came waltzing back home with that pissy look of triumph on his or her face. *Look at me, I fucked with you, ain't I just the cat's meow! Oh, yeah, you're super; now give me your cell phone and your iPod, and by the way, you're grounded for, like, one year.* Yeah, that was what Lupe hoped the MOS whose kid was AWOL would experience tonight: that teenage slap on the face that sent you to bed at dawn grateful that your baby was home safe. If not . . . well, Orlando would get the call that Mom was working overtime. It would break her heart to let him down, but he'd been there before; she'd find a way to make it up to him.

As the car pulled to a stop on Water Street, Lupe dug in her purse for the lipstick tube that once again had gotten itself lost in her tangle of stuff. Her mother always said that a little makeup went a long way, and Lupe had learned never to meet a challenge without her lipstick. It gave her strength and volume. That white couple standing there, just behind Zeb Johnson, must have been the parents. They looked wiped out, really upset. Lupe hoped that stalker the other day had been a figment of the caller's nervous imagination. She really hoped so. But then she saw a big mess of yellow paint on the street—and a footprint. *Aw, shoot.* Her antennae were getting that quivery feeling that usually meant a long night ahead.

Chapter 6

Water Street grew colder with deepening night, and the sour smell of fresh paint now seemed to permeate the air. Susan stood on a street that no longer looked familiar, her arm linked through Dave's, feeling a pool of loneliness opening within her. Some terrible story seemed hidden in each stroke and drip of yellow paint on the sidewalk and cobblestones, and now it was more necessary and impossible than ever to make her confession to Dave. But how could she just blurt it out here, in front of a stranger? Officer Johnson stood off to the side, waiting for his precinct detectives to arrive.

She sat back down on the curb and pulled her BlackBerry out of her purse.

Dave doesn't know yet. She began the e-mail to Lisa a little incoherently, she realized, but she wasn't a writer and she felt too disordered to make a solid beginning. *But I'm going to tell him as soon as I can. I wanted you to know first so you wouldn't be the last to know the biggest secret of your life. Only Mommy and Daddy and I and now you know about that time honey.*

Susan sent the message, sated with the memory of Lisa in her arms as a newborn baby, so soft and floppy and perfect it made her shiver to think she might have given her up for adoption if her parents hadn't stopped her. There was so much more to tell Lisa. She opened another e-mail.

Let me tell you about your father. His name was Peter Adkins. I haven't seen him since way back then and the truth is, my darling, the truth is the truth is he never knew about you. Go ahead and hate me. I deserve it. Facts: I was fifteen and he was seventeen when we made you, we both lived in Vernon and went to the same high school, he was popular and I was not, he was a pretty good student and I was a terrible student (except in dance, ceramics and strangely math), and you are very much like him in some ways, the good ways. Peter was an amazing boy just loaded with charm and yes Lisa yes we loved each other. He made me feel beautiful before I ever really saw myself in a mirror. But I don't have to tell you that people are complicated. When I got pregnant things began to change with us and—

Dave sat down on the curb beside Susan. She sent the second e-mail with its last unfinished sentence, and zipped the BlackBerry back into her purse's outside pocket. He glanced at her with a warm smile, then rested his arms on his bent knees, clasping his hands together. He was such a good man, honest, and truly *nice* in a way that cut through all his layers. After the horrid ending with her first love, Peter, the conundrum of Lisa appearing in her teenage life and the parody of dating she had experienced in her early

years in New York, Susan had come to distrust men—
until Dave, whom she appreciated and adored completely. She reached over and wove her fingers into
the knot of his hands. As soon as possible, she would
get him alone and tell him the truth.

A gold sedan drove slowly up the street and pulled
to a stop behind Officer Johnson's squad car. A bright
red leaf fluttered out of the car when the driver's door
opened, reminding Susan that it was autumn, and a
beefy man in black leather emerged, crushing the leaf
beneath his boot. He was followed from the passenger's side by a petite Hispanic woman in tight jeans, a
hot-pink knit turtleneck and a short jean jacket. She
paused to put on some cherry-colored lipstick, smack-
ing her lips together and leaning back into the car to
place the lipstick on the dashboard. She looked about
Susan's age, in her late twenties, and the man seemed
older. He took off his leather driving cap to tissue dry
his scalp—sweating, strangely, in the cold early-
morning air—and she saw that his pate was bald
around a halo of light brown hair.

Dave stood up, leaving Susan's left side suddenly
bereft of warmth. She got up and walked over to join
him and Officer Johnson in greeting the detectives.

"Yeah, Zeb? Whaddaya got?" The woman's voice
was high-pitched and staccato. The man stood beside
her, rubbing his hands together, then cupping them to
catch steamy puffs of breath.

"Teenage girl didn't come home," Johnson said.
"This is the family. Susan Bailey-Strauss and Detective Dave Strauss, Seven-eight."

Dave again displayed his shield. Susan was im-
pressed by the immediate response it always got from
other cops.

The woman elbowed her partner. "Yo, baby, first-class, you gotta listen to him no matter what."

The man nodded gravely to Susan and then looked at Dave. "Detective Alexei Bruno, Eight-four. Trust me, ignore this one; she's the pain of my existence." He had a heavy Russian accent.

"Son of a bitch doesn't know pain," the woman said, "but I'm telling you he will. Detective Lupe Ramos." She offered her manicured hand to Dave first, then Susan, adding a just-between-us-girls wink.

Susan tried to hold herself steady in the moment, to trust that Dave would know how to handle this situation, but these detectives worried her. She looked at Dave and squinted her eyes, trying to transmit her thoughts: They had to get some competent detectives down here. He had just stepped forward with the sober expression of someone about to climb out on a limb, when Officer Johnson began a summary of his initial investigation. Susan watched Dave as he kept still and waited, ever polite. She had always admired his diplomacy—he believed that most things eventually resolved themselves—but tonight she did not feel there was time for patience. If he didn't speak up soon, then she would.

Johnson finished his summary with, "Detective Strauss might have seen someone up there"—he pointed at the brightly lit window, three buildings down—"looking onto the street."

Bruno's and Ramos's attention veered simultaneously to the single glowing window. In that quiet moment, their faces shared a look of concentration and seriousness that surprised Susan, supplying the littlest morsel of hope.

"Johnson," Ramos said, "get the girl's stats on the

air. Tell 'em we gotta MOS family situation, could be one thing or another but we're gonna run with it. And get Forensics down here; we want prints and we want 'em ASAP. Mrs. Strauss, you're gonna show me around your house while we wait on the prints. And you, *mi amor,* take Detective Strauss over here and pay a visit to that freak in the window."

"Hell on heels," Bruno muttered, as if to himself, though anyone could hear him. "Witch on a broomstick."

"Say it if you're gonna say it."

"*That* would be unprofessional, baby."

Lupe Ramos snickered a little as she consulted her watch, with its pink leather band and rhinestone-outlined face. "Yo, Johnson. When I get back here in twenty, I wanna see bodies. Got it?"

Officer Johnson nodded. "You got it, Chief."

"Mrs. Strauss, you live around here, no?"

"It's Susan," she said, feeling helpless and glancing at Dave for guidance.

"You go with Detective Ramos." Dave emphasized *detective.* "I'll meet you back here in a little while." When Ramos took a moment to huddle with Bruno and Johnson, Dave leaned in to Susan and whispered, "I'll make a call and see what I can find out. Don't worry yet; the detective squads are filled with characters."

Susan and Lupe Ramos walked together along Water Street, quickly, not speaking at first. Except for the scratchy radio sounds of Johnson calling in the broadcast behind them, they walked into a space that felt hushed, eerily silent. The quiet surprised Susan, because in her mind Ramos was wearing—had to be wearing—stiletto heels. *Hell on heels. Pain of my existence.* She didn't feel comfortable with either of these detectives, but if she had to agree with one of them it would be Bruno, despite his malapropisms. Lupe Ramos was just the kind of person who *was* hell on wheels and had to be the bane of *someone's* existence. Susan looked down at Ramos's feet to confirm her assumption about the shoes and was surprised to see lace-up canvas sneakers, pink to match her shirt, watch, fingernails and lipstick.

Ramos noticed her looking. "They my paws," she said. "I can walk silent anywhere in thems."

"They *are* my paws," Susan said. "I can walk anywhere in *these*." She hated herself as soon as she issued the corrections; she herself was a college dropout and had no right to correct anyone's grammar.

Ramos's tweezed brows arched sharply up and she slid a dark-eyed look at Susan. "I graduated from Hunter," she said in a new, sober tone. "Got my master's in criminal justice from John Jay."

She was serious, Susan realized; all of that, before, had been an act.

"Then why do you act so . . . ?" *Stupid* was the word Susan couldn't bring herself to say. She just couldn't fathom why this woman would deliberately act ditzy when, in fact, she was not.

"It's easier playing it to the hilt this way," Ramos said. "Alexei likes it; they all do. And I get results."

They walked into Susan's lobby. Dex was still on shift at the front door.

"Did you see Lisa come in?" Susan asked him.

He shook his head and Susan's heart dropped a little lower. Dex was the most alert doorman the building had, never ducking out for a cigarette or burying his face in a book; if he hadn't seen Lisa, then she wasn't there.

The women waited in silence for the elevator. When it came they stepped in, and the surrounding mirrors repeated them both endlessly and in diminishing size.

Ramos checked every room in the loft, glanced through Lisa's things, then borrowed the bathroom. Susan used the time to get jackets and consider what she wanted to say to the detective; she felt awful about her misjudgments, yet somehow not entitled to her guilt. *You say it, you play it,* she had once heard a kid on the subway say to his friend. It seemed that tonight Susan was layering herself in hypocrisy, saying what she wanted to and wishing she could take it all back.

"Listen, Detective Ramos, I'm sorry about—" Susan began when the detective came out of the bathroom.

"No." Ramos lifted one hand, palm out, and Susan noticed how pink it was. "Not necessary."

Susan felt a trickle of gratitude but she had to say it. "This night's been so confusing; I had no right to judge you." She then noticed that Ramos was holding Lisa's blue-sparkly plastic hairbrush, a tissue separating her fingers from the handle, and Susan's newly found patience vanished. "That's Lisa's brush."

"That's what I was hoping. Anyone else use it?"

"No. She's very particular about that."

"Good. You gotta Ziploc bag or something?"

Susan didn't have to ask what she wanted it for; she had read enough in the newspapers to know that Lisa's hair contained DNA and that her fingerprints would be all over the plastic handle. She got a bag from the kitchen and gave it to Ramos, who sealed the brush inside.

"It's almost twenty minutes now," Ramos said. "Let's get back; I got some balls to bust."

Susan held the door for Ramos to pass through, which she did in full form, like a queen, and it occurred to Susan that this slight, imperious woman shared qualities with Lisa. If Lupe Ramos had been half the girl Lisa was, with gifts that had propelled her beyond obvious stereotypes into possession of a New York City police department's coveted gold shield, then Susan realized she ought to trust the woman.

"Detective Ramos?"

The elevator arrived. As both women stepped in, Ramos cast Susan an ironic but warm half smile. "Lupe to you, okay?"

"Lupe," Susan said. "How long do fingerprints take?"

"A day, maybe two . . ."

Disappointment must have shown on Susan's face; she could not possibly wait a whole day or even two to learn if Lisa herself had painted the yellow line.

"For most people. For me? Coupla hours, tops." In the mirrored cube of the elevator, Lupe Ramos smiled a few dozen smiles. "So you really don't think she ran away, huh?"

"I know she didn't." They were back on the sidewalk now, Ramos walking briskly and Susan keeping up. "Lisa's the kind of kid who would tell me if she was going to run away."

"I know just what you mean." Ramos issued a cynical snort. "I got one just the opposite at home."

So she was a mother, too. Susan felt a moment of camaraderie before a stinging question arose in her mind: Was she a mother, if she had always pretended not to be? When she thought *mother* she thought of her own mother, Carole, with two daughters; Carole Bailey, the woman who had troubled to raise both girls from birth.

"Forensics better be done dusting that door," Ramos said as she pawed her way along Water Street in the direction of what appeared to be a crowd of police. "I wanna get in there, have a look around. Plus I got me a hankering for some good, strong dark chocolate."

Lupe Ramos got right to work, shouting like a carnival barker into the busy scene in front of the chocolaterie. Susan tucked herself into a quiet pocket, off to the side. She could see Dave, down the street with the Russian detective, trying to get into the building where he may have seen someone looking out the window earlier that night. Even from a distance he looked frustrated, and the Russian looked like an angry bear.

Under the dim light of a street lamp, Susan took out her BlackBerry.

I remember you when you were five in your Spiderman costume and how offended you were whenever someone called you Spidergirl. You just can't imagine how cute you were, running around in that costume. But then I started to have this same dream: little Spiderman, running down Front Street—in the dream, a steeper slope than in real life—turning onto Water Street, while underwater-slow dream-me calls for you to stop. The distance between us expands the harder I try to catch up. The ending is always the same, with little dream-you laughing, turning the corner—and vanishing. You see, it has never been easy for me and the dream-fear is just one of the feelings I've carried around that I couldn't share with you. Well, Lisa—I named you, you know—I don't ask for easy. I just want you back.

Susan sent the e-mail with a feeling of desolation. Lisa was gone. Some deep part of Susan's soul had always feared she would lose Lisa and had tried to warn her. And now she was *gone.*

Chapter 7

Dave and Bruno stood in front of the newly varnished oak door beside which a bank of intercoms offered a button for each of the four apartments.

"It's the third floor," Dave said.

"I'm Russian, not blind." Bruno pressed buzzer number three.

Dave had never detested anyone as much. Bruno was six feet tall, about the same height as Dave, but with twice the girth and so much hot air he could have floated a blimp all the way up the Hudson. Dave was appalled in every way by this man: his arrogance, his lack of professionalism, his disrespect for Dave's rank, even his head-to-toe black leather and that idiotic seventies cap. And Bruno wore cologne, lots of it; Dave had never trusted men who wore perfume.

There was no answer, so Dave pressed the buzzer again. Without waiting, Bruno pushed it four more times in blunt succession and then crossed his arms over his chest. Dave got it, and stood back.

As soon as he could get away from Bruno——once

they had been upstairs and talked to the late-night hor- ticulturist, if he or she even existed—Dave would call the night squad captain at his own precinct, the Seven- eight, and ask him to do a little research. If Bruno and Ramos were as hopeless as they appeared, Dave would pull strings to get another team assigned to the investigation. He would take it over himself if he had to, unofficially, since he was out of his jurisdiction. They had to find Lisa as soon as possible, before . . . He stopped that line of thinking, that bad cop-habit of dark expectation. They had to find her; that was all that mattered right now.

"Answer!" Bruno stabbed the buzzer again. "It's spicy cold out here."

"Listen," Dave said. "I *think* I saw someone look- ing out the window. I'm not even sure. Maybe we should—"

"Tonight your girl is missing in a mess of paint; you see someone watching out a window—"

"Maybe."

"Maybe, schmaybe," Bruno said. "On Monday me and Loopy are down here on a suspicious-person re- port and we don't find any suspicious person. So now I'm a suspicious person. You got it?"

"Monday?"

Bruno nodded and banged again and again on the door.

"A man?"

Bruno nodded and banged.

"And you never located this guy?" Dave asked.

Bruno didn't respond; the answer was obviously no. Now Dave understood why they had gotten here so fast after Officer Johnson had called them.

Dave looked away. Fifty feet down, more police

had gathered in front of Susan's shop and factory. An unmarked gray van from CIS—Crime Investigation Services—was parked haphazardly by the curb. In front of the shop's door, a forensics technician in white rubber gloves was crouched down, carefully brushing powder over the knob and surrounding surfaces with what looked like a basting brush.

Bruno took five steps back to look up at the third floor of the brick building where the unnaturally bright light still glared. In two angry lunges he was back at the door, pressing the buzzer over and over and over.

Dave ground his jaw and kept silent. He watched the light, knowing what would happen next. And then it happened.

"The light just went off," Dave said.

"Yeah, I knew the bastard had something to hide." Bruno then stepped back and shouted in his deep bass voice, something in Russian that ended with at least one exclamation point.

Dave walked away, back toward the shop and the police force he recognized. He thumbed a speed-dial number into his cell phone; there was no point waiting any longer to make that call to Sam Trachtenberg, the night squad captain of the Seven-eight. Sam was a good cop, a die-hard detective who could be counted on to gather accurate information, and he knew everyone.

"Oh, yeah, their reputation precedes them," Sam said with a bark of cynical laughter when he heard the names Lupe Ramos and Alexei Bruno. "Word is they'd win the Most Annoying Award hands down, every time, but here's the catch: They've never failed a case. . . . Uh, sorry, Dave."

"No," Dave said, "never mind." His tone was stoic but he knew he wasn't fooling Sam. Dave had once been the Seven-eight's best hitter, the one who had never failed a case—until Becky Rothka. Last October he had asked the Rothka family all the same questions he heard tonight about Lisa and listened to the answers with the same wariness of adolescent instability he had seen on Zeb Johnson's face: tolerance, doubt. No one in the Rothka family was an MOS, but Becky Rothka was a young thirteen, a true innocent, so he had stepped on the gas.

"So you think Bruno and Ramos are up to it?" Dave asked Sam.

"Word is they are."

"Well, Sam, if you say so. Just tell me how to convince my wife."

"Sorry, pal, that's up to you. So you working this case with them?"

"I don't know yet. And Sam, it might not be much of a case."

"Right. Let's hope. Gimme a buzz if you need anything, okay?"

"Thanks, Sam."

Dave clipped his phone back onto his belt loop and walked into what had every unsettling appearance of a crime scene. He hated how this was shaping up, hated all the reminders of Becky's disappearance last year, hated that some guy had been reported lurking around these very streets just days ago. *Hated* it.

The forensics technician was finished with the front door and was now working in the garage on the tool cabinet where the paint and paintbrush had been stored. Outside, Dave listened to Lupe Ramos bark orders to someone in the CIS van, insisting he take the

first set of prints to the lab *now.* The lady had some serious nerve. The guy in the van said they should wait,
and Ramos came back with a stream of threats and in-
sults that pummeled the man into acquiescence. The
van drove off with half a job that would probably dis-
place seven others.

Yellow police tape now cordoned off a whole section of Water Street; the yellow tape and the yellow
paint were the only vivid colors in the early-morning
darkness other than the bright pink splash of Lupe
Ramos. She drove the investigation like disaster
triage, using Bruno as her right hand. No wonder he
was cranky: According to Sam Trachtenberg, Ramos
and Bruno were equals, despite the obvious fact that
she treated him like a subordinate.

It was nearly four a.m., soon to break into a new
day, but outside it was still deep night. Dave was used
to all-nighters and the raw edge of exhaustion, but
Susan wasn't, and Lisa was *her* sister. He wondered
how his wife was coping.

He found her in the office at the back of the factory. It was a small room crammed with a desk and
two chairs. Bracket shelving climbed all the way to
the ceiling, holding wire baskets of recipes, magazines, inventory records, invoices, receipts—the entire paper blizzard of a small business, neatly
organized. Two green paper tickets tacked to a corkboard reminded him that they had had plans for that
very night: *Wednesday, eight p.m., Brooklyn Academy
of Music, New Wave Festival.* (He wouldn't have
been able to go with her, since he'd rotated into the
night shift—a condition of detective work that annoyed his wife and routinely stymied their social
life—and she probably would have taken Lisa in-

stead.) Susan sat at the desk, running through the electronic pages of her BlackBerry's daily planner. Zeb Johnson sat beside her, taking notes about Lisa's schedule in the last few weeks.

"Sweetie?" Dave stood in the doorway, warming his hands in his pockets.

"They want to talk to all of Lisa's close friends."

Dave nodded; it was protocol.

"That's it, I think." Susan handed Johnson a list of names and numbers.

Johnson stood up and thanked her. "If you think of anything else, let me know."

When they were alone, Dave shut the door and sat next to Susan. He told her about his call to Sam Trachtenberg, but decided to keep to himself right now the suspicious-person business Bruno had mentioned; she was already worried enough.

"I think Ramos is okay," Susan said. "We had a little chat. The other guy, the Russian—I can't tell."

"We'll let them do their job," Dave said, "and we'll see. Sam's got good antennae." He pressed a loose tuft of her hair behind her ear. She was wearing the ruby-and-diamond earrings he had given her on their first and only wedding anniversary. "Tired?"

"Yup." She reached back to touch his hand, which had settled behind her ear. Her fingers felt so warm. "You?"

He nodded. "I'm used to it."

"Dave, we need to talk."

"I know we do."

But after all these hours, when they finally had their chance, she fell silent. He took a metal folding chair from against the wall, fanned it open and sat solidly facing her. And waited. She seemed unable to begin.

Her silence unnerved him, and he felt he had to help her, jump-start the conversation if he could.

"I think Lisa's all right," he said. "I think she's taking a long walk somewhere, fuming over whatever happened between you two. I think she started the yellow line, then changed her mind and threw the paintbrush in one of her fits, just at something she was thinking. My God, think of the hormones raging inside a kid at the age of fourteen."

"It was a man's footprint, Dave. You said so yourself."

"Someone came along and stepped in the paint after she changed her mind about the line and ran off—"

"The police are taking this pretty seriously," she said.

"Of course they are, as they should. We *have* to take these things seriously, just in case, but the thing is, Susan—"

She sat forward suddenly. "Lisa is mine." Her eyes settled uneasily on his face, waiting for his reaction.

At first he didn't realize what she was saying. Then he felt a coolness emanate from his stomach and seep into his muscles. A coolness and nausea, like the sudden illness that befell him once while riding to work on the subway. He had fainted, been checked out by the doctor that afternoon and pronounced in excellent health. His colleagues had called him "pregnant woman" and "wimp" and "old lady" because worrying over one another's health was something the guys at the precinct did not openly do. He was a man, a cop, and he didn't get sick for no apparent reason. And he did not get sick from words.

But these were not just words. "Lisa is mine," she had just said. Meaning Lisa belonged to her? Meaning Lisa was . . . He knew what it meant; Susan couldn't

have been clearer. Lisa had been about to launch a
search for her birth parents, and they had fought and
Lisa had stormed out and was missing now. He knew
what it meant.

"I was fifteen when I had her." Susan's voice was
soft; it was the same voice that whispered "I love you"
in his ear when they had made love that morning; the
voice that had insisted she was not ready to have a
baby. "I'm sorry I never told you, Dave, I just . . ."

She stopped talking. He waited. This was nothing
like what he'd expected her to tell him tonight. It had
never once occurred to him that Susan could have
been Lisa's birth mother; that concept and all that
went with it had not once crossed his mind; never.

"I wanted to tell Lisa first," she said, "but I didn't
know how, and time kept passing."

"And you told her tonight."

She nodded, keeping her expression still and her
eyes on his face. "I'm sorry it took so long. I've been
working it out. It hasn't been easy."

He got up and paced the small office, hands
jammed in his pockets, eyes grazing her, then darting
away. It hurt to look at her now, which seemed ab-
surd. She was the same person she'd been five minutes ago; nothing had changed; nothing had to
change . . . did it?

"You said you didn't know if you wanted children,"
he said, aware of a growing inner bafflement, an itch
of betrayal. "But you never said you already had one."

"I gave birth to her," Susan said in a quiet voice,
"but I didn't raise her."

"What?" He stopped pacing and faced her.

"I gave birth to her, but—"

"Okay, I heard you. I heard you." He folded the

chair back up, rested it against the wall and resumed his pacing and thinking and pushing away of the cool tentacles that were creeping through his insides.

"Dave, I wasn't ready for a baby at fifteen. I didn't raise her because I wasn't equipped to be a mother then."

"But you did raise her, in a way. You kept her."

"My parents kept her. I did what they thought was right."

"So you're telling me you didn't want her. That even then you knew you didn't want children. You got pregnant, and because your parents didn't believe in abortion they adopted her themselves."

"I never said I didn't *want* her!"

He realized his summary had sounded chilly, but wasn't it essentially true? She might have had an abortion, he thought, then hated himself for thinking that because it was Lisa they were discussing—*Lisa*—and he had come to care deeply about her as her brother-in-law . . . no, her stepfather. What was he to this girl? What was she to him? What had happened tonight in Lisa's mind when she had received this same news? Dave's imagination saw her now, the look of shock on her face, the bristle of her movements as she raced out of the loft. He could imagine the chaos of her thoughts as she walked the streets of Dumbo and painted the yellow line, then stopped painting the yellow line. If it hadn't been for the man's footprint, Dave would have walked out of this office right now and called off the budding investigation. But the footprint altered the story; their story had been one thing—a triad of love and trust and secrets—but something else had happened next.

Susan reached out to take Dave's hand, and he let

her. Her skin felt warm and dry, comforting; he felt the longing of his love for her and the coolness of his confusion.

"Please try to understand," she said. "I was very young when Lisa was born. Mommy and Daddy and I made a decision together that I should go on with my schooling and growing up and they would raise Lisa. You can't possibly know how life was in small-town Texas fourteen years ago. A teenage mother? A *single* mother? It never, ever could have happened, not in our little enclave."

She had grown up Christian, Dave knew that, and he understood the historical and cultural context of the decision she was describing to him. He understood all that—in his head. But in his heart?

"What about the father?" he asked.

"Lisa's father?"

He stared at her; obviously that was what he had meant.

"Peter Adkins." Her voice sounded vaporous but her eyes were direct, pinned on Dave's face as she let the story out. "We were high school sweethearts but he was two years older than me. We dated less than a year. I got pregnant. Lisa was born. End of story." She paused, then added, "I told Peter I had an abortion."

"He never knew about Lisa?" Dave angled forward, incredulous.

"When I told him I was pregnant, he kind of . . . reacted in a way I never really expected. It was like he suddenly owned me. He assumed we'd get married. I told him I wasn't sure and he got so angry. He scared me. So I told him I'd already had an abortion and he . . . he said he hated me. He said I should have done the right thing and married him. Then he slapped my face, very hard." She lifted her hand to her face as if she could still feel the sting.

"He hit you?" Dave's surging emotions were mixed and powerful: his desire to protect her, even against past slights, and the sense that he was only now finding out who she really was.

"If I had never gotten pregnant," she said, "he would have been my teenage boyfriend; that's all. But now—"

"Lisa's biological father is Peter Adkins," Dave said, tasting the name, rolling it around his tongue. "Peter Adkins. Does he still live in Texas?"

"I don't know where he is now."

"Do you have any pictures of him?"

"Pictures?"

"For the investigation. It might help; you never know."

"You don't really think—"

"Everything needs to be looked at, Susan, without hesitation."

It was that word—*hesitation*—that clearly stung her most. But didn't hesitation always come at a cost? He wished she had told him all this sooner, hours ago, years ago; it was something he had always needed to know.

"I don't have any pictures of Peter anymore," she said. "I threw them all away a long time ago."

"What does he look like?"

"Dave—"

"No, Susan, that's not it." He felt no jealousy, just anger and betrayal and confusion and love and coldness and nausea. If Lisa hadn't been missing, he would have preferred never knowing what Peter Adkins looked like or what he had felt like or what he had thought or what it had been like to have fathered Susan's baby. "Just give me the facts, please."

"Blond, blue eyes, about five foot nine. Lisa resembles him."

Dave filed the information into the cop part of his brain: *Description matches that of a suspicious-person report in the area just two days ago.*

"Is there anything else I should know?" Dave asked, taking a single step away from her.

"Are you leaving?" she asked, and something unintentional sizzled between them. *Leaving the shop,* he knew she had meant, but another possibility now hung in the air. It was a question he hadn't considered and wouldn't consider now; nor did he answer her or kiss her or say good-bye. Without planning to end the conversation so abruptly, he turned and left the office.

Dave walked through the factory with its gleaming machinery and nested molds stacked on stainless-steel counters. Always, a heavy scent of chocolate hung in the air here. He didn't smell it today; all he smelled and tasted and felt was the catapult of transformation. Susan had lied to him, enormously, about her past. All their talks about having a baby together, about her not being sure, would have made different sense had he known her history.

He checked his watch: It was nearing four thirty. Somehow four hours had passed since they had started looking for Lisa. Four hours of time he, as a detective, had been deprived of a set of basic facts. One and a half years as a husband. Three years as a lover and best friend. He passed through the shop, onto the cobblestone street, into the chaos of a crime scene that suddenly was unlike any other he had experienced.

Peter Adkins, Dave thought; Lisa's father and Susan's first lover. He walked forward to give Detectives Ramos and Bruno the information about Lisa's real parentage, suddenly thinking of that famous line from Tolstoy about all happy families being alike. Until his life with Susan and Lisa, he had not known how universally that idea had translated to modern times, even to reconstituted families like the Bailey-Strausses. Until today they had been happy on the simplest and best of terms, happy individually and happy together. How could it be possible for happiness simply to evaporate? It couldn't, Dave decided, and if it was in his power to save Lisa and his marriage and this family, he would do it; but already he sensed that half the fight would be within himself.

He found Ramos and Bruno standing together on the sidewalk just outside the shop's front door, silent as a stubborn old couple.

Dave kept it as simple as he could: "Susan is Lisa's birth mother. Lisa just found out tonight, which is what they argued about. The birth father was told Lisa was aborted."

"Shit!" Ramos exclaimed; no subtle professionalism there. "You didn't know either?"

"Not until right now."

"*Shit!*" Ramos looked at Bruno, who was slowly nodding his head. "Whaddaya think of that, Brunofsky?"

"Women." Bruno grimaced at her and shook his head.

"That suspicious-person report you had here last week," Dave said. "Mind telling me the guy's description?"

" 'Plain' was what the caller said," Ramos answered.

"Blond," Bruno added.

"Medium height." Ramos.

"And the scar." Bruno.

"What scar?" Dave asked.

"Pink scar on his face." Ramos. "Under one of his eyes."

"Susan described Lisa's birth father as five foot nine with blond hair and blue eyes. She didn't mention a scar, but he could have gotten it after she knew him. His name's Peter Adkins, grew up in Vernon, Texas. He'd be about thirty-one now."

Ramos flipped open her cell phone. Its purple screen was vivid in the darkness, with a cartoony white poodle prancing back and forth. She dialed her night sergeant and requested an all-points bulletin on one Peter Adkins currently, or formerly, of Vernon, Texas. "Caucasian male, approximately thirty-one years old, blond hair, blue eyes, possible scar on face."

Dave walked away before she ended her call. He needed to be alone to think, just for a minute, until Ramos and Bruno had had time to regroup. Then the search for Peter Adkins would begin in earnest; finding him now was urgent. When a child disappeared it was always the parents, both of them or all of them, whom you sought first.

Chapter 8

Susan was startled by Glory McInnis's sudden appearance at the office door, just when she was about to succumb to an avalanche of sobs after watching Dave walk away. Glory's face was streaked with tears and her short cinnamon hair was stiff and messy from sleep. Susan had seen Lisa's best friend many times, but never like this; she looked as bewildered as Susan felt. Both parents stood behind her, each with a hand on one of her shoulders as if simultaneously siphoning themselves into her while holding her in place; he was white, she was black, and Glory's smooth mocha skin was their perfect blend.

"Did Lisa come home?" Audrey McInnis asked in her gentle Jamaican lilt.

"Not yet." Susan's voice was an unintentional whisper; it was the most she could manage.

"Teenagers wander off sometimes," Audrey said, "don't they." It wasn't a question but a statement. Yes, teenagers did wander off, and they came back. *Lisa will come back.*

Susan thought of the college students, a young couple whose recent disappearance had sparked a nationwide manhunt . . . until they turned up alive and well and hardly contrite for the turmoil they had put their grown-ups through. Their families had been unable to come up with a single reason for either of them to bolt, and yet they had.

Lisa, Susan reminded herself, had a reason. In a way, her disappearance even made sense right at this moment in her life. Lisa was nothing if not dramatic; painting the line, then suddenly throwing the paintbrush could well have been part of some emotional outburst. Maybe Dave was right. Maybe Lisa had decided to paint the line and then, on a swell of anger, changed her mind.

Susan pictured Lisa alone somewhere; she saw her at the helm of the Staten Island Ferry, her long, bright hair thrashing in the night air, drinking in the urban horizons and thinking and thinking and thinking over the news. Susan forced herself to see Lisa in gentle contemplation, because it was the only way she could stand to picture her right now; the alternatives were too frightening.

Then her mind veered back to the footprint; that partial footprint made in a hurry and nowhere near Lisa's shoe size. And her heart, already cantilevered over empty space, began the plunge.

Looking at Glory's pretty, tear-streaked face, Susan finally began to cry. Glory flew into her arms and she held her, wishing it were Lisa. After a few minutes, Glory pulled out of Susan's arms to say, "She would have told me if she was going to run away. No way would she run away without me knowing. No way!"

"Glory, baby"—Audrey ran a hand down her daughter's back—"you can't keep jumping to conclusions—"

"No, Mom! She just wouldn't! And you *know* they wouldn't be doing all *that*"—Glory swung her arm toward the office door, beyond which police swarmed the factory, shop and street—"if there wasn't something really, really, really wrong."

It was one of those awful moments when there was nothing to say; none of them had the answers, and Glory's melodramatic declaration seemed plainly accurate.

Neil shifted his sleepy eyes between his wife, his daughter and Susan. "That coffee rig working out there?" He was referring to the industrial Italian coffeemaker behind the counter in the shop. "I worked in a restaurant in college. How about we supply the troops with some caffeine?"

"Yes," Susan said, grateful for Neil's suggestion. "And let's put out some chocolates. Glory, will you make up a tray? Choose all your favorites, and Lisa's too. I've got to call my parents now."

"Come on," Audrey said, ushering her family to their tasks.

Alone in the office, Susan pulled the desk phone toward her and looked at it: new lightweight plastic, slate gray. She thought about what she would say to her mother and father. They were the only other people in the world who knew the whole story of Lisa's birth, and she yearned to consult with them about the confessions. There was so much to discuss, but right now, in the middle of the night—with Lisa gone—was not the time to pour out her heart.

She dialed their number. It rang and rang and rang; both her parents were poor sleepers and used earplugs at night. Finally, her father's gruff voice answered, sounding partly annoyed and partly alarmed.

"Hello? Hello!"

"Daddy, it's me, Suzie."

There was a pause, then a statement of irrefutable fact: "It's three forty-four in the morning."

"I'm sorry, Daddy." There was an hour difference between Texas and New York, but at this time of the night it hardly seemed to matter. "Maybe I should talk to Mommy instead."

"What's wrong?"

"Have you heard from Lisa tonight?"

"Lisa?"

In the quiet of his pause, Susan could picture her parents in their iris-papered bedroom, the dark wood of their carved headboard rising behind them.

"Did Lisa call tonight?" Bill Bailey's groggy voice asked Carole, his wife.

"Lisa?" Susan heard her mother's voice, sounding tenorless from her distance across the bed. "Is that Suzie on the phone?"

Susan felt almost lulled by her parents' dreamy state of half sleep, a sweet blur so remote from the sharp edges of her own night.

"Did Lisa call you two tonight?" Susan asked. "She's not home."

"Lisa's not home," Bill told Carole.

"What?" A warble of panic had entered Carole's tone.

"What's going on there, Suzie?" Bill demanded.

"Lisa didn't call you?"

"No, she didn't call us. What the heck is happening there?" His voice had come vividly awake.

Susan didn't know how much to tell them; it seemed unkind to frighten them, across so many miles, with details about the confessions and the paint.

And she was afraid to admit the worst: that she had not adequately protected Lisa in the big city.

"If you hear from her, Daddy, please call me right away. We've got the police here; everyone's looking."

"The police!" Bill nearly shouted.

Susan could hear her mother's panic escalating in the background of her father's voice; something falling off a nightstand, the thump of footsteps, the quick opening of the closet door where her parents always hung their robes.

"Tell Mommy not to worry." It sounded as false to Susan as it felt saying it. "Just call me if Lisa contacts you."

"We'll be on the first flight we can get."

Susan sighed; what had she expected? "Okay, Daddy. I guess I'll either be at the store or at home. I really don't know; I—"

There was a click. Bill Bailey had hung up the phone, sprung into action. Susan held on to the handset before hanging it up and thought, *What if Lisa's home right now?* Her next thought was that, with police stationed outside her building, she would have been told. But what if Lisa was on her way home? Or what if, by the time her parents arrived all the way from Texas, Lisa had been found—writing poetry on napkins in a Tribeca Starbucks, pacing the wide sidewalks of Park Avenue, brooding on the boardwalk at Coney Island, wherever a fourteen-year-old imagination might lead a distraught heart?

Were they all overreacting? Susan wondered. They very well might have been, and for a moment that possibility calmed her; but then she thought with certainty that the police knew better than to overreact. She thought of the yellow line, the dribbled arc of paint across the cobblestones, the footprint. And she thought about how her own selfishness had been a catalyst for all of this: Lisa's flight, Dave's anger, even the yellow line. She thought of her parents and how they had tried so hard to let her finish her childhood when she became pregnant so young. She thought of Peter Adkins, who had swept her away like a giant wave; and how, until the wave crashed to shore, she had loved every minute of it.

Susan remembered the first time she had set eyes on Peter in high school when *she* was fourteen. He was sitting at a desk in the middle of the classroom, swayed back in his chair; an eleventh grader, he had volunteered to serve as a student mentor in a ninth-grade history class. Arms crossed over his chest, he listened to Mr. Talbot explain the French Revolution.

"Marie Antoinette was just fifteen years old when she married Louis the Sixteenth, the king of France," Mr. Talbot was saying, when for reasons unknown to Susan even now, she turned around. Her eyes caught Peter's. She remembered the confluence in her mind of a brilliant, romantic, high-strung French queen and the sight of Peter's muscled forearms, dusted with blond hair, locked across his chest. As soon as she looked at him his eyes scrunched in a smile, as if he had been waiting for her to turn around. That was the moment. The beginning.

Peter Adkins, her first love. Not tall, not heavy, but somehow he had seemed large. Honey-toned skin, blond hair, eyes the blue of a gas flame. The twang at the end of each word when he spoke to her: "How many acorns can you hold at once?" The hoarse whisper of his voice in her ear. Their sticky palms clasping. The first time they had made love he smelled of wood smoke; the second time of dampness.

Three acorns, then; her hand had been small. Now, if asked, she could hold at least five.

Peter had been a star with no real outlet; he didn't act on stage or play sports or particularly excel at academics, though he was a good student. Instead, Peter shone in the eyes of other people, whom he collected along with their adoration. For a while, Susan had been his crown jewel; his attention had elevated her. She could still feel the special aura she carried with her that year at school. What she could never explain to anyone was how, outside the limelight, Peter deflated.

Her words, describing Peter to Dave just before, had failed to explain the boy she had loved. He was vibrant, mercurial, brilliant, sensual; and at the same time he could be detached and platitudinous, a discrepancy of persona he allowed when they were alone. To say her teenage boyfriend had slapped her face when she had told him about the abortion—or lied to him, rather, though he hadn't known it—didn't capture the moment. She could still feel the sting on her left cheek. She could see Peter holding out his hand, stiff as a board, actually looking proud of himself.

"I love you, Peter," she had said to him after the slap, out of an instinct for survival that thinly served the moment. After all these years, she still felt ashamed of that slap and of her reaction to it. At the time, she had felt ashamed of what she had done to deserve it. Then, over the years, she realized she had never deserved it and had grown ashamed of loving someone who thought she did.

"If you loved me, Suzie, you would not have killed our baby. You know you'll burn in hell for this."

She had learned that when he wanted real clout, he reached into his Christian faith for imagery. But all the kids did that back then—conjuring a religious patina to cover all sorts of bad behavior—and when he'd said those words, *burn in hell,* she really couldn't see it. Though as the years rolled on, the image had gained some weight as confusion and guilt accumulated into a kind of millstone she wore inside her skin.

When Bill and Carole Bailey had decided they would raise Susan's baby, an urgent plan had been put into place. The family house in Vernon was sold and, just as Susan's body threatened to look more pregnant than fat, they moved a dozen counties away, from Wilbarger to Panola, to the town of Carthage. Bill made the move alone, relocating his independent insurance office, while Susan and Carole spent the summer in Corning, Iowa, at Carole's sister May's farmhouse. When Lisa was born in early September, Carole stayed on and Susan returned alone to a new life in a new house in a new town. She had started at her new school just a week after Lisa's birth. She remembered the bittersweet disorientation of those weeks, going to school with her breasts taped beneath her shirt to stop the milk. After that, she saw Peter Adkins only once more, four years later: She noticed him through the broad window of a 7-Eleven, clerking the late shift, as she made a rare visit back to Vernon to visit a friend.

Susan knew by now that Lisa wasn't getting any of her e-mails. She took out her BlackBerry anyway.

How do you explain love? I wouldn't know where to begin. Love was seeing you right after you were born. Love is now, this burning pain in my chest.

A scraping noise from the factory, just outside

Susan's office door, jolted her. She sent the e-mail and stood up. Audrey McInnis was sliding a tray of chocolate truffles out of the rack and carrying it into the store.

Taking a deep breath, Susan walked through the factory and the shop until she found herself outside on the dark, chilly street. More police had arrived. In a kind voice, Officer Zeb Johnson informed her of what was happening, as if it were her right to know everything. It was a simple courtesy, of course, she being Lisa's custodial adult—or mother, depending on what the police now knew. Had Dave come out here and announced Susan's confession to everyone? Stood on the curb and shouted it out? No, Susan thought, that wasn't Dave's style; he would churn the information carefully. But surely Detectives Ramos and Bruno would have to know, and she resigned herself to the slow broadcast of her life's dearest secret. She had a daughter, whom she had sheltered from the truth but nevertheless loved. Susan Bailey-Strauss was the mother of a teenage girl who was now missing.

Workers for the early shift began to appear, and one by one Susan turned them away. The cordoned-off piece of Water Street was beginning to look like a film set, as if a *Law & Order* production crew had landed there for the day, a circumstance to which most New Yorkers were well accustomed. Some of the workers hung around as if they might be hired as extras until finally Lupe Ramos raised her voice to shout, "Police investigation! Clear the area, *please!*" It was the least polite and most effective *please* Susan had ever heard.

A bank of lights illuminated the search for physical clues, burning hotter and brighter than natural day. A cadre of police officers had gone off on a street-by-street canvass of the neighborhood. Dave had left with Alexei Bruno to "dig up some information"—meaning, Susan figured, to look for Peter Adkins—and also to interview Lisa's friends. Lupe Ramos alternated between directing the investigation and assaulting the horticulturist's door, at one point shouting into her phone about a search warrant that was not being issued fast enough. And the fingerprint analysis was under way to confirm—or discount—everyone's assumption that Lisa had been here tonight.

Finally, dawn arrived in full, unpeeling steadily across an azure sky. The police lights stayed defiantly on as forensic analysts combed through the yellow paint and cobblestones and concrete sidewalks for hair, fabric threads, any telltale remainders of an as-yet-undefined event. Police photographers systematically documented the scene from every angle with an unsettling workaday familiarity. Susan kept reminding herself of Dave's wisdom to let the police do their jobs, a challenge that got harder as reporters and television crews began to arrive. The police broadcast, Susan realized, had been picked up by the media, who now waited like vultures for any sign of blood.

Chapter 9

Wednesday, 7:05 a.m.

Dave paused at the entrance of the Brooklyn Heights Promenade to watch the pale light of early morning overtake the sky. Across the East River, lower Manhattan looked perfectly still, looming, throwing out great shadows. Dave thought of Susan and how fragile and despondent she had looked when he left her in her office. He could still feel the cool air on his hand when he pulled it out of hers and the abandoned look on her face that followed. He could still feel the moment of his own retreat and his inability to stop it. She was Lisa's mother. It made no sense and yet it made perfect sense.

Dave and Bruno had spent the last two hours interviewing Lisa's friends and schoolmates. They had just woken the fourth kid on the list, made her and her parents nearly hysterical with fear, and learned nothing. Bruno was now walking heavily up Montague Street, his back to the river, lighting a cigarette. Dave had been captivated by the spasm of light behind him and a sudden thought of Susan, for whom he yearned with a new sense of unrequited future, and turned around to look across the river at Manhattan, huge and stark. It was the same view from the loft, he was just noticing when his cell phone began to ring—the same view, yet the slight shift in angle completely transformed it.

He unhooked his phone from the belt loop of his jeans and flipped it open.

"Strauss," he answered.

"Dave, it's Marie Rothka."

Always, when he heard Marie's voice, something inside him froze. Last fall, in the early weeks of the search for Becky, Marie had called him often. Then the calls trickled to occasional reminders that the groom was still at large, when he felt bored or cruel and phoned in his occasional taunts to a still-grieving mother. After a few more months, the calls stopped. Hearing from Marie today, with Lisa missing, the timing couldn't have been stranger.

"He called. Just now."

Dave turned around and began walking in Bruno's direction.

"Okay, Marie. I'll check on the trace. Maybe this time . . ." Maybe this time they'd find him. Maybe, but doubtful. Each time the groom had called he had hijacked someone else's analog cell number. They'd get a crude location from which he would be long gone.

"There's more, Dave." She paused. "He said he has a new bride. He called her Lisa."

Dave stopped walking, and listened.

"He described her as pale and light. He said she was small like Becky," Marie cried, " 'but not as good.' "

The last time the groom had called Marie, six

months ago, he had told her he would "remarry," give
Dave another chance to find him, but "next time
change one thing." Dave's mind had entertained a host
of possibilities, individual alterations to a highly plotted crime. Up to now he had considered everything,
except that he might strike Dave's own family—because that had been unthinkable. The half-year silence
alone should have warned him. Between Becky's disappearance and the last phone call, the groom had
taunted him, circled him. And then he had simply vanished. Why hadn't Dave seen this coming? All the
pieces had been there—the two girls looking so much
alike, same age and same school last year on the day
Becky disappeared—and he had been unwilling to
look because he had not wanted to see it. He had always thought of himself as tough and honest, and he
was, but he was human and therefore addled by weak-
nesses. He had failed to recognize the vulnerability of
his family because the fear of losing them had been
too great. And just as he thought that, something else
came clear: the groom's strength was the opposite of
Dave's weakness—he was completely alone, and ut-
terly ruthless.

He told Marie he'd call her back, closed his phone
and broke into a run. So this was it; so this was how
the groom would one-up Dave, plunge the hovering
knife right into his heart. It would only have been
more perfect if he had taken Susan, instead.

In minutes they were in the car, Bruno driving im-
patiently in the direction of Tillary Street and the
precinct. Dave, in the passenger seat, held on to the
dashboard to absorb the jolts.

"First of all, you don't know it's the same guy. This
one, maybe he heard about Lisa on the news, put it to-

gether, now he's copying the cat." Bruno's voice was gruff and certain, with the stub end of his cigarette hanging from his lip as he spoke.

"No way the press has the news out yet," Dave said, though he knew anything was possible.

"You saw the reporters hanging like Vulcans at the scene." Bruno turned the car onto Gold Street and screeched to a halt in front of the squat concrete edifice of the Eighty-fourth Precinct. "Maybe it's not in the morning paper, but radio and TV?" He snapped his fingers and rolled his eyes, then squashed out his cigarette in an ashtray too crammed to shut. "Come on, man, you know as well as I do the news is out."

Dave ground his jaw; he had to will away every last bit of wishful thinking. Bruno was right: The news of Lisa's disappearance had to be out already, which meant the call to Marie could have been a prank from just about anyone who knew enough about Dave's family and his past cases to put two and two together. Dave thought of the article about him in the Metro section of the *New York Times* last year, featuring the Harvard-grad cop and his lovely family. Publicity for a cop was generally a bad move, but his sergeant had urged him to do it as a way of "interfacing with the city." It was in the wake of Becky Rothka's disappearance, and city families were frightened; bottom line, the brass had wanted to put a human face on the department's failure to save an innocent girl plucked from its streets. Dave had taken the department's bravado a step further when in print he had called the groom "a pathetic loser who wouldn't stay free for long." He should have known not to vent his frustration to a reporter, and as soon as the words had slipped from his mouth he regretted them; but it was too late. The paper used his foolish, impulsive remark for the article's headline. Every time he thought of it now, he cringed; goading a psychopath was never a good idea. The public had loved it, though. For a while, after the article came out, people recognized Dave; but then they forgot him, and that suited him better. Anyone could have seen the article, learned Lisa's name, seen her picture and made the call this morning. It really could have been a prank; but Dave was certain Marie would recognize the groom's voice. It then occurred to him that the groom himself could have been a prank caller, having heard the news that Lisa Bailey—sister-in-law of Detective Dave Strauss—was missing and decided to pull Dave's chain just for kicks.

They left the car in front of the station and hurried into the precinct's small, grim lobby. A front-desk officer sat behind a sheet of bulletproof glass; the dropped ceiling was discolored by veins of rusty water; four olive-green plastic chairs with cigarette burns sat empty along one wall. Not a welcoming place, but then no amount of new paint could have cheered up a typical urban precinct. Dave had a working knowledge of the Eight-four's stats; it was a tough precinct, with highly contrasting demographics butting right up against one another: the moneyed neighborhoods of Dumbo and the Heights, seedy Fulton Street feeding into a cluster of hopeful new malls, the crossroads of two major bridges, and low-income projects across the street from Metrotech Plaza, the spiffy corporate development that was a perfect hunting ground for drugged-out perps looking for easy prey.

They went upstairs to the Detectives Unit, a big

room filled with old desks holding a motley collection of computers and typewriters. It was not unlike Dave's unit at the Seven-eight: different room, same beige walls; different faces, same expressions. Dave then noticed, in a far corner, a single hanging fern with bright green leaves; someone was watering it regularly. He looked around him and wondered who was who, here at the Eight-four; who, specifically, was nurturing optimism.

Bruno went straight to his own desk, where he landed heavily in the room's only large executive chair, spun around and picked up his desk phone. He punched in a number and breathed into the receiver while he waited for an answer. Meanwhile, he hooked a nearby rolling chair with one of his leather boots and sent it in Dave's direction. Dave arranged it by the side of Bruno's desk and sat down. He checked his watch; in ten minutes he would call the CIS tech lab to see what, if anything, the automatic trace had picked up on Marie Rothka's line.

"Hey!" Bruno spat into the phone.

Dave figured Bruno was calling Lupe Ramos, with the assumption that he reserved his nastiest tones just for her.

"No, you listen to me for once! Strauss here's got an open case, one year ago, missing girl, never found."

Each phrase struck Dave like a piano hammer, hitting the wrong note.

"The perp's a psycho, probably butchered the girl; he calls the mother sometimes; he called her this morning, said he's got a new girl. Says her name is Lisa."

Dave heard the faraway prattle of Ramos's overheated reaction emanating from the phone. Bruno held the receiver away from his ear and raised one eyebrow at Dave, confirming what he had to put up with. Then he replaced the receiver to his ear.

"He calls her to make her happy! Why do you think he calls her? He gets his kicks. Listen to me, Loopy, we gotta figure out what we got here, repeater or copying cat or goddamn cranking nothing."

More tinny chatter spilled out of the phone.

"Strauss's got all his own case files on the way over. Two plus two, baby. I'm not *stupid*. It's you, me and him."

Dave closed his eyes and pictured Lisa the last time he'd seen her: sitting next to Susan at the kitchen counter, spreading cream cheese onto half a bagel, chirping about her acoustic guitar teacher. Her white socks had glittery silver stripes.

"We just walked in," Bruno said. "We gotta check the trace Strauss has on the mother's phone, see if it caught anything. I'm telling you we just walked in! Gimme a chance to look!"

Bruno slammed down the receiver next to the base of the phone and rolled himself to the neighboring desk. Contrasted with Bruno's messy desk, this one was almost schoolmarmishly neat, with a calendar-blotter in a maroon leatherette frame, a well-stocked mug of pens, and a small photograph of Lupe Ramos and a boy about thirteen years old pressing their faces together and smiling. Her son, obviously; he looked just like her. On the blotter sat a neat manila envelope with the location code for Forensics stamped in the corner. The fingerprint results. Dave wanted to snatch the envelope out of Bruno's lumbering hands but held back. Bruno pinched open the metal clasp as he rolled back to his own desk, snorting and shaking his head at Dave for more confirmation that Ramos's bossiness was out of line. He picked up the phone before the chair had stopped rolling.

"Yeah, got it. How the hell do I know? You sure you gave him the right phone number this time, eh? You want results, you gotta cross your *i*'s and dot your *t*'s, and I mean every goddamn time." Bruno slid the printout out of the envelope, scanned it, then handed it to Dave.

There it was: four fresh print hits for Lisa, one on the alarm keypad, two on the paintbrush handle and one on the screwdriver she had presumably used to pry open the can of paint. There was no question now that she had been at the store last night.

Dave closed his eyes and tumbled backward one year into the bitter moment when he realized the groom had gotten away. It had been the most helpless feeling of his life. The thought that the groom could be back—that he may actually have taken Lisa—sent a ripple of cool, nauseating dread through Dave's body. He sat stiffly forward in Detective Ramos's chair, forcing a deep breath and along with it the convictions of a second chance. This time, he would not be helpless; he would not allow that miserable psychotic creep to control him; this time, Dave would get him.

He picked up Bruno's phone and dialed Joe Rinaldi, a CIS nightwatch tech who often worked late. Whenever he called for a trace on Marie Rothka's incoming calls he could tell by the downshifted greeting that they had lost the groom again: the pause, then a break in the tech's voice as he began to speak, then the bad news about this guy's genius and how he hijacked analog signals to elude the digital trace.

"Hey, Dave." Rinaldi sounded energized; it wasn't the usual greeting. "I just picked up the phone to call you. We made the trace! You're gonna love this: It's a landline, and it's local. Blaustein's got a unit on its way over there now."

Chapter 10

The wailing of sirens along Water Street came with the suddenness of a deluge. Susan flew down the front steps of her shop to see what was happening. In the exquisite light of early morning, squad cars jammed to a stop just beyond the yellow police tape, sending reporters and onlookers into frightened clumps on the sidewalks. The police flung open their car doors, leaving them gaping as they ran across the street into the Café Luxembourg, the new patisserie that was due to open next week.

Everyone seemed to swarm back into the street at once, and it was almost impossible for Susan to get through. Lupe Ramos stood on the café's stoop, shouting into a bullhorn: "Stand back! This is a police investigation! Anyone interfering will be arrested! Do you hear me? Stand back *now!*"

A local television van pulled up, rigged with satellite dishes pointed skyward. A man with a large camera on his shoulder jumped out, followed by a woman in a red skirt suit. They spotted Susan and rushed over.

"Are you a relative of the deceased?"

Susan came to a standstill and looked at the woman, stunned.

"What did you say?"

"Any relation to the deceased?"

Was it true? Could it possibly be true that Lisa had been across the street the whole time and that she was, she was . . .

"Let the family through!" Lupe's voice pierced the chaos. "Do not bother the family or I promise you—" She stopped speaking when Susan reached the top of the stoop.

Susan glimpsed police inside the café. One of them caught Lupe's eye, slightly shook his head and shrugged, indicating, it seemed to Susan, that his search had come up blank. A cold sweat gathered on Susan's face. What exactly was happening here?

"Is it true?" Susan asked Lupe. "That woman said Lisa was—"

Lupe lowered the bullhorn and escorted Susan into the café. The door snapped shut behind them and it was quiet. What looked like a hundred faces outside gathered together, watching through the door's glass panels.

"It's not true." Lupe Ramos looked small, shrunken to her normal size without the dual elevations of stoop and megaphone. Her eyes were bloodshot around pin-prick pupils still reacting to the bright light of early morning. "They'll throw anything at you to get a reaction, so don't react, okay? You're gonna have to deal with this now."

The cop who had signaled Lupe to come inside approached her. "Zip."

Beneath the delicate structure of her heart-shaped

face, Lupe's jaw tightened. "I didn't think she was here; that woulda been too easy."

Susan followed Lupe through the pretty space: blue antiqued floor, round marble tables on curlicue black-iron stands, a huge old mirror framed in nicked wood behind a long espresso bar and pastry display.

"Please tell me what's going on," Susan asked.

"An old case of your husband's got a call today—"

And Susan knew: Marie Rothka. She knew all about the phone calls that poor woman got from the man who had abducted her daughter. And now, she knew all about Marie's sickening fear the day her child had vanished.

"—and it traced to here."

Susan also knew that the Rothka traces never came out. For a criminal as brilliant and elusive as Dave had described him, this didn't seem to make sense.

The next thought—*Why did that psycho call today?*—brought a wave of panic that nearly forced Susan to her knees. She sat at a tan marble table, pressing her hands over her mouth, her eyes darting over the marble's map of dark veins.

Off to the side Susan heard the café's door open, letting in an audible flourish of the chaos outside, and she heard the door click shut. She heard Detective Bruno's bass negotiate the usual harangue from his partner. She heard footsteps and then sensed more than heard Dave entering the café. She turned around and there he was, looking at her. The disquiet she saw in his eyes confirmed her worst fears. She got up and rushed over to him.

"Is it true, Dave? Did Marie Rothka call you?"

"It's true." His voice was low, intimate. He glanced around the café, his attention landing on an open door leading into a backyard. "Let's go outside where we can be alone."

The café's back garden had been tiled in bluestone, upon which sat five round iron tables with matching chairs. Christmas lights were strung along the wooden fences.

"Where's Lisa?" Susan couldn't help the hysteria rising in her voice. "Where is she, Dave?"

"We don't know."

"Why are we here? Why did the police come here? Why do the reporters think she's dead?"

At the hard sound of that last word, a floodgate broke and Susan's tears overflowed once again. Dave held her until she had calmed down enough to listen. Then he pulled out chairs for both of them and sat facing her.

"So far, it's just a phone call," he said.

"I thought of Becky last night, Dave. I thought I was being paranoid because I kept thinking about her not coming home that day. I *thought* about it."

"Sweetie, I thought about it, too," he said. "But thoughts aren't facts, and fears aren't facts. As soon as the media pounces on a case, we get bogus calls. And you have to remember that the groom used to call Marie Rothka periodically—"

"The *groom?*"

"That's what we called him."

"You never told me that. Why?"

"I didn't think you—"

"No, Dave. Why did you call him the groom?"

Dave sighed. "Susan, I don't think you *want* that much detail."

The way he'd phrased it, emphasizing *want,* told her the details were painful. In fact he had told her very little about the nuts and bolts of the case; much of what she knew she had read in the papers. "Tell me the facts, Dave, *please*."

"Okay." He nodded, watching Susan closely as he said, "He called Marie this morning."

"And you're saying this was his usual call?" Susan asked. "You're saying he made his regular call to Marie today?"

"We're not sure if that's what it was."

"Why?"

Dave paused before saying, "He said he had a new bride." The sun flashed on them, momentarily blinding Susan before a shadow made Dave visible again; he reappeared with a desolation in his eyes that frightened her. "He called her Lisa."

"My Lisa?"

"Yes, sweetie." Dave leaned forward to take Susan's hand, and the contrast of his warm touch made her realize how cold she was. "Your Lisa. That's what we think he meant."

"Our Lisa," she said, looking into his eyes.

He broke his gaze away from hers and nodded silently. A breeze caught a strand of the Christmas lights and rattled it against the fence.

"Dave?"

"It could have been a prank caller," he said. "Remember that, okay, Susan?"

"But why would a prank caller call from here? Please, just give me the *truth*."

As soon as the word slipped out, it hung between them like the golden snitch. His look was searing. He said nothing, but in his troubled eyes she could almost see the machinations of a betrayal she had delivered to him just hours ago—her ill-timed confession, her own

hard truth—as it curdled into anger and transferred
into renewed rage at his nemesis, this *groom*.

"If that shithead took her," Dave said in a voice
tense with frustration, "I swear to you, I'll find him
and crush him with my bare hands."

In Dave's eyes, in his tone, it became clear to Susan
that this was worse than any of them had imagined.
Even in her own fearful imagination she had never *believed* Lisa could have been abducted, like Becky
Rothka, by the *groom*. The moniker disgusted her
when she thought of its most obvious references: a
wedding night, an innocent girl, and . . . What came
next brought Susan's helplessness into her throat,
stopped her breath. She felt her face contort against its
will as she thought of all the things she wanted to say
to Lisa, and how now . . . now it was too late.

Chapter 11

Lupe Ramos watched Dave Strauss lead his distraught wife into the café's backyard for a private chat. Nice guy, smart, but maybe not lucky. Lupe wouldn't have wanted to be him right now. She wondered how he'd navigate the return of an ugly, unsolved case, the surprise of his wife's having told him a whopping lie, and the fact that a teenage girl he was supposed to watch out for was missing with a capital *M*. If Lisa's biological father turned out to be the suspicious person lurking around Water Street a few days ago, and if it turned out he took Lisa, and worse yet, if he turned out to be this Groom character, they were all going to be in for one steep climb today—Dave Strauss in particular. Lupe was aware that she didn't know this detective very well at all, but she'd seen cops go suicidal and homicidal under stress; she'd keep her eye on him.

At this point in the investigation, nothing was clear. Lupe still harbored the scant hope that Lisa was just your standard AWOL teenager on an emotional

bender, and that it might even be possible to get home
to Orlando in time to sail the Euphrates with him after
school. Why not hope? Wasn't that the stuff you were
supposed to start every new day full of?

Right now, they had one good fact: the seven-a.m.
call to Marie had been traced to a landline right here
at the Café Luxembourg. So it had made sense to
shoot some backup over here to check for missing
girls and random psychos. It made even more sense
that the cops who did the initial sweep had found neither. There was no evidence of breaking and entering,
which could have meant anything, including the possibility that whoever made the call had a key (or had
gotten a key, or had stumbled on an unlocked door).
Hopefully the caller had left some small clue lying
around, such as a set of fingerprints on the phone.
Hope *did* spring eternal.

"I'm gonna look for the phone," Lupe told Bruno,
who was crouched down behind the coffee bar, scanning shelves of delicate white espresso cups and tiny
saucers, dessert plates, and baskets of brand-new
stainless-steel utensils. "You check out the counter
area for starters."

He grunted. He hated it when she ordered him to do
something he was already doing; she couldn't imagine
why.

"I'll check out the office. Vronsky, you wanna hit
the basement when you're done there?"

"Since when do I get to want anything, eh?"

"That's an excellent question. Hmm. Let me think
about it." She walked away, both of them knowing she
wouldn't waste a second on Bruno's chronic frustration.

She passed a gleaming copper espresso machine
and found an open door to the right of an empty pas-

try display. On the left side in a short, dark hall was a
blue door with an enamel sign, WC. Across from it was
another blue door, unmarked.

The door was a few inches ajar. With her elbow, she
pushed it all the way open, careful not to touch anything. The office was ready to go, with a built-in desk
and shelves holding just a few files. There was an in-
basket with a small stack of papers, an out-basket with
a smaller stack of papers, a desktop computer, a
framed poster of a French liqueur advertisement leaning against the wall—the kind you saw at just about
every overpriced caffeine pit stop—and on the corner
of the desk, a phone.

Correction: part of a phone. There was a base—
black plastic, multiline, with ten blank speed-dial
slots—but no handset.

Lupe picked up a pencil with the end of her sleeve
and used the eraser to press the page button on the
phone's base. The handset did not respond. She
scanned the office, front to back and top to bottom,
checking every place the handset might have either
dropped or been set down. Leaving the pencil on the
desktop (so if Forensics questioned it she could tell
them, *Yes, that's the one I touched*), she went back into
the hall. Her eyes traveled everywhere, looking for
that phone. The bathroom with its hoity-toity pedestal
sink and white wainscoting. The coffee bar area where
Bruno had already checked, though not specifically
for a missing telephone handset. The café itself, with
its cute little decorative shelves and pretty tables. And
finally the backyard, where Dave and Susan sat together. She was crying; he was watching her cry.
Could have meant anything, but Lupe wasn't about to
probe.

"Been looking around for a telephone handset," she told Dave. "Did you hear a page?"

"Handset." He stared at her, digesting the word, absorbing the idea. "It's not there?"

"It's not with the phone base in the office," Lupe said. "It's not anywhere. I checked."

Just then Bruno appeared in the yard door. "Nothing in the basement," he said.

"Made any calls lately, Bronson?" Lupe asked him. "'Cause you didn't hang up the phone."

Bruno nodded deeply, understanding. He shoved his hands into his pockets and brought out his deflated pack of cigarettes. "Mind if I smoke?" Without waiting for an answer, he lit up, inhaling deeply and exhaling in a dragon breath of smoke. He picked a sliver of tobacco off the tip of his tongue.

"How far's the range of a cordless phone?" Lupe asked anyone.

"A coupla hundred feet," Bruno said.

In a world of satellites and Wi-Fi hot spots, that surprised her. "You're kidding me. They fly to the *moon* and send back pictures."

"Not this kind of phone," Bruno said. "Believe me, I know. In Russia, I was engineer."

"You sure about that?"

"Yes, I'm sure! I know who I am! I was *big* engineer—"

"No, Brunofskaya, I mean the range of the phone."

"Oh. Well. No." She watched the irritation pass over his big Russian face. She *loved* this guy. "Without the phone I'm not one thousand percent sure—"

"So we don't really know," Lupe said, "where he made the call from. And we don't know if that face you maybe-maybe-not saw in the window last night,

Strauss, is real. And we don't know if Lisa's right here or if she's on the other side of the city or the other side of the country by now."

"What we know," Bruno echoed, "is that we don't know."

"In a nutshell," Lupe said, shaking her head. "What time did Mrs. Rothka get her phone call?"

"Seven," Dave answered.

She checked her watch. "Over an hour ago. *Shit.*"

Dave stood up and it seemed like his whole body went rigid, like he was an arrow that was about to shoot.

"Listen," he said with the kind of tight voice that told her he wished he didn't have to take the time to explain all this. "He doesn't stay local; he leaves the area, that's his pattern. We've probably only got sixteen hours, tops, if it's the same guy who took Becky. Around midnight of the first day he had her, he planned to do some kind of ceremony with her."

"The *groom,*" Bruno grumbled. "A *marriage.*"

"That's how he thinks of it," Dave said. "He waits for nightfall, but midnight's the deadline."

"Why midnight?" Lupe asked.

"Something he said to the mother the day after he took the girl." Dave kept his voice low and his eyes off his wife, who looked to Lupe like she might vomit any second. "He told her he would kill Becky at midnight, but marry her first."

Susan buckled over, her arms folded over her waist, and wept.

"How we doing on our APB on Adkins? Anything yet?" Lupe asked Bruno.

"Peter had nothing to do with this," Susan managed to say through her tears. "I haven't seen him or heard from him in years. He never even knew about Lisa."

"Yo," Lupe said to Dave, just spat it out. "You didn't tell her?" Would it hurt Susan to know that some guy who looked like her old teenage boyfriend was spotted lurking around the neighborhood just two days ago?

"Tell me what?" Susan tried to wipe her face dry with the palms of her hands, but it was useless.

Like the nice guy Dave was, he hesitated before answering. *Sweet,* Lupe thought, *how these two hold so much back, always saving each other from life's ugly truths.* In her own romances she'd always taken the tough-love approach; but then again, look where it'd gotten her: alone.

"Ramos and Bruno answered a suspicious-person call on Monday," Dave said oh-so-carefully to his stunned-looking wife. "A man whose description matches Peter Adkins's was seen hanging around on Water Street. He wasn't there when the detectives arrived."

A deep vertical line appeared on Susan's forehead. "You think it was Peter? Here?"

"We don't know exactly what to think," Dave answered her. "We're collecting information right now, following any possible lead. But we have to keep open to the chance that it might have been."

Susan shook her head, saying nothing. The quiet after that was painful.

"Okay then," Lupe said, "let's get back on track here. Let's try to find the guy, for starters, and let's try to find the phone handset that made that call. Then we'll get some fingerprints if we're lucky. Then we'll know."

"If we're lucky," Bruno echoed.

Susan stared into space; poor woman. Over the

years, Lupe had dated her share of jerks, but at least the boy who'd gotten *her* pregnant when *she* was fifteen had had the good sense to die young and leave his memory intact. Not so Susan Bailey's first boyfriend, this Peter Adkins—stalker, groom, whatever.

Lupe took out her cell phone and keyed in an autodial to her sergeant. "Let's run a full Amber Alert on Lisa Bailey; you got the stats."

The precinct's conference room wasn't much to look at—a windowless, rectangular room with pea green walls and a dry-erase board that stretched across one whole wall—but Lupe had used it before as command central for tough cases. You needed a room big enough to hold a lot of people and to really spread your files out, and this was going to be it. Her sergeant sent her five detectives out of the rotation pool, and they arranged themselves around the long table.

Bruno, meanwhile, wheeled in his executive chair and parked it at the head of the table. Lupe rolled it around the corner, to the side. Then she put the biggest of the padded conference room chairs at the head and sat herself down. He glared at her, standing behind his oversize chair, but leave it to the big, tough Russian to say nothing about her little coup. Really, she *loved* him.

"Do me a favor, Bronski," she said, "and see if we got anything good off the call-ins yet."

A special police phone number had been broadcast for potential witnesses to call in any tips on the case. All the local television and radio stations had been airing the number since the Amber Alert went out. There were bound to be plenty of calls, there always were;

contrary to reputation, New Yorkers loved to get involved.

Bruno aimed two heavy breaths right at her before stalking out of the room. Dave Strauss either didn't notice or didn't want to notice. He sat down with the pile of manila folders and envelopes he'd had sent over from the Seven-eight and began to look through them.

A secretary came in with nice fresh yellow pads and plastic cups filled with sharpened pencils, which she dotted along the table's center. Ramos was about to get started briefing the other detectives when Bruno burst into the room, his mood brightened. He held a stack of papers listing a transcription of each and every phone tip. It looked like they already had at least a hundred.

"The power of publicity, baby!" Bruno plopped the papers on the table in front of Lupe's chair.

She gave everyone a quick rundown of what to look for, and between them all it took just a few minutes to pull out the interesting calls.

A couple who lived in Dumbo had seen Lisa in the park at about ten thirty last night, when they were out walking their dog. They said Lisa was alone, sitting on a bench, and seemed to be watching a man who was skipping stones into the river. The man was blond and average size, about thirty, but she didn't seem to know him. The couple did not see Lisa again after they left the park.

The next set of witnesses was a group of five young women. One of them, by mutual agreement, had placed the call to the police. They had finished dinner at the restaurant on Main Street at about eleven o'clock. They'd all had a little too much to drink but remembered that a medium-height white man with blond hair, wearing a brown canvas jacket, had been standing on the curb across from the restaurant. He seemed to be waiting for something, or thinking something over, and he seemed nervous. As they walked up the street on their way to the subway, they talked about him. One friend said he reminded her of a guy she'd recently been set up with on a blind date, and if this guy was on his way to a blind date now, he'd do the woman who was waiting for him a favor by not showing up. The friends had broken into laughter and were still laughing when they reached the corner of Main and Water streets. They all noticed a girl sitting alone on a curb. One of them had made a comment about her seeming young to be out alone, but the women were preoccupied trading stories about bad blind dates and they forgot about the girl as they continued to the subway. As soon as they heard the news reports this morning, they immediately called and e-mailed one another to confirm their memories of last night.

"Let's bring them all in, the couple and the friends," Lupe said. "We'll stack them into the interview rooms and get their statements." Her mind landed back on Peter Adkins: Old flame comes back to find his birth daughter and dole out a helping of revenge. It made sense, but was it true? *Was* Adkins the groom? It would be convenient: two birds with one stone. But Lupe didn't go for convenience; in her dinners, yes, but not in her work. She looked over at Dave Strauss. How exactly did *he* fit into all this? He was the guy who hadn't found the groom in the first place, and now it almost seemed like the groom had come back to provoke him into something . . . but what? And why? She wondered if the psycho was punishing the detective for calling him a loser in the *New York Times*. The entire NYPD had gotten a charge out of that one. Was that partly it? Had Dave Strauss wounded the groom's overstimulated ego? But there *had* to be more.

Chapter 12

"Two girls. Two Octobers. One year apart."

Five detectives Dave didn't know from the Eight-four kept their eyes on Lupe Ramos, standing in front of the long dry-erase board that stretched nearly all the way across the wall of the conference room. A metal lip at the base of the board held red and black markers and a roll of tape. On the left side of the board was Becky's name, in red; on the right side Lisa's, in black. Between the names, lines were forming, webbing their stories.

Dave glanced across the table at Marie Rothka, Becky's mother; he hadn't seen her for nearly six months. Her long dark hair had gone gray and been chopped short. She looked smaller now, fragile, though the day he had first met her last October she had struck him as a buoyant, earthy woman, the kind of busy mother you appreciated but ignored. For the past eight months she had volunteered at the National Center for Missing & Exploited Children, and when she had shown up at the precinct this morning, insisting her experience might prove useful, Dave had been unable to turn her away. He had learned that victims' families tended to react in one of two ways: They either withdrew in anger and pain at their loss or became determined and often effective helpers. Marie was the second variety. As the mother of a missing child, she held special status as a perpetually questing soul in search of answers. Dave had let her stay because he had come to like and respect her, and he refused to judge her desperation; he also recognized that she might in fact be able to help in some as-yet-undefined way. Looking at Marie now, so alone at the table of detectives, Dave's mind skipped to another helpless mother: Lolita's mother, Charlotte Haze. He wondered how her daughter's plight would have transformed *her* had she not been hit by a car just at the moment she'd understood the truth about her new husband's intentions for her daughter. Would she have managed to banish Humbert and save Lolita? Obviously Nabokov had *had* to kill Charlotte or there would have been no story, a mother being a child's fiercest protector. Just as Dave's mind skipped another step to Susan—was she a mother or not?—and the digression of his thoughts began to swallow him, Marie caught his eye and brought him back to the moment on the starkest terms. Her presence was a constant reminder that his failure to find Becky may have somehow led to Lisa's disappearance. The questions were how and why.

Ramos pulled a piece of tape off the roll and stuck Becky Rothka's photograph to the board. "Becky Rothka, last year, thirteen years old," she said. Next to Becky's photo, she taped Lisa's. "Lisa Bailey, fourteen. A year ago, thirteen. Same age. Similar physical appearance. Last October they were both eighth graders at the same school, but they didn't know each other. Another coincidence, or whatever; Becky was adopted and Lisa was adopted. Strauss, you wanna explain that? Dave Strauss here's got a gold shield from the Seven-eight over in the Slope," Ramos said by way of introduction. "He's been working Becky's case and he's also a family member of Lisa Bailey, the second missing girl."

The other detectives appeared to grow more alert at this information; they all now looked at Dave.

Dave felt sick seeing Lisa's and Becky's pictures side by side, their names connected by the undefined deeds of an evil man no one knew. He ground his jaw, hating himself for not seeing the connections sooner, but it was too late for regrets. The two investigations had merged and he was officially on the case now. Disciplining himself to focus his attention on the facts, he leaned forward and began the simplest way he could, with the basics every detective wanted to know first about a missing child.

"Lisa's mental state was excellent when we last saw her yesterday. She's been living with us for a little over a year, going to school. Well behaved, nice friends as far as we could see, no real signs of teenage rebellion except the usual verbal stuff. She's a freshman at LaGuardia High School in Manhattan, where she majors in singing. She's a good student, a good kid, generally does what she says she'll do." He leaned back into his chair, folding his arms across his chest, and continued. "Here's where it gets complicated. Lisa was adopted; that is, she grew up thinking she was adopted at birth by my wife's parents, Carole and Bill Bailey. They were her parents, my wife Susan was her sister; that was the family story. But the truth is this: Susan gave birth to Lisa when she was fifteen—and Lisa was told this just last night. The birth father was a boy named Peter Adkins. He was seventeen at the time, which makes him thirty-one now. He was told Lisa was aborted, so presumably he doesn't know about her."

Ramos wrote Peter Adkins's name in black on the board and underlined it twice, saying, "Adkins matches the general description of a suspicious-person call we got just this Monday, same area of Lisa's disappearance. White guy about thirty, medium height, blond hair. An anonymous caller complained about this guy loitering a long time on Water Street for no obvious reason. Man with a scar under his eye. We don't know yet if Adkins's got a scar, so that's one thing we gotta find out."

Three of the detectives sitting at the table scribbled that note; the others just listened. One of them raised his hand but didn't wait to be called on before speaking.

"Did Adkins have a facial scar back when Mrs. Bailey knew him?"

"I don't believe so," Dave answered. "But we'll double-check that."

The hand stayed raised. "Did we talk to this Adkins fellow yet?"

"Still tracking him down," Dave said. "CIS found out he left Texas nine years ago. They're doing a national search in the DMV database to locate him now."

"I'll do more," Bruno offered. "I'll get into some chat rooms, put it out there."

"Good," Ramos said. "Better check voting records, and go to the IRS if you have to. He might not drive."

"Every teenager in Texas learns to drive," said another detective, a young white man with a blond crew cut who looked like he would know.

"He might not drive *now*," Ramos said, "if he lives in the city. We get anything yet from family and friends?"

"None of Lisa's friends know squat," Bruno said. "No enemies, no big problems, she didn't tell anyone she was planning to run away."

"She didn't run away," Dave said.

"No," Ramos echoed, "she didn't."

"Lisa's verbal." Dave sat forward, hoping to create an accurate portrayal of Lisa, to make her real to these people who knew so little about her, to make finding her as urgent to them as it was to him. "Running away, avoidance, would not be her style. If anything she'd want to vent, really let Susan have it for not telling her the truth until now. Of course, it would be impossible to say for sure, but I can't see Lisa running away, and the yellow paint, especially the footprint, supports that sense of her."

"Ditto," Ramos said. "But listen, Dave, you know we're gonna have to dig anyway. LaPierre and Shabbaz, I want you two down at the home. Check out all the kid's stuff, get into her computer. Look for a blog or a paper diary or whatever and read back as far as they go."

Two detectives, a large black man in an orange shirt and a skinny Middle Easterner wearing a Yankees cap, rose from the table and left the room.

"Lafferty"—Ramos addressed the young crew-cut detective—"grab a partner and get over to her school, LaGuardia, up at Lincoln Center. Talk to the principal, her teachers, anyone you can get."

"Will do." Lafferty followed his colleagues out.

"I'll talk to the parents." Ramos looked at Dave when she said it. "I mean the grandparents. They on their way, Strauss?"

"Should be landing soon," Dave answered.

"Good," she said, turning to the board to touch a manicured forefinger to Becky's two-dimensional face. Dave was struck once again by the girls' similarities: Both were small with blond hair, green eyes and a dusting of pale freckles across their noses and cheeks. The photographs also showed the difference a year and different temperaments could make. Becky, captured by her father's camera in a bright summer sun, looked angelic, while Lisa's image hinted at rebellion, with her bare midriff, belly-button stud and dash of mascara.

Small like Becky but not as good. The groom's words of that morning resonated in Dave's mind. Lisa *was* good, though; having lived with her, Dave could attest to that. She was a complicated, bittersweet girl with a mind of her own, but she was *good*.

Dave's eyes hurt; he rubbed them but they only hurt more. His attention settled on the bulging files in front of him: a paper trail of Becky Rothka's disappearance. Lisa's high soprano seemed to rise out of the files; he couldn't stop hearing her voice.

The silver thread of a Joni Mitchell song Lisa had sung last week at a freshman recital at LaGuardia wove through his mind: standing alone on stage, drenched in spotlight, playing her guitar and singing. Lisa had mastered most of Mitchell's songs, and for reasons Dave didn't know she had chosen to sing "Woodstock." He remembered Woodstock—seeing it reported on the evening news, anyway; he was just four years old at the time—but for Lisa and her generation the passions of the sixties and seventies seemed to inspire an odd mixture of boutique recollection and yearning for meaning in a chain-store world. On stage, Lisa's voice had sailed beyond the proscenium arch and filled the auditorium, and for the first time, Dave really got it. He got her talent, her gift; why she had to sing; why she had had to come to New York. Sitting in that packed auditorium next to Susan, Dave had felt the first stirrings of real love for Lisa. Since that night, the song had hummed through his mind. And now, inexplicably, it made him recall a moment he had long forgotten.

Years ago when Dave lived in Manhattan, in another life, he had lain in bed with his girlfriend Claudia, in the Fifteenth Street apartment they had shared for five years, singing a Leonard Cohen song. He couldn't remember which, something poignant about a lost love. Dave and Claudia had sung together, tripping over the words and laughing at themselves.

Just two weeks later, he returned home from nightwatch to find that she was gone.

He did not pause to wonder if she was merely out; he knew she had left him. They had been arguing a single point for over a year: She wanted to get married; he wasn't sure. She had become passionate on the question of how he could live with her for five years yet not want to marry her. Dave, in a classic failure, had been unable to explain.

When she left, he was struck by how little he cared, deeply at least. He cared superficially, realizing he would have to move, since technically the apartment was hers. And he cared in that there had been a time he had felt he loved Claudia, and in some ways he would miss her. But they had never formed that essential, unassailable bond that a couple needed to hold them together. He had come away from his life with Claudia wondering if he was incapable of such a bond.

For the four years before he met Susan—during which time he had altered his life completely: making detective, changing assignments and even boroughs— he had dated many women but nothing lasted. One of his girlfriends told him, in parting, "You're great, Dave"—what was her name? Mia?—"but some men aren't built for commitment." He had come to agree with Mia; attracting women and courting them was never a problem, but walking away was a little too easy, and always tempting.

Then, when he found Susan—standing next to him on a work shift at the Park Slope Food Coop—she magnetized him in every way. He was bagging olives and without thinking he offered her one. A green, garlic-stuffed olive. She opened her mouth and tasted it; they both agreed it had a nice flavor, "Kind of a bite," she had said. From the first moment, everything between them was effortless. Loving her and marrying her were the simplest and the best things he had ever done. But did they have that unassailable bond? He had thought that they did—but did they?

From Susan, he had wanted everything: love, a home, a family. His desire for children had blossomed out of their love, and he had assumed she would feel the same way; but when he asked her, she hesitated. "I don't know if I'm ready to have a baby," she had told him, "or if I'll ever be ready." He had respected her need for time to think it over, but now the entire orbit of that conversation had tilted, and he couldn't understand how she could love him and live

with him and marry him, yet not share with him per-
haps the most significant fact of her life: that she had
already had a child. What else, he wondered now, had
she kept from him?

Still, despite the stinging sense of betrayal, the
thought of losing Susan shook him almost as much as
Lisa's disappearance, and the two potential losses
began an entwinement in his mind. Somehow, he had
to find Lisa, and to make his way back to the implicit
trust for Susan of which, just this morning, he had
been convinced.

Dave wondered where to begin and thought, *Anywhere.* He glanced at the file nearest him: a tattered
manila folder with phone numbers and names pen-
ciled across the top. Then he stood up and walked
around the table to the board. Ramos stood to the left
of Lisa, Dave to the right of Becky.

"We don't have much time," Dave said. "If the
phone call this morning really was from the same man
who took Becky, and if he really does have Lisa—if it
wasn't a prank from some nut—then we have until
tonight."

"It was him," Marie said. "I know his voice."

There was silence a moment; then Dave continued.
"With Becky, his pattern was this: The morning after
she went missing, Marie got the first phone call; later
that day, she got a letter. It was overnighted from a
drop box in the Bronx, signed in her name but not in
her handwriting. The letter was not, I repeat *not* di-
vulged to the public, so if we get a letter again this
time, I'd say the game is on. If we're dealing with a
repeat of the same crime, he may follow the same pattern, or not. I stress *if.* There are some obvious
conclusions we could make right now on the spot, but

I want to caution us not to do that. We'll have to trust our instincts today, but at the same time we need to process the facts." He turned toward the photographs of the girls. "They look alike. Both were adopted, or ostensibly adopted. They're the same age. The first thing we've got to do is boil down the essentials."

Bruno drummed his tobacco-stained fingers on the tabletop and leaned slightly forward. "Why this phone call today to Marie? Why not to your wife?"

It was an excellent question, and Dave did not have an answer. "All I know is that for the last year, the groom has made it a game to taunt Marie. We can't say right now how the game might be changing today. We'll have to see."

Ramos sat down at the head of the table and ripped off the top sheet of her legal pad. She began to make a list, the headers of which she recited aloud: "Birth dates, birth places, birth parents. Let's start right there."

"Becky's birthday was . . . is September sixth," Marie offered.

"Lisa's is September second," Dave said.

Ramos wrote the information neatly on her pad. "So when Becky disappeared, she just turned thirteen."

"Yes," Marie said.

"And Lisa at that time, a year ago, was also just thirteen."

"That makes them not possibly blood sisters," Bruno said.

"Not *full* sisters," Ramos said. "Not the same mother."

"Could be the same father, though," Bruno said. "This Peter Adkins, maybe he got around."

"You know anything about that, Strauss?" Ramos asked.

"No," Dave said, discomfited by the thought that Susan's young lover might not have been faithful to her.

"Where was Lisa born?"

"Texas, as far as I know," Dave answered; though the truth was, he had never asked.

"What do we know about Becky's birth mother?" Ramos asked Marie directly.

Marie took a deep breath, the tendons arching out of her thin neck. She unwove her hands, placed them flat on the table and sat forward. "Becky was born in Lawton, Oklahoma, to a woman with three children and a husband who had just died of emphysema. We ran an ad saying we wanted a baby and were willing to pay well, and Carla answered it."

"Lawton," Ramos said. "That share a border with Texas, by any chance?"

Marie nodded, glancing quickly at Dave.

He remembered now how close Lawton, Oklahoma, was to Texas; right over the border, not too far from Vernon, where Susan had grown up. And he remembered how Loder Hull, Becky's birth father, had jumped onto their radar screen when it turned out there was no death certificate for him at the Lawton City Hall. He'd flashed on their screen pretty hotly for as long as it took to determine that his death certificate had been misfiled under *L* instead of *H*. It had been an innocent mistake, but in the hour-long interim when the dead man became a real suspect, Dave's imagination had processed dozens of scenarios. Loder Hull had become a monster in his mind, a father with hidden depths of rage against his own flesh.

"Birth father's death was confirmed?" Ramos asked.

"Yes," Dave said.

"How old were Carla Hull's other kids at the time Becky was born?"

"We never met them," Marie answered, "but I believe they were all very young. When we spoke on the phone there was always crying and shouting, you know, chaos."

"Any of them ever come looking for their baby sister?"

Marie shook her head. "No."

"We pretty well established that no one in the Hull family had anything to do with Becky's abduction," Dave said. "We talked to them all. Everyone checked out."

"Who were your suspects at the time?" Ramos asked Strauss.

Dave didn't have to look at his files to recall the roller-coaster ride through the hall of mirrors those days and weeks following Becky's disappearance; the names and faces that took on gruesome dimensions before vanishing from view; the dizzying heights when he thought he was onto something and the plunging disappointment when he realized he wasn't.

"We looked hard at one of Becky's teachers who was trafficking in pornography on the Internet," Dave said, "but he wasn't interested in kids and he had a solid alibi. We also tried to find a guy the mailman saw lurking around the outside of Becky's school that day. Guy was zipped up in a red sweatshirt, wearing the hood, long sleeves, long pants. We couldn't get much on him and he wasn't seen again. All we know about him was that he was average height, and white."

The detectives remaining in the conference room traded glances and nodded. Dave knew what they were thinking, because he was thinking it too: an average-looking white man, probably with blond hair under his red hood and possibly a scar beneath one eye. They were all fixing on Peter Adkins as Ramos and Bruno's suspicious person and Dave's groom. Maybe they were right. But what if they were wrong?

"Then?" Ramos asked.

"Nothing," Dave said. "By night, we had nothing."

Ramos faced her table of detectives. "We got two girls born the same week in the same general area. Both adopted out. Similar physical description. White guy lurking around Becky's school. White guy lurking around Lisa's neighborhood. And we got the phone call this morning."

She paused to let her gaze jump from face to face to face, commanding full attention in the room's sudden quiet.

"Okay," she said, "let's just say the groom is Peter Adkins, Lisa's birth father. Let's say he's trying to get his due as a father, or maybe he's out for some kind of revenge since he was told his baby was aborted and he found out she wasn't. Let's just say he was looking for Lisa the first time but took Becky by mistake—easy, since the girls at thirteen looked a lot alike, their birth records probably trace to the same part of the country, and they went to the same school. Let's say this guy's not quite right in the head and he's got Lisa now, and for whatever sick reasons of his own he plans to do to her the same he did to Becky."

Dave glanced at Marie, whose face had gone pale at the straightforwardness of Ramos's analysis: two girls caught in the same web, with Becky taken, simply, by mistake.

Ramos walked over to the board, picked up the red marker and circled PETER ADKINS, adding a floating question mark beneath it. Then she drew a red tendril reaching to Lisa's black name.

Watching Ramos, with the first blossom of Becky's and Lisa's twining maps in red and black behind him, Dave felt an unwelcome yet familiar impulse. An image of Peter Adkins began to form and hover in his mind—a man he knew almost nothing about, who therefore could be capable of anything. Dave's thoughts kept turning back to Loder Hull. In the hour he had been a suspect in Becky's abduction, the man had been many things. He had been a hardworking father whose death truncated a happy family life; and he had been a stalker, a rapist, a killer of young girls. Now as Dave thought about Peter Adkins and who he might be, his mind veered similarly in all directions. Not knowing enough about him was what crawled under Dave's skin. His mind swerved between the two men, between Peter Adkins and Loder Hull. A year ago he had spent whole minutes wrapped up in the possibility that Loder Hull had never died, that he had come back to harm his own daughter. Then he had been wrong. Was it wrong now to think that Peter Adkins might have done the same?

"What's happening with our warrant for Seventy-seven Water Street?" Ramos asked Bruno. "We got to find out what that freak upstairs saw."

"Still on the DA's desk." Bruno snorted. "I been calling them, believe me you."

"Call Johnson's cell," Ramos told Bruno. "Find out if he's been able to keep the building sealed. And tell him to keep ringing doorbells. This warrant is taking too long; we gotta get inside."

"Lisa won't be in that apartment," Dave said, knowing Ramos didn't think so either. If any of them really thought Lisa was that close they would have broken down the door hours ago. The face Dave thought he'd seen in the window was growing vaguer, and he felt increasingly certain he had imagined it; a ghost in a bright light, it evaporated as soon as he tried to remember it. Still, the missing handset from the Café Luxembourg was a concern; the call to Marie had been made from someplace nearby. Ramos was right—they needed to get inside that building, if only to cross it off their list—but Dave's gut told him they would not find Lisa there. "His pattern before was to get her far enough away, somewhere that felt safe to him but someplace close enough to get to relatively quickly. Remember, Becky's letter was sent from the Bronx, and that was where we found—" Dave stopped himself.

"You can say whatever you have to," Marie said softly.

He didn't need to say it; they all knew what had been found of Becky in that Bronx Dumpster: tiny green beads from her necklace, soaking in a marinade of blood.

"If it's Peter Adkins," Dave continued, "he's close, but not that close."

"We got the Amber Alert covering the whole tristate area," Ramos said. "Transit, Housing, Port Authority, Aviation, Canine—everyone's on alert. How far away could they be?"

Chapter 13

Lisa woke up in a cold sweat, knowing something was missing. Something was wrong. That feeling of having forgotten something—like her keys, or her tampons, or to brush her hair before leaving the loft—came over her in a panic.

And then, bit by bit, her mind oriented itself to where she was. She could smell and feel and hear things: mold, a scratchy rug, the drone of motion.

She was in a car. In the trunk of a car. Lying on her side. Her arms and legs were collapsed together in front of her and they were tingly; she tried to stretch them but there was no room in the trunk. It was dark in here, and smelly. She remembered now.

It was a small red car. The back bumper was smashed in on the left. He had put a gun against her spine and made her get into the trunk.

The trunk was sealed tight and her eyes couldn't adjust to the dark. But her mind was waking up. She remembered now: She had been so afraid.

The loner guy had stopped in front of her.

"What's the yellow line for?" he had asked her. He stood there in his tan canvas jacket with a dark brown corduroy collar, passing a stone back and forth between two hands. She had felt afraid of that stone; it was her first signal. He had a high forehead, wispy blond hair, a dimpled chin.

"People park here that shouldn't," Lisa said. "Block us in."

"Who's *us?*"

He tossed the stone between his hands. She stood up. The paintbrush dripped by her side but it seemed unwise to take her eyes off him.

"Me and my parents." She told it as a lie, then realized it was true: If Susan was her mother then that made Dave her stepfather, and technically they *were* her parents.

He kind of smiled then; a thin-lipped smile, almost a smirk.

"So where are they now? Letting you out all by your lonesome this late."

His words had the same Texas limp hers did. He sounded like a local, displaced here in Brooklyn, like her. Only here she felt more at home than she ever had in Lindsay, despite the comfortable life Mommy and Daddy had given her.

Like a real New Yorker, she stared him right in the eye. She drew herself up tall and stepped forward, over the yellow line, into the street.

"What do you want?" She didn't see why she should let him bring it up first.

"What I want," he said. "What I *want.*"

That was when he slipped the stone into his pocket and took out the gun. It was not even a good-looking gun: it was blunt-nosed and rusty.

"No way, loser." Lisa threw the paintbrush at him but missed; it landed a good foot to his left and splashed yellow onto the cobblestones. She ran as fast as she could in the direction of home, but he was taller than she was and each one of his steps brought him closer. She heard the squish of his shoe hitting the edge of the yellow splotch and saw the footprint he left just before he reached her, and she thought, *Good*. Dave always told her that a detective needed one good clue.

As soon as he got the gun into her back, she was smart enough to stop. Or dumb enough. That was what she couldn't decide now, pressed into the dark, stinky trunk that was going, going, going somewhere. The sound of a road was endless when you couldn't see it. You could hear every pebble and every notch on the asphalt, and you could even hear if the driver lost his nerve: He slowed down just a little, then sped up, changing his mind.

Never get into a car with a stranger, Mommy had often told her, sounding paranoid; why on earth would she even consider it?

Never get into a car with a stranger, Dave had instructed, sounding authoritative, because he knew things regular people didn't know. Like that girl Becky, who vanished last year, *poof,* right off the street near their school. Dave had imagined aloud if a car had pulled up next to her and offered her a ride on her way home. "One minute she was there," he had said, "and then she wasn't." Lisa wondered why she was thinking about that now, but *knew* why she was thinking about it, and tried to push it out of her mind.

She remembered last night. There it was, parked up the street from the chocolate shop, a red car Lisa hadn't noticed lately. It was always parked there, it seemed to her, and so had blended into the scenery; she had stopped seeing it after the first time, months ago, but now it was the only car on the street and it was bright red.

He took her to the car, keeping quiet while she talked to him.

"What are you doing this for?" she said. "You don't really want to do this. What if I was your mother or your sister? Please, sir, think about *that*." Yes, she had actually called him *sir. Dufus,* she thought now. *Idiot.*

That ugly gun made a cold, hard ring on her spine.

"I saw you skipping stones before," she said. "You got better. It just takes practice."

He popped open the trunk with his free hand. "Get in."

She got in. As simple as that. Saying, "You still have time to change your mind."

He slammed shut the trunk door.

It was so dark she couldn't see her watch. She had no idea what time it was, how long she had been here, how far he might have taken her. Was it still night-time? Was it day?

She would try her voice: "Help!" It filled the trunk, resonating inside her body.

She felt around for an inside trunk latch. They said that some of the newer cars had them for just this reason, or if you got stuck inside your trunk *by mistake.* Well, who got stuck in their trunk by mistake? No one did. It was just that there were so many carjackings these days. And kidnappings. That was what this was: a kidnapping.

There was no trunk latch and no light. She felt around for anything else but it was completely empty. No one kept their trunk this empty unless they cleared it out on purpose. He had prepared, then; planned this.

"Help!"

She pounded on the inside of the trunk. Pounded and pounded. She could practically see all the cars whizzing past, drivers listening to their radios and CDs and iPods. No one knew she was there, inside the trunk of the little red car. She pounded and pounded.

But all her shouting and pounding seemed useless. She felt dizzy and a little sick. She thought of Meg in *A Wrinkle in Time* and how she felt herself getting sucked inside out when she time-traveled at first. She felt her body crackling apart, and was surprised when she came out whole on the other side. It was Lisa's favorite book of all time and she'd read it through twice. It was about a girl, age fifteen, who wasn't nice and had trouble concentrating in school, who lived with her mother and two brothers, and who was obsessed with finding the father who had left them two years before. She met some strange people and ended up on another planet, where her hotheaded obstinacy was the very thing that saved her and helped her find her father, who against his will had been held captive on the evil planet, and who had wanted nothing more than to see his family again. So Meg's bad start was her happy ending. The end.

"Help!" she tried again.

And then she felt him decide something: The car swerved gradually to the right and began to slow down. The tires hummed a little as they took a curve—were they exiting the highway?—then gained some speed on another straight road. It wasn't long before the car took another curve, a sharp one this time, then pulled to a stop.

Lisa wondered if the loner guy planned on opening the trunk, now that they had stopped. Then she realized he wasn't a loner anymore, technically, since he had her. He would need a new name, but she couldn't think of one that could fit a person who would do such a thing. People named Orville or Lamont or Wendell always worked hard to be normal. This guy probably had an average name, a name he'd worn all his life like a mask over his gruesome nature, something like Bill or Bob or Dick. No one was named Dick anymore, so that would be it: Dick.

Would Dick let her out right here, wherever they were? Lisa supposed he would, if they were alone, and suddenly she didn't know if she should be more afraid of being taken out of the trunk or staying in it.

"Do I need a key?" she barely heard a man's voice asking.

Someone answered something about a hook and a door. It was hard to make out exactly what they were saying from inside the trunk. She thought she heard some distant footsteps, and the sound of a door opening and closing, and the hum of a car driving off. She heard another car pull up.

They were at a gas station.

She punched her fist on the underside of the trunk, feeling the sting of metal on flesh each time she hit, hit, hit. The sound it made wasn't loud enough, so she started to yell.

"Hey! Someone! Get me outta here! In the red car! He locked me in the trunk! *HELP!*"

Her voice boomeranged inside the tight little space and she had to quiet down a minute to see if anyone had heard her. The lull was so complete, she thought someone was listening.

"HELP ME. I'M INSIDE THE RED CAR. PLEASE DON'T LET HIM TAKE ME."

There were some more voices; then the red car shifted its weight and her whole body reverberated with the slamming of a door. The motor revved. The car swerved backward, paused, moved forward and began to pick up speed.

Chapter 14

Susan listened to Dave's voice crackle on her cell phone, trying to make out his words through a tunnel of static that had suddenly engulfed the conversation. As she began to lose him, she saw—through the window of her chocolaterie—Officer Johnson help her mother and father out of a yellow cab. Glory, Audrey and Neil McInnis sat with her at one of the small front tables, drinking cocoa; Susan's was untouched, with a brown film floating across the top.

"Dave? Are you still there?"

He had asked her about Peter Adkins and she had started to answer as calmly as she could, her mind fighting the suggestion that the boy she had known and loved might have turned into a kidnapper—or a killer. Susan could hardly believe the police were making such a wild leap. Yes, he had slapped her in anger, but just that one time. Peter Adkins had been a popular, fun-loving boy, the life of the party; they had loved each other; there was no way he could have taken Becky and now Lisa; there was no way Peter

Adkins, Lisa's biological father, was the groom. It had
to be a coincidence that a similar-looking man had
been spotted on Water Street the other day. How many
blond thirty-one-year-old men must there have been
walking the streets of New York City? Tens of thousands, Susan would have guessed.

"Susan? I want—"

Dave's voice crumbled and then fell to silence as
their connection dissolved. She wished she knew what
he was thinking and that she could share her thoughts
with him right now, but there was such a distance between them. He was a cop doing a job. She was a
woman striving to understand what exactly was true
and real. She was so terrified for Lisa she could barely
think.

Dave's voice returned. "Susan?"

"My parents are here."

"We'll need to talk to them."

"Of course."

"Susan, I—"

"Dave?"

Their connection dropped out completely this time.
Susan wished she knew what he had been about to
say: "I love you," or "I'm not coming home," or simply, "I'll see you later."

A throng of reporters gathered around Carole and
Bill Bailey. Susan watched questions being thrown at
her stunned parents as Johnson shook his head, refusing comment on their behalf, and pulled them forward.

They hadn't brought any luggage, but her mother
had her enormous purse, which might have counted; it
was a big, brown leather tote she took everywhere.
She huddled against Johnson as he guided her through
the media circus. Bill followed, head down. They

were a quintessential Southern couple in their late fifties: lean and handsome, neatly groomed, wearing perpetually stoic smiles that normally promised confidence but now, in this context, looked dazed. Carole's short, teased hair had gone slightly blonder but was still well within the bounds of good taste. Bill's silver hair had thinned. Susan was shocked to see how much older her parents looked since last spring.

Johnson opened the shop door to let her parents in, pulling it quickly closed behind them. Outside, he shook his head at the reporters, then turned down Water Street in the direction of the building the police had been trying unsuccessfully to enter.

"Suzie." Carole lifted a hand to gently touch Susan's face. "All those police. Have you heard from her?"

"Not yet, Mommy." The hum of her own voice sounded thin and small, and the little-girl *Mommy* coming from a grown woman rang with contradictions: If Susan was to be a mother now, how could she still be a child?

They fell into each other's arms. Susan reached a hand out for her father; the shoulder of his wool overcoat felt hard and cold. He smiled and touched a chilly finger to her hand.

"Let's don't lose faith, Suzie," he said.

As a child, she used to call her newly sober and born-again father "the minister" behind his back, though in fact he was an insurance salesman. The one time he had caught her saying it, his refusal to be offended—in fact, his insistence on taking it as a compliment—had shamed her. "I'm proud of my faith, Suzie," he had said, "and you should be, too."

"I won't lose faith, Daddy."

"Let's pray for Lisa."

Susan, Carole and Bill huddled into an embrace, their heads tilted into a gently touching triad. Susan closed her eyes and listened to the murmur of her father's voice, asking for Lisa's fast and safe return. Behind them, she heard Audrey join the prayer. In the whispering moment Susan began to feel comforted, but then she had the loneliest thought of her life: *Our prayers are selfish, contradicted by reality.* As soon as she thought it, she hated herself for thinking it, but it was too late. The voice in her mind was too strong to ignore; it was Lisa's voice, insisting Susan take another look.

Like Dave, Lisa was a nonbeliever, though unlike him she was an agnostic holding out the slim chance of a power greater than herself. Each minute that passed without her now brought her voice more desperately into Susan's consciousness. Lisa was adamant that God had abandoned her at birth. For the first time, Susan began to wonder if that could be true, and if in fact she herself had abandoned God by abandoning Lisa. She may not have literally abandoned her baby, but she had bargained with motherhood, and didn't that basically count as an abandonment of faith? Because if you couldn't live authentically, how could you expect innocence from a mean world? And if you couldn't expect innocence, forgiveness, how could you maintain a faith in God?

Until last night, as far as Lisa knew, she had been turned away by her birth mother; that was *her* truth. How could Susan have expected her confession to reverse Lisa's long-held truth of her own abandonment? How could Susan hold on to the faith that God had her best interests in mind when so many of her judgments and actions seemed patently mistaken?

Susan felt almost violently confused and pulled away from her parents, taking her seat at the table with the McInnises. Carole rested her large purse on the table to Susan's right and waited for someone to tell her what to do; it was a rare thing to see her mother out of her Texas milieu, without direction.

"Maybe it's time for us to go home now," Audrey said. Susan had appreciated the McInnises' insistence on keeping her company, but it was in fact a little awkward now that her parents had arrived.

"Thank you for being here, Audrey," Susan said. "And Neil and Glory—thank you."

"I don't want to go." Glory's voice was stubborn, her eyes bloodshot. "I want to stay until they find Lisa."

"But honey—" Audrey began, cutting herself short at the sight of her daughter's stubborn expression. "All right. I'll stay with you. We'll all stay right here; there might be some way for us to help."

Susan looked at her parents, standing in the shop after their long journey, no idea what to do next. She couldn't just keep them here, anxiously waiting amidst the chaos.

"Mom? Dad? You haven't seen Lisa's room since we painted it."

"Lavender," Carole hummed, remembering.

"Come on," Susan said. "Let's go home."

Carole picked up her purse. Bill slid his arm through hers and they started toward the shop door. Outside, the mob of reporters gathered, sensing motion.

"I'll go first." Susan stood up, strode past her parents and opened the door.

As soon as they walked into the loft, Susan heard sounds coming from Lisa's room.

"Lisa!" she called. "Lisa?"

Carole and Bill followed Susan down the short hall. Lisa's bedroom door was open, and as they got closer the sounds got louder: clicking, like someone was tapping on a keyboard. Susan went in first, flooded with relief and joy at the certainty that she would find Lisa sitting at her computer, IMing friends or maybe even reading Susan's e-mails, beginning to understand and possibly to forgive.

But it wasn't Lisa. It was two men. One, in a bright orange shirt, was at Lisa's desk scrolling through her computer documents; the other, in jeans and a Yankees cap, was sitting on the edge of Lisa's lavender-quilted bed, flipping pages of her personal diary.

"Who are you?" Susan shrieked at the strangers in Lisa's room. "What are you doing in my home?"

"Whoa, calm down! We're police." The man at the computer reached into his wallet to produce his identification. "Detective Ramos sent us down; didn't anyone tell you?"

"No," Susan said, but it immediately made sense: They were plainclothes detectives searching through Lisa's private life for any possible clues to her intentions for last night and today. It was something Dave routinely did on cases.

Their ID told Susan that the one in the orange shirt was Tyrelle LaPierre; the other one was Mohammed Shabbaz. Both were detectives from the Eighty-fourth Precinct.

"Sorry about that, ma'am," Pierre said. "Mind if we just finish up?"

"Of course not," Susan said. "And I'm the one who's sorry."

"Well, I've never seen anything like this," Bill fumed. "In Texas, this would never happen."

"In Texas, the nice man would not have apologized," Carole said, taking her husband's hand. "Bill, come with me." She dragged him out of Lisa's bedroom.

Susan noticed La Pierre staring at her now. "You're the one's been sending her all those e-mails?"

"Yes," Susan answered quietly, too exhausted to feel ashamed.

One side of La Pierre's mouth dimpled and he nodded slowly. "Well, sorry again."

Susan worried that now, because the e-mails had been opened, Lisa wouldn't receive them if she tried to from wherever she was.

"Would you mind . . ." she began, faltered and began again. "Would you mind forwarding them back to her when you're finished? That way—"

He stopped her with a crisp, "Will do." He didn't need an explanation; he was a detective; he got it; and probably he loved someone and got that, too.

Susan left the detectives to do their work. She felt flat, depleted, after the surge of hope and the shock of seeing strangers in Lisa's room. She had a sense now that this could go on not just for more endless minutes and hours but days, weeks, or longer. And her e-mail messages to Lisa would float untethered in cyber-space, drifting like thin white clouds that never become rain. Life without Lisa would be unbearable.

She went to the kitchen and made some coffee while her parents waited at the dining table, admiring the birthday roses, which had opened. As the coffee brewed, steaming its fragrance into the kitchen, Susan stood in the doorway and looked at her favorite wedding photo, a black-and-white unplanned shot she

and Dave had had blown up to poster size and framed
in white-lacquered wood. They were married by a
justice of the peace on a dock in Red Hook. Immediately after the ceremony, as they walked arm in arm
along the dock, a strong wind had surprised them.
Dave, in a black tuxedo, had his arm around Susan's
waist and pulled her closer as her dress billowed up
and out, revealing her bare legs and the sneakers she
had assumed would stay hidden beneath folds of
white satin. The expensive pumps she had planned to
wear had stayed home in their box—during the rehearsal, she had discovered that the heels got caught
in the slats between the dock's wooden boards. In the
photo, they were both laughing. She remembered that
as one of the two sweetest moments of her life; the
other being the first time she ever saw Lisa, moments
after her birth.

  She got her BlackBerry from her purse and keyed in
an e-mail to Lisa.

  *Love = your newborn face, the soft, soft feel of your
brand-new skin. You were the most beautiful flower
girl in the history of weddings in your long yellow
dress at the end of the dock with daisies in your hair.
That one daisy kept sliding down and you ignored it
and when it finally fell it was caught by the wind and
flew out like a feather over the ocean. It was such a
windy day. Love also = Dave. Maybe having you both
in my heart and life and days was too much to expect.
Life has a way of hitting back at us (doesn't it?) and I
have always been a little too selfish.*

  When the coffee was ready, Susan brought a tray
with two filled mugs, a small pitcher of milk and a
bowl of sugar to the detectives. She wondered if Detective LaPierre was reading her e-mail right now;

reading it, and sending it back out to Lisa. Susan returned to the kitchen, prepared her parents' coffee and carried another tray to the dining table. Sitting down, she told them about last night.

"That's why she ran out, then." Carole's expression softened, shedding a layer of panic. "Any teenager would respond that way."

"She's run away," Bill said. Bill and Carole looked at each other and seemed to mutually exhale. "She'll come back," he added. "They always do. You did, Suzie, remember?"

Susan had run away for one day when she first learned she was pregnant, before returning home to tell her parents everything.

"I remember," Susan said. "But Lisa probably didn't run away. This is different." She carefully explained first about the yellow paint, then about Becky Rothka and finally about this morning's phone call from the groom. She did not mention the lurking man who looked like Peter; she just couldn't believe it had actually *been* Peter, and the suggestion would upset her parents too much. "Dave will be here in a little while. He's working with the detectives and they need to talk to you both."

"Okay," Carole said.

"Anything we can do, Suzie." Bill nodded. "Anything."

"The thing is"—Susan picked up an advertising flyer she had dropped on the table yesterday and nervously rolled it into a tube—"I just told Dave this morning about Lisa."

"Oh, Suzie," Carole said, but gently, "you never told him before? We always assumed he knew."

The heavy stone of her mother's disappointment

sank low in Susan's stomach. "I wanted to tell him so many times, but—"

"Well, that was a mistake, young lady," Bill said, "from every point of view."

Bill's tone was the one he had always used to straighten her out whenever she did something wrong. The tone with which he had solved her pregnancy: "We will raise the baby as our own."

"I know, Daddy," Susan said. "You're right, but—"

"No *buts,* Suzie—"

"Bill, please let her talk."

Susan glanced at Carole and the two women—Lisa's two mothers—wordlessly agreed that Bill's need to commandeer the moment would have to be overlooked. His wife's rebuff sent him deeper into his chair. He glared at Carole and she ignored him.

Carole leaned foward, reaching across the table so she could take her daughter's hand between both of hers.

"Darling, I don't think you need to worry about Dave. He's a good man and I believe he will handle this just fine."

"I know, Mom. I should have told him sooner, but I wanted to tell Lisa first. It seemed only right."

"Of course it was right."

"I hoped it would make her happy."

Carole smiled sadly. "It's a big helping of information all at once."

"Maybe it was too much; maybe she would have been better off not knowing; maybe—"

"She was going to look. She would have found you. You just spared her the trouble."

Spared her the trouble by dumping another trouble right on her, Susan was thinking when the doorbell rang. She opened the door and looked into the hall, but no one was there. On the floor, propped against the baseboard, was a flat cardboard FedEx envelope. She picked it up and saw that it was addressed to her. The return address was nothing but a messy blue scrawl in the upper left corner: *Bronx.*

She sat down at the table and pulled the paper zipper across the top of the envelope. She wasn't expecting anything, but sometimes she got business mail at home. Across the table, her father's spoon clinked against his cup. Her mother jostled the roses into a prettier arrangement. Susan reached inside the envelope.

Inside was a single sheet of lined yellow paper, frayed across the top. It was a letter, dated that very day.

Dear Susan,

By now you know I'm gone. I am not alone. I am with the only man who will ever really love me. Tonight we will marry and then we will be joined for eternity. A closed casket will be best. I belong to Him now.

Lisa

Susan felt light-headed as her eyes skipped across the unfamiliar script, round and upright like rows of eggs. There was a wispy quality, as if someone had applied only enough pressure to make the words visible on the page.

"What's wrong, Suzie?" Bill said. He scraped back his chair; Carole followed, and they came around the table to stand behind Susan and read over her shoulder. Soon Carole's wailing voice filled the loft as she buckled into Bill's arms.

Susan reread the letter carefully.

A closed casket. To hide what? Mutilated bodies sped through her mind, torn from a lifetime of accumulated imagery. Her brain was a TV turning thousands of channels; a magazine flipping decades of pages; billboards flashing past for years; headlines and lyrics and footsteps plodding on a deserted street; unheard screams. The images poured into her consciousness at an astounding rate. She hadn't known they were inside her, and now she couldn't push them back. She squeezed shut her eyes and tried and tried not to see Lisa's body taken apart bit by bit, by *him,* in some twisted revenge.

But was Peter really capable of such violence?

She thought of Becky Rothka and became confused: Did this mean that he, Susan's first lover, the father of her only child, had killed a girl before? It was impossible to believe. And yet . . .

She dropped the letter onto the table and ran into the bathroom. Kneeling over the toilet, she retched out her insides, all of them: stomach, brain, beliefs, hopes, intentions. After splashing her face with cold water and rinsing her mouth, she returned to the dining table and picked up the yellow sheet. She read the letter once again.

"Mom? Does Peter Adkins's name ever come up back home?"

"We live so far away now," Carole answered. "I almost never run into his people. As far as I know he got a job somewhere, moved away."

"Moved where?"

"Well, I don't know. Away."

"Do either of you think there's any chance Peter found out about Lisa?"

"We bent over backward making sure that boy never found out!" Bill said. "What are you saying, Suzie?"

"You don't think it's *him?*" Carole asked. "Suzie, you knew him best. Could he really do something like this?"

"I never thought so," Susan whispered. "I have no idea."

Back then he had seemed capable of anything, which was largely what attracted her to him; he was powerful and he had enormous dreams.

Carole's tears started again and the two women succumbed together, reaching for each other's arms, drawing close. Behind her, Susan heard her father leave the room. He returned a moment later with the two detectives and gestured to the letter, which lay crooked and ugly on the table. They read it silently.

"Anyone call the chief yet?"

"I'll call Dave," Susan said. She wiped her eyes with the backs of her wrists. No more tears for her; she wasn't allowed any. She had brought Lisa into the world, spun trouble for her and had no right to feel sorry for herself. She crossed into the kitchen and picked up the cordless phone off the counter.

Chapter 15

Wednesday, 12:15 p.m.

Dave walked into his home to find his wife and her parents huddled together on the couch, their faces swollen from crying. All the windows in the loft were closed, and the air felt as oppressive as the inside of his brain. That Susan had received a letter, perfectly timed and from the Bronx, was terrible news. Only those with inside knowledge of the Rothka case had known about the first letter, last year—insiders, and the groom himself. Dave could still recall the sour smell of Becky's blood, her tiny green beads, found in the Dumpster just two blocks from the FedEx box where her letter had been dropped. The smell, of course, was probably garbage, not her blood—there had been only traces of it, not enough to transmit an odor—but the smell and the free fall of hopelessness that day had merged permanently in his mind.

He kissed Susan's forehead and Carole's cheek, and shook Bill's hand. Then he went to read the letter.

It sat on the table, a duller yellow than the paint, but

still yellow—a color Dave was coming to loathe. The top of the paper was jagged from being hastily ripped from a pad. Dave stood there and read it through three times. Becky's letter had been on smaller white paper, written in blue ink, in a similar rounded penmanship also applied with the lightest touch. He remembered comparing Becky's letter to a sample of her own handwriting, which was denser, smaller, filled with impulsive corrections. Dave recalled how Marie had known instantly that her daughter hadn't written the letter; not just the handwriting but the sentiments had been off-key. He now had the same reaction to this letter. He lived with Lisa and knew her handwriting, which was rushed and slanted reliably to the right. And she never would have referred to *Him* without irony. Clearly, someone else had written it and signed it with Lisa's name.

Ramos stood next to him, reading the letter and shaking her head. When first Susan and then Detective LaPierre had called them at the precinct about the letter, they had jumped. Dave and Ramos had headed right over to see it for themselves and to talk with the Baileys, while Bruno had stayed behind to surf the Internet for any flotsam and jetsam the groom may have floated in cyberspace, and also to pursue the search for Peter Adkins. Lifting her eyes from the letter, Ramos gave Dave a look that could have been interpreted in various ways: *There goes my day* or *We're gonna catch him this time* or *Don't you just hate it when the psychos come out of hiding?* She then went down the hall to Lisa's room to confer with LaPierre and Shabbaz. Dave was glad she hadn't voiced her thoughts with his family so close.

Marie, who had insisted on coming along, took a

seat quietly at the table. He had tried to talk her out of coming, she had refused to take no for an answer, and he had lacked the fortitude to insist she go home. She was a mother, a lost mother, trying to help in any possible way. Dave realized that Marie still had hope for Becky's return, which both concerned and amazed him, yet he was beginning to find her hope infectious and even a little inspiring.

Susan dried her eyes, came over to the table and stood in front of Marie. Dave introduced them. "She's hoping she'll be able to help."

"If that's all right with you," Marie said gently.

"Yes, of course."

Susan sat beside Marie at the table, joining her hands into a single knotted fist that caused Dave a jolt of sadness. Susan seemed to be hanging on for dear life. He was about to walk around the table to comfort her when Marie laid a hand over hers. The personal nature of the gesture surprised Dave, but it was not the first time he'd seen women who were strangers dig deep, immediate channels to each other. He could practically see his wife relax a notch, and for that alone he felt grateful Marie was there.

Ramos reappeared and took a seat at the table beside Dave.

"Let's get started," she said. "We've all had a look at the letter now. Same handwriting—probably—Forensics will tell us yes or no. Meantime let's work on the birth father. Mrs. Strauss, anything you can tell us, this is the time."

"All right." Susan straightened in her seat.

Dave looked behind him, to his in-laws. Carole was sitting on the couch, legs crossed and arms folded self-protectively. Bill sat beside her, hands splayed open on his knees, staring into space. His pale eyes were shot with red.

"Carole? Bill?" Dave said. "Would you please join us?"

Carole rose and Bill followed. They sat at Susan's side of the table, facing Dave and Ramos.

"Detective Ramos is going to ask us all some questions," Dave said. On the way over, they had agreed that she would do the questioning, as this was his family; or, as she had more bluntly put it, "You don't wanna shit where you eat, Strauss, right?"

"Let's start with where Lisa was born," Ramos said. "The hospital, the town."

"Mercy Hospital," Bill answered. "That's Corning, Iowa, where Carole's sister May lives."

Iowa? Dave was surprised; he had always assumed Lisa was born in Texas. He had heard of Aunt May in Iowa but had never imagined . . . any of this.

"Suzie and Carole spent the summer there before Lisa was born," Bill continued. "Suzie came home first and started at her new school. Carole came later with the baby. That's how we did it. While they were gone, I moved us from Vernon to Carthage. No one knew us there; they had no reason to think the baby wasn't adopted."

To Susan, Ramos asked: "Your name is on Lisa's birth certificate?"

Susan nodded. "But it was a closed adoption; the records were all sealed."

"Why'd you bother with all the red tape? Why didn't you just take her home? I mean, she was already yours."

"Because," Bill said in the same authoritative tone he had just used to outline his master plan, "we didn't want to confuse Lisa if she ever went looking into her birth records. The paperwork would just say she was adopted and no more information was available."

"I see." Ramos nodded and frowned and drew a smaller circle within a larger circle on her pad. "Susan, was Peter Adkins ever violent with you?" Ramos asked suddenly. "Before you got pregnant? Any signs of unusual anger?"

"No, not before," Susan answered. "Just when I told him."

"Violent?" Bill shifted forward in his seat.

"Just a little, Daddy. I didn't want to worry you at the time."

"Worry us?" Bill looked at his wife. "Worry us!"

Susan took a deep breath, and continued. "Peter was very sweet most of the time; he loved me and I believed I loved him. I was just fifteen years old. I didn't know anything about love." She looked at Dave. "What were *you* doing at the age of fifteen?"

Dave's memory fell open to that moment of his life. At fifteen, he had seen the first two of his three sisters leave home. He had taken over their shared room and devoted it to posters of rock stars, hockey players and girls in bathing suits. He had his parents' old lava lamp and a shag rug he never vacuumed. He spent his time doing what fifteen-year-old boys did alone in a room. That, and he wrote poetry, which he hid between his mattress and box spring. He was a virgin until eighteen, so one thing he knew he did not do at fifteen was father a child. Essentially, though, life at fifteen swept him along, consumed him. That was the answer she wanted, but now was not the time to give it. He met her eyes and tried to tell her silently that they would talk soon—about everything. Her lies, and his. He realized that not telling her about Becky's letter, trying to protect her from its horrid implications, had opened her up to a worse shock than if she had been able to prepare herself. At some point in their marriage, they had failed to be fully honest with each other. That would have to change.

"Tell us whatever you can remember about Peter, Susan," Ramos said.

Susan drew another deep breath, exhaling this one slowly. "He would wait for me outside our house, even when I wasn't expecting him. I guess he was a little controlling, but I didn't see it that way then. He was sweet. But then when I got pregnant—"

Carole finished for her. "She grew up five years in one day. It broke my heart to see it."

"I was sad I had to give up my baby."

"But you didn't give her up, darling," Carole said tearfully. "You never did."

"How was it Peter never found out you were pregnant?" Ramos asked.

"She didn't really show until she was six months along," Carole answered. "I was like that, too. She looked like she was letting herself go a little, that's all."

"And you're sure Peter never knew?" Ramos asked.

"We *were* sure," Susan said with a slight waver in her voice. "I mean, my family moved all the way across the state. I went to a different school, had new friends. We never saw each other at all after that, and as far as I know he never made any effort to find me. Peter had plenty of friends and all the girls liked him. I just assumed he moved on with his life."

"He knew your parents adopted a baby?" Ramos asked. "I mean, he must have known."

"Not that I'm aware of."

"But people talk in small towns, no?" Ramos's pink nails drummed the tabletop.

"Ma'am," Bill said, "let me tell you that where we come from, one county is as big as your city here. We moved twelve whole counties away. We're talking hundreds of miles of land. The chain of gossip gets broken in a twenty-mile radius, wouldn't you say, dear?"

"Yes," Carole agreed. "I'd say so."

"So you moved," Ramos said, "and life went back to normal. Sort of."

Dave watched Susan's face as she struggled to recall the chaos she must have felt at fifteen with a life suddenly bereft of any real normality at all.

"Yes," Susan said quietly. "I finished high school and left for college. My parents raised Lisa."

"It was the idea of the abortion," Carole explained. "It may be legal, but down where we're from, back then especially, it wasn't done. At least, it wasn't talked about."

"That boy never looked for us after we moved to Carthage," Bill said. "Not one time."

"No," Susan agreed. "Never."

"Suzie made the best decision she could at the time," Bill said. "We all did."

An exhausted lull spread across the room, and then Susan said, "This probably isn't important, but Peter had pretty bad rashes."

"What kind of rashes?" Ramos asked.

"Skin rashes," Susan answered. "Eczema, all down the insides of his arms. He'd scratch it like crazy and sometimes it would bleed."

"His arms could look pretty bad," Carole said.

"Sometimes, even in the heat, he'd wear long-sleeved shirts to hide the rash," Susan said.

"Not just to hide the rash." Bill's tone was firm. "Suzie, you've got to tell them about the rest of it."

Carole nodded heavily, as if the rest was unpleasant but needed to be heard. "Tell them about his *sorrow.*"

"I will, Dad," Susan said. "I was going to." But then she seemed to flounder. Dave smiled gently at her; she smiled back, took a breath and got started. "He had an older brother, Robbie, who died the year before I met Peter. There was a big swimming hole in Vernon. All the older kids swam in it summers; the little kids weren't allowed, because it was deep. Robbie and Peter were there alone one afternoon, and Robbie fell in and drowned."

"He was a good swimmer," Carole said.

"That's right," Bill said. "Hearing the story, it never made a lot of sense that such a good swimmer would drown in calm water."

"Peter was the only one there that day," Susan said, "and he said Robbie slipped on a mossy part of the big flat stone over the water and fell in."

"He idolized his big brother." Carole's voice had grown soft, remembering.

"Yes," Bill said in a sharper tone. "He certainly did. Go on, Suzie, tell them."

Dave leaned forward. "Go on."

Susan looked from Dave to Ramos. "Peter cut his wrists after his brother died. He just tried once, but there were scars."

"Peter would not discuss it," Bill said. "All of us, the whole town, kept silent on the matter."

"And the mother," Carole said, "well, she was just destroyed."

"Not that we knew these people," Bill said, "until Suzie and Peter started dating. But their story was common knowledge."

"Was there a father in the picture?" Ramos asked.

"He died when the boys were very young," Susan said. "Cancer."

"Did Peter ever try to kill himself again?"

Susan shook her head no, but Dave thought she looked uncertain. How *could* she be sure, not having seen him since he was seventeen? "By the time I knew Peter, it seemed like he had worked his way through it."

"We all thought that boy got all the luck in that family," Bill said, "considering. He was basically a solid young man, and we liked him. He overcame some real hardships, losing his father and his brother so young."

"We never knew Robbie personally," Carole said, "but Peter used to mention him from time to time. He adored his big brother, and I got the impression that when he died . . . well, I always figured that under Peter's high gloss he was a little bit shattered."

A little bit shattered, Dave thought; just a little bit. He wondered what had really happened at that swimming hole.

Ramos put down her pen and leaned back in her chair. "Did Peter ever get any help for his problems?"

"He had some creams for his eczema," Susan said, "but they never could cure it."

"There is no cure, as far as I know," Carole added.

"What about his mental problems?" Ramos asked. "The suicide attempt. He see a psychiatrist? Take meds for depression? Anything like that?"

"Not that he ever mentioned," Susan said. "His moods *were* a little shaky, though."

"I admit I always wondered," Carole said softly, "just in the back of my mind, if Peter might someday run into trouble. Sometimes you could see the weather changing in that boy's eyes."

"Look at that letter." Bill made a sweeping gesture with his hand toward the letter, his voice stoked with anger. "I'd say he *is* trouble if he wrote that."

"No one said he wrote it," Ramos said.

"Well, isn't that what this is all about?" Bill's face went sharply red. "You just can't tell me, Detective, that this chat about Lisa's birth father, *right now,* is your idea of socializing."

"I don't socialize much." Ramos wouldn't succumb to Bill Bailey's forcefulness; a good decision, Dave knew from experience. "Susan, I know this isn't easy for you."

Susan went stony, just managing to hold herself together. Dave leaned across the table to rest his hand on Susan's and Marie's, which were still joined and had grown warm.

Ramos clipped her pen to her pad and stood up. "Come on, Strauss, let's get to work."

"Marie?" Dave pulled away, standing. "Can we drop you at home?"

Marie hesitated. "Maybe I'll stay a little longer."

"You sure?"

"If it's all right with you," Marie asked Susan.

"Yes," Susan said, "please stay."

Bill got up, crossed the room and systematically threw open one window after another. Wind now sped through the open space, wind and the grind of construction that would crescendo into the afternoon. The crisp air was a relief; Dave took a deep breath of it.

"Yo, boys!" Ramos shouted down the hall. "Come on, we're outta here!" Detectives LaPierre and Shabbaz appeared from Lisa's room and followed her to the door. "How'd you do?"

"Nothing," LaPierre said.

"Ditto." Shabbaz.

Dave got a Ziploc bag from the kitchen and slid the letter into it. He would take it over to Forensics himself, then back to the Eight-four to see what Bruno had turned up. If any of the witnesses had arrived, they could start questioning them.

"Keep in close touch with us, Dave," Carole said.

"I will."

Dave felt Susan watching him and turned to look at her. His beautiful, beloved, emptied-out wife. For one quiet moment, their eyes settled into each other's; he felt awful leaving her but he had to go to work. He needed to find Lisa. And now he also needed to find Peter Adkins, whether or not he turned out to be the groom. Dave's mind was filled with this man he had never known existed until today and who now seemed to be dictating his entire future. His job and his marriage, and possibly Lisa's life, were all suddenly predicated on who this man would turn out to be.

Chapter 16

Outside the loft building on Washington Street, Lupe Ramos put Strauss in a squad car with LaPierre and Shabbaz and sent them over to Forensics with the letter, then home. Home being the Eight-four—she spent so much time there. Her real home was in her son Orlando's heart, she'd told her boy once when she'd been caught on a case for two days and nights straight. He was nine then, angry at her when she walked in the door after so much time alone with Grandma-who-couldn't-even-speak-English, and she'd told him, "Look, baby, there's no piece of ground that can separate me from my true home, and that home is you. Got it?"

"Yeah, Mom, got it."

She chucked him on the chin with the back of her hand and he flew into her arms. They cuddled on the couch for a full twenty minutes. He was the one man in her life who forgave her for how she looked, smelled, felt or where she'd been all night; this little man demanded her love, and she gave it. Something she figured by now she'd never find in a grown man.

Lupe thought Mrs. Susan Bailey-Strauss was lucky in her husband. Dave Strauss was confused as hell right now, but anyone could see he was crazy for her. Lupe wondered what she would do if someday she met a guy like that, a full-grown man who could really love her. Would she tell him all her secrets? She had plenty; her early years were no picnic. But she'd never met a man who really wanted to know the dirty under her sweet-and-sour. Love was like that, and if you wanted love, you had to hold tight to your side of the covers.

When the car was gone, she went back inside to talk to the doorman. Burly guy about sixty, wearing a black toupee and a nametag reading EDUARDO. Her head barely came up past the tall counter that looked like some kind of fake green marble. Eduardo was looking down, reading something, and he didn't notice her. Pick any reason you want; on the job, he was off the job, "Which is why he's a doorman" she would have told Orlando.

"Excuse me!" She deliberately made it a statement instead of a question, and brought out her badge. Now he saw her.

"Yes, Detective, what can I do for you?" He had a crick in his voice, telling her he smoked. The yellow stains on his fingers, when he reached over to shake her hand, confirmed it.

"Got a few questions about a FedEx delivery this morning," she said in Spanish.

"Okay," he answered in kind.

"You remember it?"

"FedEx and all the rest come in and out of here all day long," the guy said.

"What time you started working today?"

"Six. I'm here until two in the afternoon."

"'Bout eleven thirty this morning, FedEx came with something for Susan Bailey-Strauss."

He shrugged and smiled, his small eyes nearly vanishing in the folds of his skin.

"You remember or not?"

"Sure, I remember. I'm here, no?"

Good question. "Can you give me a description of the guy?"

The sides of his mouth dipped in an imitation of thought. "Listen, these guys are in and out *all day,* bunches of them, every size, shape and color. They're like lollipops." He chuckled at his own wit.

"Lollipops," she said in a flat voice, staring at this loser. "Let me make a note of that." She did not take out her notebook. "How long was this one lollipop upstairs?"

Eduardo pursed his lips in more deadly thought. "About five minutes." Meaning: *Taking a pee break or a cigarette break or a nap on my desk—no idea.*

She slipped one of her business cards over the top of the high counter. "You think of something, you let me know."

"Will do." He took the card.

She would have liked to have gotten a look behind his counter, but could have guessed: crushed cigarette pack, coffee-stained paper cup, empty soda can, old gum balled up in a paper wrapper.

He came around the counter, buttoning his navy blue blazer, and opened the door for her.

A couple of cops she recognized from the Eight-four were stationed outside the building and she asked them the same questions she'd asked Eduardo. Their memories weren't much better.

"We didn't know we were supposed to be looking for FedEx," one said.

"A little warning woulda been nice." The other was a genius, too. "I mean, FedEx comes and goes all day, everywhere. They're like—"

"Lollipops, I know."

Lupe walked away, thinking *useless* and *interesting* and *I* will *make a note of that: No one actually saw anyone make a delivery to the Bailey-Strauss loft.*

She walked down Washington Street and into the Empire-Fulton Ferry State Park, in exactly the same direction Susan Bailey-Strauss had last seen Lisa go. Some things were crystal-clear right now; others were murky as old bathwater. She needed to *think,* which for some people meant taking a walk and for her may have been just a little bit more. She *prowled;* that was what she called it. Her colleagues at the Eight-four knew that about her by now: "Loopy's on the prowl!" someone might shout when she headed out without purse or appointment. "Loopy's hopping on the Ouija board. New York City, watch out!"

Prowling opened her; it helped her mind to work out problems—problems like missing girls, footprints and suspicious persons who looked like long-lost fathers. Sticky, knotty problems.

Her pink sneakers crunched along the pebbled path. She smelled the pungent air of the river and watched bubbles jump out of the froth left by motorboats as they trolled past. This was how she did it: by letting her mind go calm and open to whatever she needed to know. She was a single mother, a detective, always busy; but she had learned that if she slowed down, she could hear things beneath the surface, and this was where she—the being who was not woman or mother or cop—came alive. She couldn't explain it, exactly, but it was a component of how she solved all her cases. Too much noise, and she couldn't read the signals.

She found an empty bench and sat down, turning to look behind her at the huge warehouse building, empty as a ghost, that faced the Strausses' building on Washington Street. She wondered what went on in there at night, or in the day, for that matter. The cops had been all through it this morning: no Lisa, no one, nothing. She closed her eyes and imagined life on the waterfront a hundred-plus years ago, before bridges blocked the sky and the quiet, when the place hummed with immigrant factory workers. She wondered what it would be like here a hundred years from now. "Flying cars," Orlando would say.

Lupe got up and circled out of the park at Main Street. She could feel the cobblestones through the thin rubber soles of her sneakers. When the rail tracks surfaced, they felt cold underfoot. She walked them. She thought of Lisa, and how teenagers let time peel away like a waterfall, figuring there'd be an endless supply of it later. She thought of Lisa last night, tried to *feel* what it might have been like to be her. She felt lost and she felt found. She was a happy girl with a new piece of information about her past. A surprise answer to a question she had long considered asking.

Lupe remembered being a teenager herself. At fourteen, she herself was always out alone. At fifteen, like Susan Bailey, she was pregnant.

Orlando's father, Hector, had eyes the color of sand mixed with ocean, unusual in a person of color. He was excited to be a father and went into the drug trade to make some money, got killed before he even saw his baby. Broke Lupe's heart. Orlando carried a shadow of Hector on his face, and once in a while she visited her teenage lover in those eyes, but not for long.

Besides getting pregnant at fifteen, Lupe's and Susan's histories were opposite. In the world of Lupe and her friends in East New York, Brooklyn, girls got pregnant and had their babies all the time. Grandmas raised them. It was their way. Now some of Lupe's teenage girlfriends were grandmas themselves, sitting on the bench, living on assistance, wondering if they had missed a moment when they might have fought the undertow. Lupe's moment was simple. Riding on the subway one day, sixteen years old, cradling sleeping baby Orlando in her arms, she read an ad for police recruits. It said you needed to be a high school graduate. So she became one. The more she tasted, the more she wanted, the more she got. She didn't resent being a single mother. She felt steely inside, but did not swallow anger or spew it at the world in general; she gave it to her work, as a gift for the bad guys of New York City.

Turning onto Water Street, she came into the crime scene. A couple more TV vans had joined the wait. At this point the forensics techs were gone and cops were guarding the scene from gawkers; you never knew when you'd have to go back behind the yellow lines and look for more clues. Yellow lines, yellow paint. Before sunrise the scene had looked like a bumblebee, the black of night striped and splotched with yellow. Now, in full day, it looked like tired chaos.

Just hours ago, Lisa had been here. The yellow paintbrush had flown from her hand. Lupe's eyes followed the arc of drips landing in a now-dried paintblot filling the seams between cobblestones. She stood above the partial footprint, yellow, and let it into her mind. The shoe's sole had a particular pattern, already matched by Forensics to a common work boot. Size nine. A small foot for a man. Last night, in the dark, they were here together. Agitation showed in the half-finished yellow line, the splatter of paint, the hasty single footprint. Lupe felt a cool autumn humidity hanging in the air like the remnants of fear.

She ignored the reporters who tried to talk to her, waving them off with a, "Later, pals," and moving along the street to Officer Zeb Johnson. He was standing on the sidewalk in front of Seventy-seven Water Street, perfectly still. Coulda been asleep on his feet, but she doubted it. She took him for about twenty-one, a kid. Liked him. He was handsome, too, but she wouldn't go there; she had a hands-off policy at work.

"What you got?" she asked when she was close enough not to shout.

"No one's gone in or out. Where's that warrant?"

"Bureaucracy, baby."

"So you don't think she's in there?"

"Strauss doesn't. He knows the perp better than anyone, without knowing him, if you know what I mean."

Johnson's smile was television white.

"I'm pushing for the warrant," Lupe said, "but if you get a chance to go inside on the quiet, do it, and call me." She winked.

The smile was gone and he nodded. "You got it, boss."

She said good-bye-for-now and continued her prowl along Water Street. She had a strong gut feeling about this place, that there was something here for her to discover, but she couldn't put her finger on it. Not yet. So she'd keep prowling, keep looking. Up ahead, cobblestones gave way to asphalt, curving past the River Café with its strings of white lights and waiting limousines. She bought herself a chocolate ice-cream cone from the homemade place on the wharf, and licked it as she pawed her way to the end of the pier that faced lower Manhattan. In the summer, on a weekend, she'd brought her mother and Orlando here for ice cream. They'd watched as, one by one, nine Asian brides arrived like butterflies with their wedding parties to be photographed against the city.

Chapter 17

Dave found Bruno hunched at his desk, thick fingers flying across his computer keyboard. His hair had gotten greasy, and Dave now understood why the driving cap never left his head: The job's hours routinely inflated without notice, like today, and without his morning shampoo Bruno's halo of hair would be swimming in oil by night—the hat was his style statement as well as his policy against a bad-hair day. He had also developed a body odor. Dave had always loathed bullies and felt sorry for the people on whom they preyed, and big, smelly, lumbering Alexei Bruno, in his head-to-toe black leather, suddenly became that sad little boy in the playground trying hard not to crumble in front of the other kids. His rapidly deteriorating physical state quickly took Dave through reactions of pity and sympathy to, almost, fondness.

"I got nothing yet from the DMV or the IRS," Bruno said, "but here's what I found so far on my own." He swiveled to hand Dave a piece of paper on which seventeen phone numbers and five addresses were scrawled. "Go for it to town. I'm in the chats and the blogs with the crazies."

Dave looked at the sheet of paper Bruno had handed him. In large, flowery handwriting, he had listed information for any and all Peter Adkinses ranging across the United States. Instead of spending hours chatting with all the Peter Adkinses in the country, Dave decided to see what the hard-core techies could do with Bruno's list.

Dave sat at Ramos's desk and picked up her regulation cream-colored phone. He knew Joe Rinaldi's number by heart and dialed it even though Rinaldi's shift at CIS would have ended by now. Whoever picked up the phone would know Dave, so long as he wasn't new.

It was Patty Orenstein. "Dave Strauss!" she said. "I saw your name on last night's log. Rothka's active again?"

"Unfortunately."

"Shoot."

He read all the numbers and addresses Bruno had collected off the Internet. "We're looking for a Peter Adkins originally from Vernon, Texas, and who may have ended up in New York. Can you draw me a short line between a phone number and an address, as local as possible and as current as possible? Then I'll take it from there."

"Reach you at the usual?" she asked.

"My cell."

"Gotcha."

Patty was one of the fastest techs in the department; she could retrieve a wide range of information from landlines and digital sources, and had never made him wait more than ten minutes for an answer when he asked for it stat.

Dave rested his elbows on Lupe Ramos's neat desk and thought about Peter Adkins. It seemed he had loved Susan, before hating her, with the volatile passions of adolescence. Everyone went through that, and most grew up and let it go. Was there something different about Adkins that had made him cling to old wounds? Did the early deaths of his father and brother somehow play into it? Did the *manner* of his brother's drowning, and Peter's suicide attempt, fit in somehow?

A map appeared in Dave's mind, highlighting the line where northern Texas snugged up against southern Oklahoma. Texas, where the Baileys lived, and Oklahoma, where Becky Rothka was born just four days after Lisa's birth in Iowa. Two baby girls put up for adoption at the same time, beginning journeys in different directions. It might have been easy for Adkins to mistake Becky for Lisa; if he had been looking for an adopted-out baby born anywhere near the Texas–Oklahoma border during the first week of September, Becky would have fit the bill. Yes, that part made sense. And if Adkins had then seen the newspaper article about Dave—picturing Susan and Lisa—he would have realized Becky was the wrong girl. That, too, made sense, and yet it seemed too coincidental that Becky had been Dave's case and Lisa was his sister-in-law . . . no, his stepdaughter, making him a father of sorts.

Dave could not get square with how he fit into the picture. His presence in both scenarios—one professional, one personal—was too neat, almost predictable, to make any real sense.

And if the groom *was* Peter Adkins and if he *had* mistaken Becky for Lisa the first time and if he *was* now trying to correct his mistake—*why?* What was the point? If he had wanted to meet his birth daughter, why hadn't he just asked?

The tangle in Dave's mind reached a dead end and the strands disassembled. It did not make sense, not enough sense, and not in the right ways.

"Don't you hear it?" Bruno turned sharply to stare at Dave, who only now felt and heard his cell phone vibrating and ringing on his belt loop. He answered the call.

"Ready with a pencil?" Patty greeted him.

Dave picked up the nearest ballpoint pen from Ramos's desk and ripped a sheet off the top of a clean pad of paper.

"Ready."

"Peter Adkins and Donna Klein, Four-sixty West End Avenue, Manhattan. That'd be Eighty-third Street. Want a landline, too?"

It was almost two o'clock, and Donna Klein answered the door in her robe. It was pale blue and unclean, Dave noticed, with a tear at the shoulder. Her short strawberry-blond hair was messy; her feet were bare.

"I'm working," she said bluntly, meaning, *State your business and get lost*.

Dave and Bruno displayed their gold badges. She squinted at them, then reached into her robe pocket for a pair of glasses, which she put on. They were much like Susan's reading glasses: tortoiseshell rectangles. Donna stared at the badges for ten long seconds, as if memorizing them or convincing herself they were real, then stepped aside so they could enter.

She led them through a small foyer with a polished

black-and-white marble floor and into a medium-sized living room painted taupe. A brown leather chair was angled across from a puckered-leather couch, which was flanked by wood-and-glass end tables with nothing on them. A box of tissues sat on a matching coffee table. On the wall directly across from the couch was a painting of a vaguely familiar yet unspecific outdoor scene. The place was antiseptic, soothing. She had to be a shrink or a professional patient.

Venetian blinds were partially open, slanting strips of sunlight across the beige carpet. In one corner of the room an office credenza gaped to reveal a computer, messy piles of paperwork and a phone. Donna Klein sat down at the black office chair in front of the computer. A yellow happy-face screensaver darted around the screen.

Bruno stood in front of a bookcase with neat rows of hardcovers and clusters of tiny crystal cats. He extended a forefinger and touched one of the glass figurines. Dave wished he wouldn't, but then Donna spoke.

"Those are my pets." Her tone dripped with sarcasm. "My husband wouldn't let me have a real pet—he has allergies—so he got me those."

Wouldn't. Not *won't.*

A sheaf of papers slid off the small desk, scattering on the floor. Donna leaned over to pick up the papers, stacking them just as messily as before.

"Insurance paperwork," she said. "My assistant quit last week. What can I do for you?"

"I take it your husband's not home."

"We're separated. Peter hasn't lived here for almost two months."

Dave sat on the couch. Bruno joined him, holding

one of the crystal kittens in the meaty palm of his hand.

Donna stood up and walked over to the leather arm-chair, in which she sat. She crossed her legs, making sure the robe covered them, and rested her full attention on her visitors. *And how does that make you feel?* Dave half expected her to say.

"Lisa Bailey." Bruno tossed it out like a pebble dropped into a well, then waited, listening for it to hit bottom.

Donna looked quizzically at Bruno.

He elaborated: "Your husband's daughter."

Donna sighed and dropped her face into her hands.

"How much do you know about her?"

"About a year after we were married, Peter told me he had a daughter he had never met. He had just learned she existed. He was struggling with the idea of finding her."

"So did he?" Bruno asked.

"Not that I ever knew of."

"How long were you married?" Dave asked.

"Just two years. We didn't have children of our own. Peter wanted to; he was *desperate* for children—"

The emphasis on *desperate* bothered Dave; it sounded like Susan describing him to himself: "You're desperate for children, Dave, I know. But I'm just not there yet." What lengths would a man go to, to satisfy his desperation? Adoption, maybe. But kidnapping? For an instant Dave wondered where his own impulses might take him were he to learn he had a child; that somewhere in the world lay the answer to his desperation. He would yearn to know his child, yes, but he would never do anything to frighten her. Could he?

"—but I could never conceive."

"He walked out on you," Bruno summed it up, "to find himself someone young and febrile."

Donna looked bewildered for a moment before indignation swept across her face. "I'm only thirty-two. And I think you mean *fertile*."

"That's the one." Bruno set the kitten down on the coffee table.

"Peter didn't leave me," Donna said. "I wanted him to go."

"Would you mind telling us why?" Dave asked.

Donna hesitated, deciding where to begin. "I'm a psychiatrist, an MD. Peter is an LSW—a licensed social worker. The gap between our degrees was just the beginning, you know, the soil where the seed could grow. When the seed's putting down roots underground, you don't see the growth. And then the first little green sprout appears above the soil, and the stalk, and then a flower."

Dave could tell she had practiced this speech, maybe just to herself lying in bed late at night, or maybe to friends, or maybe in her own therapy sessions. Everyone created metaphors for their lives, even Dave—everyone.

"I began to notice Peter's erratic behavior soon after our marriage," Donna continued. "But I'm human; he was my husband; I tried to ignore it."

Was. They couldn't be divorced so soon, but clearly she had buried him along with their seed.

"Eventually it became clear he was bipolar. Do you know what that is, Detectives?"

Dave and Bruno both nodded; criminals often had manic-depressive tendencies, to say the least. Every bad guy was a genius—master of the perfect, undetectable crime—until he got caught, and then he was suicidal. Rage and repentance, that was the usual cycle. Dave thought of Peter Adkins's teenage suicide attempt; he thought of the questionable drowning of his older brother, an excellent swimmer; and he thought of love. From everything he'd learned about Peter, it seemed that love accentuated his volatility and possibly his rage and subsequent remorse.

"Well, it turned out he'd been medicated for years," Donna continued. "I know what you're thinking: How could a psychiatrist marry someone and not know they're mentally ill? Well, isn't it the ultimate game to fool your psychiatrist? Even better to marry one, don't you think? Once my eyes were open, I began to wonder if Peter's condition might be complicated by schizophrenia. There seemed to be some delusional thinking developing," Dr. Klein went on. "I urged him to change medication. He did for a while and he stabilized. But then . . ." Her foot began to shake almost spasmodically. "*Then* he decided to have a messiah complex."

Again, Dave noted her choice of words: *decided.* Did people decide to be mentally ill or to think they were God any more than they decided to be moved by love? Personally Dave thought that insanity and evangelicalism were one and the same thing: a lethal fusion of helplessness and absolutism tyrannizing a mind or a family or a society into all manner of unwinnable battles. Lately he'd begun to think this was the very conflict at the heart of terrorism, reaping death and destruction for the love—the *love*—of God.

"So you asked him to leave."

"More or less."

"Meaning?"

"I had to wait for the right moment." She recrossed her legs in the opposite direction, stilling the quaking foot. "I was afraid he'd explode, Detectives. I was *afraid.*"

"Guy ever hurt you?" Bruno asked in his cut-to-the-chase way. Dave was beginning to appreciate the contrast between their methods: he smoothed, Bruno jolted, resizing the platelets of a settled conversation. He was starting to understand Bruno's usefulness and wondered if his gaffes and malapropisms were more orchestrated than accidental.

"No," she answered. "But he threatened."

"So finally he left," Dave said. "Then what?"

She sat back in her chair, relaxing at the very thought of Peter Adkins vacating her life. "I had the locks changed immediately, I can tell you that."

The phone on her credenza began to ring.

"I'm sorry, gentlemen, but I have a patient in half an hour and I haven't showered."

At her desk she opened a small drawer and from a chaos of papers extracted a business card. The phone rang three more times before stopping, presumably answered by a service.

"Any chance you have his old calendars or a list of his patients?" Dave asked.

"He took all that with him." She smiled professionally, showing them the proverbial door. "And even if he hadn't, I couldn't show you. Doctor–patient confidentiality."

"His daughter is missing, Dr. Klein."

She thought a moment, and nodded. "He used to back up his calendar on the computer. I can print that out for you. Can I get back to you a little later with that?"

Dave could tell she was the type who slowed down the more she was pressured, the kind of person who didn't like to be told what to do. People like that worked best independently, and this woman, by the look of it, was very much alone. He wondered how decisively her work had trained her to distance herself from others, and if she realized that Lisa was real and that her life was actually in danger.

"As soon as you can," he said, squelching the desire to insist they needed it five minutes ago, not sometime this afternoon. "Maybe you could e-mail it to me in the next few minutes?" He walked across the room, pausing at the credenza to exchange business cards. Bruno meanwhile put the tiny glass kitten on the coffee table and waited at the door. "And if you can spare any photos of him, that could be helpful, too."

Donna reached into a drawer and began to pluck out photographs. She rifled through them, removing the ones that included her, and handed Dave three. "They're all yours."

Dave held the four-by-six prints in his hand, resisting the urge to look too closely before leaving the apartment, though he was eager to see the man Susan had loved, the man who had fathered Lisa. And he wanted to see if Peter Adkins had a scar beneath one eye. He glanced at the top photo and saw a fair-haired man sitting on the very couch he himself had just vacated, smiling, one arm stretched along the back cushions. If there was a scar, Dave didn't see one.

"One more question," Dave said. "Did Peter have a scar on his face? Under one of his eyes?"

"No," Donna said. "But I haven't seen him in two months. I guess he could have had some kind of injury since then." She sounded completely disinterested;

but at this point, Dave was hardly surprised at her lack of concern for her soon-to-be ex-husband.

"Do you know where he is now?"

"You said one more question."

"Two."

She smiled. Then she shrugged her shoulders; finished with Peter, finished with them.

"Don't you forward his bills somewhere?"

"Brooklyn," she said. "Seventy-seven Water Street, near the waterfront. I've heard that area's really coming up."

Chapter 18

Wednesday, 2:28 p.m.

Back in the gold sedan, with Bruno at the wheel weaving lanes across the West Side Highway, Dave called Ramos to tell her about their meeting with Donna Klein.

"She gave us an address for him, Seventy-seven Water Street." He said it simply, knowing she'd hear it in boldface, and was not surprised at how quickly she reacted.

"I'm on my way there right now." She breathed in heavy beats as she spoke, as if she were running. "Johnson's already inside. I just got a call the warrant's in. I want you to get it from the precinct and meet me on Water Street, like, *yesterday.* Tell Bruno to stay at the precinct and get updated on the witness interviews, and tell him to bug Forensics about the letter—*anything* they find on that piece of paper, we want to know. You hear me?"

Dave translated Ramos's orders into simpler, calmer language, but Bruno's seasoned ears interpreted the rant right back into it, and he snickered. "Oh, yeah, baby, whatever you say."

They pulled up in front of the Eight-four, where Tyrelle LaPierre was already waiting outside with the warrant. Bruno barely stopped before they were off again. The warrant snug in his pocket, Dave watched through the passenger window as the urban scenery morphed and morphed again. From the projects that housed the precinct like a bunion, their short journey flowered past the slick growth of Metrotech Plaza and its midday corporate hubbub, devolved into the tricky vein of Flatbush Avenue, sliced the unspoiled tip of the Heights and then tumbled into the burgeoning Dumbo waterfront.

They sped down Front Street toward the turn onto Water.

"Pull over here," Dave told Bruno. He didn't want to draw reporters' attention; even in the city of cities, child abductions were rare, and when they did happen the press ate it up—and they ate you up along with the story. Cops learned to keep a distance from the press until they had something worthwhile to say, a lesson Dave had learned the hard way.

Bruno stopped and Dave got out, slamming the door. He turned to see Bruno nod heavily, the leather cap dipping over his eyes, and the sense of fondness overcame Dave again.

"Good luck," Bruno said, then pulled into a wide U-turn and was gone.

Dave ducked under a barricade and walked quickly, but not too quickly, along the broken asphalt and cobblestone patchwork of Water Street. He could see that a cadre of reporters had gathered in front of Seventy-seven. It probably meant that Ramos was already inside, that they had seen her go in and swarmed up from Susan's shop. As he approached the building, he

was surrounded by cameras and microphones. Dave
arrowed through the half-tired, half-hungry reporters,
issued a tight smile and the requisite, "No comment,"
and pressed the intercom button for apartment number
three.

"Dave," he announced himself.

After he was buzzed in, he made sure the door
clicked shut behind him to stop the reporters getting
through. He walked evenly up the hall until he
reached the foot of the staircase and, once out of sight,
bounded up two steps at a time.

He was met by an elderly Hispanic woman who
guarded the third-floor apartment door with a packed
key ring jangling in her arthritis-bent hand. Assumedly
she was how Johnson had gotten inside, and hanging
around now was her big payoff. Her eyes were black
seeds tucked into the leathery folds of her skin, but
when she smiled warily at Dave as he entered the
apartment, he saw the ghost of a lost, supple beauty.

Zeb Johnson was standing in the living room, if you
could call it that. The only furniture was a single
wooden folding chair and a telescope whose lens
speared through a tangle of greenery hiding the window on the right.

Dave nodded at Johnson and, passing him, put the
folded warrant into his hand. Keeping his back turned
to the woman, Johnson slipped the warrant into his inside breast pocket and withdrew a piece of chewing
gum. Now he turned to her and offered her half. It was
a slick move, offering to share the gum. With the warrant snug in Johnson's pocket now, the woman would
never know he hadn't had it before.

"Thanks, Officer," the woman said—was she
blushing?—"but I can't with these dentures."

Johnson smiled and nodded. He unwrapped the gum and put the entire piece into his mouth.

From another room, Dave heard Ramos's high-pitched voice. "Friggin' true believer's no different than any other friggin' man I ever known in my friggin' life!" Then she kicked something, hard.

But before Dave could follow his ears, his eyes caught on a mosaic of papers covering every inch of wall space. Pages ripped from books and magazines. Newspaper clippings. An old dimestore photo strip showing Susan's teenage face check-to-cheek with Peter Adkins—a younger, brighter version of the man in Donna's photographs. Dave's gut cramped at the sight of the two of them together and then cramped tighter at what he saw next: recent photographs of Susan, Lisa and Becky, cut up and overlaid with images of Jesus Christ.

"And we thought the guy liked plants," Dave said to Johnson, who raised his eyebrows and shook his head.

Halfway up the wall was the article about Dave, its two photographs dead center: as a young beat cop on the street, and more recently with his lovely family. The nauseous tickle he had felt just before the article came out had been a warning he should have heeded, but he had respected his sergeant's wishes and cooperated with the reporter. *Loser,* he had stupidly called the groom. And now he knew, without a doubt, that exposing himself and taunting his nemesis had been a terrible mistake.

On the wall above the article was a photograph of Dave and Lisa together, taken on Water Street. He remembered the day: It was summer, he had picked Lisa up at Glory's house on his way back from work and they were stopping by the shop to visit Susan and discuss that night's dinner. Lisa, he recalled, had mischievously suggested a meal of chocolate. You could almost see that day's heat in the photo; it had the fuzzy, unfocused quality of a ninety-degree afternoon.

Dave's eyes drifted from the photograph down past the article to a hand-scrawled caption below it, written directly on the wall in black marker.

I am slain in the spirit.

Slain in the spirit. He had heard that somewhere before.

"Do you know what this means?" he asked Johnson.

Johnson came up next to him and read the words.

"It kind of means you've died to make room for Jesus in your heart." Johnson shrugged. "The guy's born again."

There it was, Dave thought, the toxic fusion of love, insanity and religion. So Adkins was born again; no big surprise there. What confounded him was why any *sane* person would be so willing to accept the blunt fallacies of a promised redemption.

He scanned the wall, trying to pull the clutter of images into focus. Was it a clutter? Or was it some kind of puzzle constructed by Adkins's God-addled mind? There were so many pictures of Susan and Lisa, especially Lisa. The photos of Becky were small, grainy and few.

He turned around to look at the window where he had first noticed the light of the grower's lamp and the ghost of a face withdrawing. Perched on a shelf was a timer; so the light had turned off on schedule before, not because of Bruno's shouts from the street. Presumably the timer had turned the light back on, since it was glowing now. Dave also noticed that only one of the two windows was festooned with greenery. The other window was empty behind a drawn white shade, the plastic kind that curled at the edges and snapped up when you least expected it.

He then noticed that the telescope on the tripod in front of the single chair was in fact not a telescope. It was a camera with a telescopic lens. This way, Adkins had been able to do two things at once: watch the street for his prey and gather their images. Photograph them. Document their existence.

Susan and Lisa.

How long had he been watching them?

"You live here?" Dave asked the woman at the door.

"This is Evelyn, Detective," Johnson answered for her. "She lives downstairs. Her son does maintenance in the building."

"You know the guy who lives in this apartment?" Dave asked Evelyn.

"Of course," she answered somewhat primly; he could tell the activity excited her, that she was lonely, and he understood that.

"Who is he?"

"David Strauss," Evelyn answered, obviously proud to bear forth the information. "A professional photographer. A very pious man. A *good* man."

Those three statements, following his own name, struck Dave as pure dissonance.

He nodded, glancing casually at Johnson with a silent admonishment to wipe the surprise off his face. It was a poker game; you could afford to give nothing away.

"Could you tell me," Dave calmly asked Evelyn, "what this David Strauss looks like?"

"Oh, sure. Blond, blue eyes, not so tall and not so handsome like you, Detective, sir."

It was a compliment difficult to absorb at the same moment that Dave's mind tried to process the information that, for some reason, Peter Adkins was trying to mask himself in Dave's identity.

"Goddamn motherfucking son of a bitch!" Ramos's high-wire voice squealed into the living room, followed by a loud scraping sound. She shouldn't have been touching anything, let alone destroying it; she had to know that.

Dave followed the noise. As he got closer, he smelled the revolting yet familiar odor of rotted flesh. He had been sure the groom would follow his pattern and take Lisa away. But could it be possible? Could Lisa be *here?* He denied that appalling possibility with the next, worse thought: It would be too soon for her body to have generated such a rancid stench.

The bedroom was a shock of carnival color. Jesus and Madonna statues of all sizes and types cluttered the floor alongside a similar variety of porcelain dolls dressed to frilly perfection. Amidst the crowd of figurines, a double bed was neatly made with a green-and-blue-striped blanket and two pillows.

"You any good with locks?" Ramos asked.

She was crouched in front of a cage, the source of the awful smell. Inside were a dozen or so dead kittens along with three barely alive ones; limp and shriveled, they were the hairless breed Dave had heard of but had never actually seen before. By the look of it, Ramos had thrown piles of clothes off the cage and dragged it out of the closet.

"We gotta get them outta there, give those babies a chance." Ramos jammed a pen into the lock but it didn't budge. "He takes better care of his plants. Now, *that's* a crime."

"Why does he want the kittens?" Dave wondered aloud.

"They cute like me." Ramos gave up on the lock and stood up. She gestured to the display of figurines. "Any chance Lisa liked dolls when she was little?"

"I guess so."

"Any chance she likes kittens?"

"She's allergic to cats."

"She'd be allergic to cat *fur*," Ramos corrected him.

Of course: sometimes the fur, sometimes the dander, sometimes both, was what incited allergic reactions, not the cat itself. Dave felt disgusted by how simply Peter Adkins had summed Lisa up. What little girl didn't like dolls and kittens? And now, as a teenager, what did he expect of her?

"It's called ob-jec-ti-fi-ca-tion." Ramos hammered each syllable. "I ain't no dummy. They all do it, every friggin' psycho I ever arrested and even the ones I tried to love. They think they know exactly who you are and what you want but they don't know nothin'."

It was a rough interpretation, but Dave had to agree. Everywhere in this creepfest of a room, where a man had yearned for a girl, Dave saw *his* three girls: Lisa and Becky and Lolita. He saw them helpless on the neat bed before their self-appointed savior-monster as he designed the annihilation of their innocence; saw their sexuality stolen and turned against them, hidden behind the bland frozen faces of the virginal Madonnas; saw their quiet agony in the three barely living kittens whose scrawny backs were pressed against the inside mesh of the cage as they struggled for breath.

"He's a freak, all right." Dave kept his voice low, just above a whisper.

"Listen to me, Dave," Ramos said. "After we catch him, I want him first. I *want* him. But I figure you want him even badder."

"I do," Dave said. She had seen the collage in the living room and the surveillance setup. She knew as well as he did that, by necessity, Peter Adkins—the groom, if he *was* the groom—was going to be Dave's.

"Johnson!" Ramos called to the main room. "You any good at picking locks?"

Footsteps headed to the bedroom shrine just as Ramos's cell phone began to ring with a disco beat.

Zeb Johnson entered the room, covering his nose with a cupped hand. When he saw the pile of mostly dead kittens, he stopped short and his eyes seemed to droop at the corners. He knelt down to inspect the lock. His hands briefly searched his pockets, apparently finding nothing by way of a tool.

"Whoa," Johnson said, glancing around the room at the Jesuses and Madonnas and frilly dolls. He looked at Dave, who looked back without a trace of real shock. Dave hadn't seen exactly this before, but he had seen different and he had seen worse. Johnson plucked a fake flower from the fist of a plastic Jesus, using its wire stem to quickly pick the lock and free the three living kittens. Dave meanwhile kept an ear cocked on Ramos's call.

"Christ-all-friggin'-mighty," she said. "Mr. Adkins ain't no good at this game." She held the phone away from her face to speak to Dave, "Bruno says you got someone who does phone tracking fast, special for you."

"Patty Orenstein." Dave recited her phone number from heart, and Ramos relayed the information.

"Jesus freak left us a pretty ghost on Lisa's letter." Ramos flipped shut her phone. "A phone number, somewhere upstate. Nine little numbers lined up like target practice."

Nine numbers. One was missing, then, and upstate New York was a big place; you could drive nine hours north before you hit Canada.

"Did they get the area code?" Dave asked.

"Eight-four-five."

Ulster County, he thought. From beginning to end, the drive could take anywhere from two to four hours. He tamped his excitement; it was just the imprint of a phone number, written on a page above, and possibly had nothing to do with this case.

It was three long minutes before Ramos's phone rang again. When it did, she listened intently before speaking.

"Okay, Brunocello, call Aviation, order a copter; that's the fastest way. I want you and Strauss to go together." She ended the call without a pause in her talking—no chance for Dave to ask where he was going or exactly why—and shifted her attention to him. "Rental house, upstate New York. Town of Gardiner. House rented last year to one Mr. David Strauss."

She smiled an *are you thinking what I'm thinking* smile that Dave read instantly: Peter Adkins was dropping crumbs, luring Dave to him, and there was no doubt in any of their minds that Dave would follow the trail and go.

"Bruno called the local cops," she said. "They'll go take a look right away. Meantime he'll meet you at the copter."

"You're staying here?"

"Yeah. I got a feeling one of us should stay behind, supervise this end of things, and I'm it."

"I'd better get going then," Dave said. It would be a good twenty minutes on the highway, with no traffic, to Floyd Bennett Field at the far end of Brooklyn where the police department kept some helicopters ready to go in an old hangar.

"Yo, Strauss, they're sending you up in the Bell Four-twelve," Ramos said. "Ever use it before?"

"Nope, not yet."

"Me neither. Tell me how it rides—I hear it's a doozy of a bird."

She winked good-bye to him and he nodded good-bye back. He knew her well enough by now to know she wasn't giving up a chance to ride in the PD's fanciest copter or to get in on the upstate action out of any sense of altruism. She was thinking something, staying back for a reason. He didn't know what it was, but he had started to trust her instincts enough not to question her.

It was thirty minutes before the helicopter was in the sky, carrying Dave and Bruno above the far edge of Brooklyn into a crisp blue horizon. The pilot's mumbling code-talk with air traffic control became a buzz as Dave's thoughts veered to Lisa; he hoped with every iota of his being that this flight would bring him closer to her, not farther away. Then he thought of Lisa and Susan, their similarities and their differences, their life together this past year and his life with them as a family. In a certain simple way, it had been Lisa's bad fortune to have been fathered by Peter Adkins, and Susan's bad fortune to have loved him. Blind bad luck. The truth was you never really knew the capacities of the people you loved until they were tested. Now, the more Dave learned about Peter, the less stinging Susan's confession became. Her adolescent error had gone very wrong; couldn't he forgive her for that? She had intended to tell him about Lisa; everyone made mistakes; and no one could plan a catastrophe like today. One thing Dave had learned in his nearly forty years was that if love was transformative, it was also transformable; that it was meant to change and you were meant to adjust. He remembered reading once that the hallmark of a healthy mind was flexibility, and that long marriages adapted over time. Yes, they would survive this . . . if only he could bring Lisa home. Alive.

The blades roared above their heads, chopping lowdrifting clouds that had appeared as they headed north. Dave looked to the left and felt liberated by the endlessness of the view. Up here, flying in a bubble through the sky, he didn't belong, he was nothing, and this sense of his own inconsequence lightened and comforted him.

Bruno sat beside him, sucking on the filter of an unlit cigarette. In this confined space his ripe body odors were peaking. He turned to Dave and spoke through the half of his mouth not clutching the cigarette.

"It's pretty up here."

Dave nodded, staring out the window.

"The Gardiner cops are probably there by now," Bruno said. "This house, they knew it. But did anyone know this renter, this David Strauss?"

It was a strange, rhetorical question, and Dave didn't try to answer it. He glanced at Bruno's grinning face, cheeks fat like a chipmunk having a bad-facial-hair day, then set his eyes back on the cloud-wisped baby-blue sky.

"Who are you, my friend?" Bruno asked.

"You just answered yourself."

"What does he have against you?"

Dave allowed a small smile. "I got the girl."

"You mean the girls," Bruno corrected him.

Of course, Dave thought. Susan *and* Lisa.

So that was it: He got the girls.

Chapter 19

Lupe Ramos's cell phone erupted with its disco sere-
nade moments after Strauss took off for Floyd Bennett
Field and his fancy copter ride. It was the kind of call
she liked, showing her that her colleagues were doing
their jobs, tracking down hard evidence: They had
found the telephone handset missing from the Café
Luxembourg.

She took two steps for every one of Zeb Johnson's
long strides, her pink sneakers pawing soundlessly to
the *squish, squish, squish* of his big rubber soles. She
was getting used to navigating the uneven cobblestones and could swear she moved quicker now than
this morning. They hiked a left onto Main Street,
where they were met with a rush of wind and so much
sunlight it was like a door had opened. Bridge ramps
to the left and right bookended the open space: pale
blue sky, green lawn and a steely river calm from no
boats frothing the water at the moment. Lunchtime
was well over, and fewer people than before lolled in
the park. Kids were getting home from school,

making her keenly aware that just about now Orlando was realizing she wasn't home to help him with his social studies project; she'd already left him two voice mails promising to make it up to him with pizza and a movie Saturday night.

Cops were clustered at the Washington Street entrance to the Brooklyn Bridge Park. The silver CIS van was already there. A rubber-gloved tech was kneeling over the rowboat-shaped sandbox, where the phone handset had been found by a two-year-old digging for treasure. The playground fence was traced with yellow police tape.

Brooklyn Bridge Park, a sweet little playground between Main and Washington Streets. The jungle gym built like a ship in homage to the river. A stone's throw from the Bailey-Strauss loft.

Lupe's mind couldn't stop ticking. She *knew* there was more to this than Peter Adkins, knew it in her bones. A couple of short blond hairs had been collected from the street in front of the chocolate shop and from the Water Street apartment, but it told them little; they'd need DNA to prove they were Adkins's hair, and that took weeks. What they could do today was identify fingerprints found in the apartment—and on the handset.

The black handset was crusted with sand. The tech shook it gently over the sandbox, then carefully placed it in a brown paper bag, which he creased shut at the top like it was lunch. It was a different tech from the one she chewed out this morning, but she recognized this guy, and apparently he recognized her too.

"Got it, boss," he said. "I'll tell them to process it stat. Get back to you in about three hours."

"Wrong!" Her voice rang out over the playground, the park, the river. "One hour, tops! You got that?"

She felt how everyone around her froze for a split second. Felt it, and didn't care. When you were five feet tall and weighed a hundred pounds, your voice was one way you made an impression.

Fifteen minutes later they were back at the precinct. For hours now the task force detectives had been questioning witnesses, asking questions, having them stew alone in their respective interview rooms, then returning to ask the same questions and see if the answers stayed the same. Now Lupe was ready for her crack at them.

She sprinted between room A, where she'd stashed Evelyn Sanchez, self-appointed proprietress of Seventy-seven Water Street; room B, where she had Donna Klein, high-falutin wife of the man they were mostly after—apparently her conscience had activated and she'd shown up with an armload of Adkins's old papers; room C, where she had the dog-walking couple who had seen Lisa last night; and room D, where the five women who had also seen Lisa were still assembling. Lupe wanted to know everything everyone had noticed, large or small. She wanted to hear all about Evelyn's David Strauss and Donna's Peter Adkins, if only to confirm for the record that they were one and the same man. In between interviews, she let the other detectives go back in, ask their own versions of the same questions—again. Some of the guys called it Cat and Mouse; personally, she liked Tenderize and Terrorize. You exhausted the person, then bored them with the same questions and exhausted them some more. You offered them a coffee or a soda and you didn't bring it. Then you acted like you didn't know they really wanted something—man, they were really thirsty now, or tired, or hungry, or they had to pee—and you sat down and asked the same questions one more time. Eventually, if they were lying, a crack appeared and you stepped right in. If it didn't, you'd bring the drink or escort them to the bathroom or both, then let them go.

After a while she'd offered so much coffee, she herself got a craving for it. Between jackhammer sessions, she detoured into the conference room, where someone had mercifully set up a coffeepot, a stack of Styrofoam cups and some packets of sugar. An energy buzz hovered in the room, keyboards clacked, voices hummed into telephones. It wasn't often you saw so much focus from a bunch of cops who prided themselves on who could tell the best joke or slack off the longest on a slow day.

She prepped her coffee the way she liked it: black and all the way to the top. Sipping away a margin so she could walk with it, she let her attention fall on the web she and Strauss had drawn together on the board. *Becky Rothka* was written in red, center left. *Lisa Bailey,* in black, center right. Just above the two names, dead center, were *Peter Adkins* and then *Dave Strauss,* where the black and red lines tracing the paths of the two cases intersected. Becky's red line sprouted up from there, ending in midair at a date in October one year ago, with the subset headers *Bronx, Letter,* and *Phone Call* shooting thin red fishing lines right into Lisa's world. Her black line, snagged up and down with red hooks, hovered unfinished at today.

Bronx, letter, phone call. Those were the three pieces they needed to unite the two sides of the board. Lupe had Federal Express working in-house to person-by-person track the letter; without confirmation that a FedEx worker had actually delivered it, and that it came from where the slip said—simply, *Bronx*—there would be no Bronx. And until they got the fingerprints on the phone, well, there was no phone call either. Lupe wondered what would happen if those connections fell apart. She mentally erased the horizontal red lines from the map. No red lines—no Bronx, letter or phone call—no connections between the girls . . . except for Dave Strauss.

She did not want to think that an MOS could have anything to do with this. But why was Strauss's name on two addresses now connected to this case: Seventy-seven Water Street, and the rental house in Gardiner? And why, she kept wondering, had the Rothka case been the only one Strauss had failed to crack? Why was his name turning up everywhere?

Dave Strauss, she thought. What were the chances? Johnson had met Strauss at two that morning. His wife had seen him come home around midnight. Lisa was last seen just past eleven o'clock. That gave him about an hour—for what? He said he worked to the end of his shift, so there had to be someone, somewhere, to vouch for him. Maybe it would be a useless exercise, maybe Lupe was being paranoid, but on the other hand there could be something revealing, something she was missing, in the Lisa-Peter-Susan-Dave connection.

Lupe added it to her mental list: alibi for Strauss for that single hour. She wondered if he'd reached Gardiner yet. And why the local cops hadn't called back with a report on that rental house. She needed to finish the interviews and get to her desk. She took a long, fast sip of the bitter coffee and started walking.

Chapter 20

Wednesday, 3:59 p.m.

They bumped along gravel for a long time, then shimmied to a stop. A door opened and slammed shut, swaying the car. Lisa listened to the crunch of footsteps. It would be easier if she hated instead of feared him. *Dickie. Dickwad. Dickface.* She had wet herself, and she felt hungry and cold, but the frozen feeling in her core was something else. It was the kind of cold that didn't come from weather.

The footsteps got louder, then stopped. Lisa heard a rattling of keys. One slid into the trunk lock and turned. Metal popped.

A horizontal thread of light broadened into a band, dragging open a bright, blinding space. He was all silhouette, all shadow swallowed by light, standing in front of her with one hand high on the trunk door. The fast light hurt her eyes, but she wouldn't cover them, because she had a feeling he wanted her to. She had a feeling he craved her fear. She wished she knew karate, or how to dematerialize, or could fly, because then she could zip right past him and get away.

Behind him a cloud passed over the sun and she saw him. In the daylight he looked older than last night in the dark, with pasty skin sagging around droopy blue eyes. His thinning blond hair covered a shiny bald spot.

When he reached into the trunk, she flinched, but his fingertips on her face felt soft. Up close she noticed his nails were dirty. There was a trace of yellow paint embedded in the lines of his forefinger's skin.

"Hello, baby," he said to her in a voice dry and grainy as sand.

I'm not a baby, Dickwad, in case you didn't notice.

She said nothing.

"Let's get you out of there."

He gripped her arm and tugged her out. She had figured he would come at her with the gun or an ax or something right away and her adrenaline would be pumping and she'd fight like hell, but it seemed this was going to be a different kind of battle.

"I hope you weren't too uncomfortable in there, honey."

Oh, boy, he was *nuts.*

"Not too bad," she answered sweetly.

They were somewhere in the deep countryside, at the end of a dirt road that emerged from woods into a clearing of grass. Set back on the lawn was a medium house with a wraparound veranda and a wicker swing. It looked like a commercial: perfect, welcoming and white.

He kept a tight grip on her arm. As he walked her toward the house, she thought about bolting. Then she thought of the rusty gun. It was so quiet here; they seemed to be all alone. If there was somewhere to run, she couldn't see it through the trees. But shouldn't she do it anyway? Did it matter where she went, or even if she was shot, so long as she got away from him before he got her into that house? She realized that she had no idea what to do and would have to improvise.

"What a pretty place," she said.

"Do you like it?" He stopped pulling her and they stood still, looking at the house. It probably was a nice house, but all she saw was a house she didn't want to enter.

"Is it yours?"

He didn't say anything, and Lisa wished she had answered differently, something simple like, "Yes, I like it," instead of answering a question with a question. It was one of her many bad habits. Her best friend, Glory, had once told her that she had a tactless habit of blurting out whatever was on her mind and asking too many personal questions.

"I like it," she corrected herself.

"It's nice inside, too." He began to tug her along again, closer to the front steps of the house.

Lisa began to cough violently. "I have allergies," she said. She buckled over at the waist, hacking like she'd been around a high-dander cat—that was her only allergy; trees had never bothered her—but he still held tightly to her arm. Immediately she wondered why she had chosen allergies when she might have used something contagious, like the flu, or better yet, HIV. Something that would have made him feel disgusted and afraid; something to give her a little power.

"I have allergies, too!" The coincidence seemed to please him. "Allergies, eczema, the works—I'm a mess. I have an inhaler in the house; you can use it."

She began to feel nauseated. The house sat to their left, the car to their right, and behind them—woods.

She wasn't sure if running into the woods would be a good or bad idea, but she had to go somewhere.

"I'm feeling a little better." She demonstrated with a deep breath. "Sometimes it comes and goes, just like that."

"I'm glad it passed," he said. "Mine usually last longer."

"Could we stay outside? The fresh air helps a lot."

Ignoring her request, he gently laid his free hand on her shoulder, still gripping her tightly with the other hand. "Lisa." His voice was pliable as licorice; sweet and twisted, the black kind. "Lisa, I have to ask you something."

How did he know her name?

They were standing so close now, just a foot of country air between them. He wasn't much taller than her, and she saw specks of aqua hiding in his blue eyes. She got the strong feeling that he wanted her to like him, ludicrous as that was. He was looking into her eyes like he actually felt something for her. Maybe, if she had met him in other circumstances—if he had been a teacher, or one of Susan's employees boxing fancy chocolates and ringing up the cash register—she wouldn't have found him so hideous. But how could she see him otherwise? When she looked at him, she saw a monster.

"Lisa, are you saved?"

"Saved?"

His face relaxed with what back-home church folk might have called a "beatific smile." It was how they imagined Jesus on the cross. Like he'd be *smiling*. Lisa didn't know how to answer. *Lie,* she heard Glory whispering in her ear. *Just tell the freak what he wants to hear.* But *saved?*

She shrugged her shoulders and her eyes slipped away from his. Immediately, she felt a heat come off him, frustration or anger or some bitter alchemy of both. If she were an escape artist, she quickly thought, what would be the exact right move for now?

She jerked her arm up suddenly, then twisted it backward, trying to throw him off balance. But he was stronger than he looked and didn't let go. He spun her around with such force that she thought her arm would snap in half. She understood in that moment that strength and hazard and intent were not things you could recognize in a person's face. This pale man with flecked blue eyes, happy for the camaraderie of their allergies, this man who seemed genuinely interested in whether or not she liked his house and liked him and was saved, was dangerous. Dangerous to her, specifically. As she went down she saw his shoe: a brand-new work boot edged with yellow.

She must have fainted, because the next thing she knew she was lying on a bed, on top of the covers, with all her clothes on. When she noticed this it surprised her, and she realized what she expected, and then it deepened: the worm of fear. As her mind awakened to the present she became aware that she couldn't move. Her wrists and ankles were tied to the four bedposts with rope, and she was splayed open. Why hadn't he undressed her, then? She had never felt so grateful for her clothes, but she wished she were wearing something that covered her better. Between her low-rise jeans and the bottom of her shirt, her belly was exposed. Naked. She didn't like it now. The little diamond stud in her belly button looked pathetic, begging for attention she didn't want.

"You shouldn't have done that before, Lisa."

She turned her head. He was standing in the doorway, kind of smiling, kind of not.

"I just want to know you," he said, stepping into the room.

Her wrists and ankles burned, he had her tied down so tightly. He stepped around to the foot of the bed and crouched down, with his knees on the floor and his elbows on the mattress. He pulled off her right sock, then the left. Her bare feet felt cold in the chilly air.

She squeezed shut her eyes and pretended he wasn't doing what he was doing to her feet. Counting her toes, one through ten. Then counting backward, ticking off the numbers toward zero. She wondered how many other girls he had tied to this same bed, or if she was the first.

"I never got to count your toes," he said.

Well, I never got to count yours, either. She hated him. "Hate is a strong word," her mother Carole once told her. "Let's try 'don't care for.' " Her other mother Susan—still a girl herself—stood in the background of Lisa's memory, rolling her eyes.

"I want to get to know every part of you."

Lisa had always figured that when her birth mother gave her away, she had paid all her life's dues at once and nothing bad would ever happen to her again. It had seemed only right and fair. Now she wondered if something had folded over in the universe of fairness last night when Susan had told her the truth, and *this* was the scale righting itself, trading one injustice for another.

But no, that couldn't be true either; getting kidnapped by some lunatic couldn't possibly count on anyone's scale of justice. This was just *wrong* and *bad*. Her mind vaulted back and forth, trying to find someplace safe to land; and as he touched her toes in careful order, she flew backward in time to last night, to a raw edge of reality that was still much much better than *this*.

She replayed Susan's words, the familiar sound of her voice: "I am your birth mother."

I am your birth mother.

Meaning Lisa had always known her birth mother.

Meaning she had never been unloved or abandoned.

Meaning the worst that had happened was that she had believed a lie. Like Santa Claus or the Easter Bunny or the virgin birth of Jesus Christ. All petty lies to bring you up through childhood; then when you were ready, one by one the lies were peeled off you like too many winter clothes. She had learned the truth about all the other false idols. Now she knew the truth about another one: The mysterious mother wasn't a mystery at all.

She began to feel a warm rivulet flowing inside her chest, almost a physical sensation, like a vein relaxing. For a moment, her mind drifted farther away, and she could feel Susan feeling her, loving her, and she loved Susan with every bit of herself.

She thought of the yellow line and wondered if Susan had seen it and if she had understood what it meant; the endeavor of Lisa's forgiveness: implicit love.

Then she thought of their argument, before she had decided to paint the line. She had been cruel when she asked Susan if she knew who Lisa's father was. Even if Susan had slept around, which Lisa doubted, she wasn't the type to lose track of who or when or where. Lisa pictured the kitchen at home, the factory, the office, the perfect stickers and bows on every item in the

front shop. Every single thing arranged just so. Maybe
Susan had experimented when she was fifteen years
old; Lisa could understand that. Just wanting to *do it*
to see what it was like. She remembered reading in
Maya Angelou's autobiography that that was what she
had done when she was seventeen, and the result of
that one careless attempt at experience was a son, her
only child. Unless Susan had had a real boyfriend, as
Lisa had herself often fantasized about, someone very
special who loved only you. She could see it having
happened that way, too. Whom had Susan loved when
she was fifteen? What boy had been special enough
for that honor?

"One, two, three, four, five."

Dickwad.

"Six, seven, eight, nine, ten."

*Are you convinced now that I've got all my ten
toes?*

Within her secret mind, another vein popped open.
It was something her brain shouldn't have wasted any
storage space on, but there it was: some pregnant
woman across from her on the subway telling some
lady next to her that when her baby was born, the first
thing she would do would be to make sure it had all its
fingers and toes. At the time Lisa had thought that was
inane; weren't there more important things to worry
about? Like blindness or deafness or Down syndrome
or microencephalitis or cystic fibrosis? The list went
on and on. Ten fingers? Ten toes?

Each time he touched the tip of one of her toes, ac-
counting for it, she felt a tingle. She had almost lost
sensation in them from the tight ropes at her ankles.
Her fingers were floating away, too. Her ten toes and
her ten fingers, leaving.

210 **Kate Pepper**

She opened her eyes and dared to look at him.

I just want to know you.

Want to get to know every part of you.

Never got to count your toes.

Your toes.

"Wait a minute," she said. "Who are you?"

He stopped counting and looked at her, surprised she had asked; he reminded her of the nerdy guy at her middle school who tripped in the hall when Glory said hi to him one day. The guy actually fell on the floor while the two girls moved away in a burst of giggles. With Dick's blue eyes stuck on her now, quiet and staring, she felt a chill laddering up her body.

One of his cheeks bunched up a little, but it wasn't exactly a smile.

"I'm your father."

Now the smile flourished on his face and she noticed his dimpled chin, exactly like her own.

It couldn't be true. Her mind filled with white noise, desperate to block and scramble his words: *I . . . am . . . your . . . father.* He stared at her with his pupils turned to tiny black dots even though they were inside the house, out of the direct sun. She wondered if he was on some kind of medication; obviously something was wrong with him.

For the first time in her life, she was speechless. She could *not* do this. She could *not* be here now. This man could *not* be her birth father. She laid her head back on the pillow and let her eyes drift to the room's single window. It was the old-fashioned kind, with a top and a bottom and eight panes of wavy glass. The view was all forest, blurry and distorted, and she thought—*No.*

Chapter 21

The loft's broad windows drank in a vast blue sky in which Brooklyn went on forever. Blue-blue without a streak of white. It was a hovering, drifting sky; the kind that made you dream, or on bad days saddened you. A chilly breeze sharpened the air. The skin on Susan's arms stiffened with goose bumps, but she ignored it and turned another page of the photo album she had tucked away years ago.

Carole sat on Susan's left, warming her side. Marie sat on her right, separated by a three-inch gap. Bill prowled the creaking wooden floor behind the couch.

"She was a pretty baby," Marie said.

"Wasn't she?" Carole managed a faint smile.

In the photo, a mature but younger Carole cradled infant Lisa, who in her striped cotton jumper could have been a little boy. Susan, as a baby, had been dressed in pink frilly jumpers with matching bonnets and booties. She wondered now if, raising Lisa, Carole had tried to correct earlier mistakes, making Lisa tougher from the start, hoping she would not turn out as vulnerable to charm as Susan had been. In the background of the picture, taken on the lawn in front of their new house, was half of a teenage Susan, sitting cross-legged on the grass, her long hair blown across her face by a sudden wind. She remembered that moment: twirling a spent dandelion between her fingers, watching her parents dote over the family's new baby, feeling bewildered.

Lisa arching up from a blanket on the floor with a big smile on her little face. Her peach-fuzz hair was so slight you couldn't see it in the picture.

Susan later that year, on a horse she remembered was called Last Laugh. Her right hand held the reins and her left grasped a gold trophy. First place for jumping.

Susan holding sleeping Lisa, looking directly into the camera, smiling.

Lisa as a toddler, kneeling on the grass, reaching a straightened forefinger at something invisible that floated in the air.

A few years later, Carole and Bill holding Lisa's hands, swinging her through the space between them. Susan remembered taking that picture herself, home on a visit from college.

She hadn't looked at this album for years; the memories were too bittersweet, too confusing. Now she felt as if the images were floating away from her, and she wished she could reach back in time. She could have kept Lisa as her own, stayed in Vernon and faced everyone's judgment and wrath.

As she turned the final page of the album, the paper end page crumbled and fell away from the spine, and a photograph Susan had forgotten about fell onto her lap. Without looking, she knew what it was, and hesitated a moment before turning it over. She had told Dave the truth before when she said she'd thrown away all the pictures of Peter; she had simply forgotten about this one, slipped behind the end page many years ago. She remembered now: She had taken the photo of Peter out of its sleeve to look at it closely, and then her mother walked into the room. It had been quicker to slide the photo under the end page than return it to its tight-fitting plastic sheath.

She turned it over now and set it down on top of the last glossy page.

"Peter."

Susan had taken the picture one Thanksgiving, in the late afternoon. Meals finished, they had left their family gatherings to be together. He wore a brown corduroy jacket, unbuttoned at the neck; his Adam's apple was sharp under his skin. In the photo he looked directly at Susan with his clear eyes imploring her, and for the first time in years she remembered the question that came right after she took the shot.

"Why can't you?"

"It'll get too late. You know how Daddy is."

"It's just a movie. If it goes long, I'll call him myself."

"Maybe tomorrow afternoon."

"Then let's take a walk."

They had walked a long way that afternoon, into dusk, which came early. The neat sidewalks of Susan's suburban neighborhood blended into torn-up countryside being made into a new development. There, in a half-finished house, they lay together and made love with their jeans pulled down to their ankles. Afterward, they wiggled their pants back up and she lay in the crook of his shoulder, on the gritty floor, staring up into a darkening sky.

"No stars out tonight," she had said.

"Supposed to rain tomorrow."

"A movie would be good, then."

He turned to her and she inhaled the corn-bread scent of his skin that afternoon.

"I love you, Suzie."

It was not the first time he had said it; he told her every time they made love. What she wanted more than anything was for him to say it when they hadn't.

"Peter Adkins used to seem like a nice boy," Carole said.

Behind them, Bill stopped pacing and looked at the photo. Then he huffed and continued wearing down the floorboards.

"We were so young." Susan touched the edge of the photograph. "We thought we were pretty smart, too."

Marie was staring hard at the picture. Susan took in her profile: lean and finely etched, a roughness to her skin. She wondered what this woman was thinking, looking at a photograph of the man who might have taken—*killed,* Susan thought, in a betrayal of hope— her daughter. Then Susan realized that Marie was probably thinking and feeling much as she herself was: a deep, aching hunger to see her child again; a wish to reverse time to that moment before the girl walked out the door and to say, "Wait for me; I'll come with you." Susan realized that she was on day one of a journey that Marie had simply been on longer.

Looking at Peter's young face now, recalling his charm and his energy, Susan felt nothing but shame. Had she really loved this boy? Yes, she recalled; desperately. She had been like every other teenage girl she knew then—a fanatic animal, a deep feeler, a truth seeker. They were probably right about most things, but they grew up—Susan had grown up. She only wished her past could have been reduced to mere recollection; instead, it had been the planting ground for all *this*.

She turned from Marie's gaunt face to the row of windows that stacked neat squares of baby-blue sky one against the next. It was like a film strip caught in a projector, the images floating by anyway. Clouds. Memories. Peter. Lisa. Susan felt herself slide out of her body and drift toward the windows, nudged right, then left at every breeze; while her other body—her real body—sat on the couch, heavy as stone. Then, at the touch of her mother's warm hand on her arm, Susan returned to the here and now, the place that would normally be called reality.

Carole was eyeing her keenly, her face soft with the fine lines of a woman aging gracefully. Even now, after all these torturous hours, her pale coif was still perfectly in place. She took the photograph of Peter, slipped it between two pages of the album and shut the book.

"The past is the past," Carole said with the Southern snap of authority Susan found so comforting. "We can't just sit here."

"Yes, we can, Mom."

"Well, we *shouldn't*. Where's your Scrabble board? Marie, do you play?"

In minutes, the three women were set up at the dining room table with Susan's old Scrabble board spread open between them, doling out the little letter bricks. Susan had always loved the smooth feel of the wooden squares as she arranged them on their stand. Her tattered paperback Scrabble dictionary sat between mother and daughter. Back in Vernon, Carole had started Susan on the game as a way to help her with her reading troubles, in the hope it would make school easier. "If your word jumps around," Carole would instruct in her bright inspirational tone, "you just take it apart and put it back together again." In the end, the word practice didn't help Susan much in school, but she got good at the game and she and her mother became formidable opponents. Tuesday nights Carole played bridge with her lady friends, rotating houses. Thursday nights were reserved for Susan and Carole's Scrabble games. This set had been a parting gift when Susan went away to college; it had lived with her for one and a half semesters, until she grew exhausted from deconstructing words that wouldn't stay put, and she dropped out; it had moved with her at nineteen into the rough unheated loft, where it waited lonely nights on the shelf while she waitressed and then worked in restaurant kitchens and then endured the long hours and apprenticeships of culinary school. Through all those years, through all the transformations of Susan's work life and personal life, through the loft's makeover from old to new, whenever Carole came to visit the Scrabble board had come out. Ditto Texas, where they still used the lovingly worn set Susan had grown up with.

Bill paced around and around the three women as they played, eyeing their letters silently before moving on to shadow the next player. He didn't like Scrabble and never joined in. Marie was a good player, but with her there Susan and Carole minded their manners more than they normally would have. It didn't matter; the game helped pass the torturous minutes of waiting. It helped Susan to not continually check her watch and her BlackBerry, though even as she composed words from her random letter bricks, her mind turned the words into obscure love poems she memorized for the next moment she could be alone and start e-mailing Lisa again. *I ponder* you *with* **exquisite ardor. Ripe avenues** *dig* **maps** *in my* **heart. Overflowing mutinous memory. Boys build toys** *while* **girls** *swallow* **pearls**. A woman who had always hated writing and reading, she now wanted nothing but to compose verses to her daughter.

They had played one full game and started another when the intercom buzzed. Susan abandoned a fresh reverie spawned by the word *cache* and got up to answer it.

"Mrs. Strauss? Mr. and Mrs. McInnis and their daughter are here to see you," announced Alan, the late-afternoon doorman.

Susan didn't hesitate before telling him to let them up. She returned to the table to complete her word, *cachet*, then joined Bill at the open door until Audrey, Neil and Glory McInnis got off the elevator and came inside.

"Any news?" Glory immediately asked. She looked so wan and frightened.

"Not yet, honey," Susan told her.

Glory fought back tears. "Is it okay if I go into her room for a while?"

Audrey's expression turned pleading on behalf of her daughter, but Susan would not have denied Glory anything.

"Of course," Susan said.

Carole and Marie welcomed them to the table, saying they had been about to take a break from the game anyway. Neil and Audrey sat down and Susan brought them all mugs of coffee. She picked up the small milk pitcher from where it had been sitting all morning, to take it back to the kitchen for a refill.

"Let me do that." Audrey pushed her chair back and began to stand, but Susan stopped her.

"It helps me to keep busy."

"This must be awful for you," Audrey said. "We won't stay long. Glory insisted we come over."

"No, I'm glad you're here. The more the—" She stopped herself; not *merrier,* certainly. There were really no words for this situation.

Susan returned to the kitchen with the pitcher, opened the refrigerator and took out the milk. Back in a pocket of solitary quiet, a fresh blossom of pain overtook her. *I love you* she wanted to write to Lisa. *I LOVE YOU.* But she had left her BlackBerry on the coffee table and didn't want to get it in front of everyone; suddenly she was crying again, and she didn't want them to see her now when she had been holding herself together so well. Then, from nowhere, she heard a loud, angry shout.

From her meager privacy in the open kitchen, she looked out at the others at the table—her mother was sitting next to Neil, her father between Marie and Audrey—and the hushed tableau told her that no one else had heard the shout. Her gaze landed on a teaspoon someone had left on the counter, a brown coffee spot dried in the curve.

It was Lisa's voice she had heard; she was sure of it. Lisa was trying to reach her, probably telling her to stop expecting the worst.

She filled the pitcher, then opened the refrigerator to replace the milk, keeping the door open too long as an excuse to turn her back on the others and think for a moment. On the bright, cold shelves she observed the bottles of yogurt Lisa liked for breakfast, the raisin-nut bread Dave sliced thin and toasted to a crisp, the chicken she had taken out of the freezer last night to defrost for tonight's dinner. It was all a museum piece now; hunger had left her. She was free of any desire for physical satisfactions, aware that only a restoration of love could begin to fill the canyons of loss that had become her soul. The love of Lisa and of Dave, one intertwined with the other. She had the stark awareness, looking into the refrigerator, that the life its contents represented was already over.

The haunting voice returned and was singing now as wisps of spicy incense curled through the open windows. It looked like cartoon smoke. No one else seemed to notice it. And no one heard the voice singing "The Circle Game"—that mythic child moving around and around the wheel of seasons. Lisa's high, bright voice sailed through Susan's mind. She had practiced that song recently.

Abandoning the pitcher of milk along with her efforts at hospitality, Susan closed the refrigerator door and padded barefoot down the hall to Lisa's bedroom. The door squealed when Susan opened it. Glory was sitting cross-legged on the bed, reading something— it was Lisa's newest diary, the blank book with a green watermarked cover. Dave had picked it up for her at Kate's Paperie a few months ago, suggesting that Lisa try to write her own songs. Susan hadn't heard Lisa practicing any original songs and had never asked her what she had decided to do with the blank book. It had been enough that Dave had thought to give it to her and so like him to choose something beautiful from a specialty paper store instead of the kind of utilitarian notebook Susan would have bought in bulk at Staples.

"She'd want me to read it," Glory said, placing her hands over the exposed pages. "I know because I'd want her to read mine, if it was me who . . ."

The inevitable reference faded into silence. The idea of Lisa vanished, missing, taken was too laden to fit into speakable words. It was unnecessary to point out the obvious. They all knew Lisa was gone.

"What's it say?" Susan stepped into the room, her toes digging into the pile of Lisa's blue carpet.

Glory shrugged. "Nothing I didn't already know."

"But you don't know anything that could be important, do you, Glory?"

Glory hesitated, briefly misunderstanding the question, then shook her head.

"I told everything I know to that cop before, I swear."

"It's okay, honey."

Glory lifted her hand from the open diary and her attention fell back to the pages, where Lisa's script flowed like waves upon waves upon waves.

In the slatted light that came through the blinds, Glory looked older, more chiseled than Susan had seen her before. Yet Susan felt she *knew* this moment. One after another, every detail in Lisa's room became a déjà vu, the last slipping into the next like a dream of a hand that could not stop entering the same glove. Susan felt a headache coming on. She closed her eyes and pressed her fingertips into her temples. Then she crossed over to the bookshelf to look for Lisa's song-practice CD. She found it in the compact silver boom box on the floor in front of the bookcase.

Lisa's voice announced itself self-consciously:

"This is me, Lisa Bailey, and this is my practice disk, so whoever you are, if you're listening to it—well, you're probably not supposed to be listening to it, but if you are—this is a test, just a test."

Glory looked up from the diary and listened.

Susan lay back on the carpet, legs stretched long and body propped on her elbows. She let her head hang, feeling the pinch in the back of her neck and the stretch at the front of her throat, as Lisa's voice filled the room.

After a few minutes, Susan heard the plunk of Glory getting off the bed and felt the air move as the girl stepped over her. Susan kept her eyes closed, listening to the singing on the practice tape. The door clicked shut behind Glory.

"The Circle Game" was followed by "Raised on Robbery," then by something else, by a newer songwriter whose name Susan didn't know. Unless Lisa *had* written her own song. Susan opened her eyes, alone now, and listened closely; it was beautiful. Only days ago she had wondered when the Joni Mitchell obsession would be edged out by something new; not that Susan didn't like Mitchell's songs—she loved them—but she had been getting just a little tired of hearing the same ones over and over.

Today Susan could endlessly listen to Lisa's voice spin out the sweet harmonies. There would be no such thing as annoyance or excess ever again, if Lisa could only be brought safely home.

The new song ended and Joni's "The Last Time I Saw Richard" began. Susan listened closely to the words, the poetry, and on a rising lyric toward the end, her heart swelled and she lost control.

She let the tears bleed down her skin, giving herself

to the pain that had completely filled her. She wished
for a deep inner knowledge that Lisa was still alive,
wished for that elusive connection parents spoke of
when a child was gone, the invisibly joining cord. But
the innocent trust required by both love and faith
eluded her now, much as she wanted to fold herself
back into their familiar comforts. She wished she
could return to yesterday, to the known patterns of a
happy family and also—it hit her now with force—to
an old, lost faith that had hovered quietly within her.
She realized now that she wanted God back as much
as she wanted Lisa and Dave back. Her faith had always been an island of comfort for her, regardless of
what her husband thought of it. But today, she wasn't
sure if she deserved any of them—Lisa or Dave or
even God—because she had drifted too far into a life
mined with failures, failures she could no longer pre-
tend weren't there.

She had failed at her childhood by growing up too
fast.

She had failed at motherhood by not seizing it when
it came to her.

She had failed at love by denying Dave the full
truth of her.

She had failed Lisa in every possible way.

She had failed God by lying her way through life.

Susan tried to close her eyes again but they
wouldn't stay shut.

The incense scent returned—no, it was something
else this time, a cooking smell seeping under the
closed door: stewing onions, garlic and thyme. Her
mother had found the chicken and was making the Famous Whatnot Stew both Susan and Lisa had grown
up on.

Standing up, Susan wiped her palms over her tears, then dried her hands on her red pants. She walked into the hallway and slipped her feet into the pink flip-flops Lisa had left out; they were two sizes too small for Susan, and the backs of her heels fell off the ends. The sandals slapped the wooden floor as she rejoined the others in the living area.

"There you are." Bill scraped his chair away from the table, leaving Marie and Audrey with an empty space between them, and came toward her. "Your friends and I've been talking and we just don't think your old sweetheart would hurt Lisa—she's his own flesh and blood. As I recall, Suzie, that boy really loved you at the time."

Susan glanced into the kitchen, at her mother, for help. But Carole was in there for a reason: She was avoiding Bill's energetic attempt to commandeer his—and everyone else's—sense of helplessness by hiding out in the kitchen and teaching Glory to make the stew.

"Peter only loved himself," Susan said, that precise notion finding her for the very first time. She realized now that it was what had made him so exciting to her as an insecure teenage girl. If only she had been able to recognize his narcissism then, none of this might have happened . . . but the thought of no Lisa—*no Lisa*—was impossible. And in the same moment that she understood the incapacity of Peter's love for her, she banished all regrets.

"Well," Bill said. "Marie here's been remembering something your old friend said to her on the phone about half a year back. 'The apple doesn't fall far from the tree.' Do *you* have any inkling what he meant by that, Suzie?"

Was he talking about the groom's periodic calls to Marie? Had Bill's doubts fully surrendered to the likelihood that Peter really was the groom?

"He wasn't my friend, Dad."

"Come on, Suzie, you know what I mean. Now *think*."

Susan looked at Marie, in front of whom sat a pad of paper covered in doodles of triangles within circles within squares and the barbed wire of curlicues surrounding it all. Within the chaos, a string of words had formed: *The apple doesn't fall far from the tree*.

"I don't know where the memory came from," Marie said. "But I *do* remember him saying it. He said it two or three times in one phone call. It didn't make any sense to me at the time. It still doesn't."

Susan glanced at the letters remaining on Marie's Scrabble stand: *PLWPEAT*. *Peat* jumped out at you, but a longer look showed you *apple*.

"I don't know what it means, either," Susan said. Peter, the groom's calls to Marie, all these random memories. Susan felt she had to go outside and get some air—alone.

"I'm going to take a walk."

"What?" Bill stepped closer to Susan, as if he would block her from leaving.

"Let her go, Bill." Carole was standing in the kitchen entrance, wearing Dave's black-and-white-checked apron, holding a metal cooking spoon that was about to start dripping stew juice onto the floor.

Susan picked up her purse from its usual spot on the coffee table and zipped her BlackBerry into its outer compartment. Shoving her bare feet into well-worn suede loafers by the door, she slipped into the fifth-floor hallway. The elevator was already there. She couldn't face the multitude of her own reflections in the mirrored elevator and kept her eyes down on her feet. She descended quickly and passed through the lobby and onto the sidewalk, where a couple of policemen nodded at her as she walked by. Afternoon was simmering in the air, pulling down the sun, preparing for another night.

She headed for the factory, thinking that if she *did* something, busied her hands, it might free her mind. She could do the office filing, the task both she and her assistant most disliked, and which therefore rarely got done; it would occupy and punish her at once, and that felt right. Or she could cut ribbons into foot-long sections. Or she could wipe out candy molds that had gathered dust on the top shelves in the factory. It didn't matter what.

At the corner of Washington Street, she turned right onto Water. A lot of people—police, reporters and sundry vultures keen on the misery of others—were clustered in front of her store and also in front of the building Dave and the police had been watching so closely all last night. Her instinct was to avoid them, to protect her privacy, but instead she marched directly into the crowd near the store.

A reporter standing in front of the shop swerved suddenly in her direction. The man's avidity repelled Susan, inspiring her to break into a trot, passing the shop and the factory, realizing that what she really wanted was to see what was inside that building everyone was so interested in. That she wanted to know exactly what the detectives knew came to her with clarity as she reached the front door of Seventy-seven Water Street.

"Excuse me, lady, but where do you think you're going?" The voice seemed to sail up from below. She looked down and saw a policeman, a dwarf, looking up at her.

"Inside," she answered him.

Behind her, another officer emerged from the crowd. This one was tall and skinny with a pronounced Adam's apple. "Sorry, but you can't."

"Please," she said, "I'm Susan Bailey-Strauss!"

Sudden camera flashes blinded her, voices flew, and she twisted around to shield her face.

Chapter 22

Wednesday, 4:57 p.m.

Lupe Ramos sat at her desk, arranging and rearranging her pens, pencils, pads, paper clips and file folders; she flipped her Rolodex to the first *A* and closed the plastic cover; emptied her pencil sharpener; changed the angle of her phone.

The Gardiner police had just reported in. Traces of Lisa were in the house, though she herself was still unaccounted for; it looked like he'd had her in one of the bedrooms, then moved her. The locals were organizing a search party to canvass the area. They'd also learned that a car parked in front of the rental house was registered to Peter Adkins, so their instincts about him had been right; fingerprints in the car had already confirmed it.

Meanwhile Donna Klein had been a treasure trove of information. Like her husband's size-nine foot and his taste for work boots. And better yet, that big envelope she'd brought with her, crammed with printouts from Peter's hard drive before he moved out, along with some handwritten notes. One was a lined yellow

sheet with a phone number to reach him if he wasn't
at the Water Street apartment . . . a number in Gardiner, New York. The phone number on that note,
placed on top of Lisa's letter, had made a perfect
handwriting match, like a ghost getting sucked back
into the body that had spawned it. That was the
clincher for Lupe: having the page in her hand, and
knowing who wrote it.

So now they had Lisa pinpointed, and they knew
who had her, and Dave Strauss and Alexei Bruno were
about ready to land. Good. Thing was, Lupe wondered
if her radar was failing her—if Lisa Bailey was upstate, what was this *feeling* nagging her about Brooklyn? Why was she sitting here, out of the action?

And what did "the apple doesn't fall far from the
tree" mean? Marie Rothka had just called that one in;
she said she'd tried to call Dave first but his cell was
out of range. She said the apple ditty was something
the groom had repeated to her a couple times during
one of his phone calls to her. *The apple doesn't fall far
from the tree.* If the investigation hadn't shifted some
of its focus upstate, Lupe would have discounted it as
just another misplaced memory—everyone had them
and you couldn't dwell. But *apples,* autumn,
upstate . . . She tried calling Dave herself but his cell
was still out of range and so was Bruno's.

She turned her mind back to the evidence. Evelyn
Sanchez had positively identified Peter Adkins as the
man who lived on the third floor. She'd taken one look
at Donna Klein's photos of Peter and said, "Oh, yes,
sir"—Lupe let that one slide—"that's David Strauss."

Score one for the real Dave Strauss. Score two
came moments later when PO Morgan Schnall
vouched for Strauss last night between eleven and

midnight. Lupe had felt an uncomfortable kind of personal relief at the news. She tried never to want any particular answer, but still, confirming that Detective First Class Dave Strauss was in the clear was right up there with reconstituting Santa; it was a piece of good news she couldn't help but wish for.

So Peter Adkins had taken the apartment and the house in Dave's name. Okay. Next, Lupe wanted prints off the phone handset found near Strauss's building; she wanted to know if Santa's beard was real, too.

It had been one hour and thirty-seven minutes since the forensics tech had driven away with the café's handset. Half an hour ago, Forensics had promised her results asap. She had called them back three times since then and had nothing to show for it but more balls to break when she was done with this case.

She picked up the phone and tried her contact at Federal Express. His voice mail answered; she left her fourth message in the last half hour even though he'd promised some answers within the proverbial five minutes. Five minutes—right. All she needed from him was confirmation of what time the FedEx letter was picked up in the Bronx and the exact location, and the name of the carrier who had delivered it to the Bailey-Strauss loft that morning. She didn't like that no one had seen him enter the building or that Susan hadn't been asked to sign for the package. Lupe wouldn't feel good about linking it to the Rothka letter—which had been trackable from pickup to delivery—until she had the paperwork. What the hell was taking so long?

She lifted the base of her phone and blew away a puff of dust. Damn incompetent fools. She flipped open her calendar and checked the dates: nowhere near her period.

She had sat down with intent to think, but thinking in the busy squad room was just about impossible. Here was where paperwork got done and backlogged phone calls got answered. Here was not where her mind could roam. She would give it five more minutes, she decided, before getting back outside. Anyone could reach her on her cell. She'd have someone else handle the nitty-gritties from here.

A true five minutes later she was heading out the squad room door when her desk phone began its heavy-bells jangle. She caught it on the second ring: it was Forensics, finally, with analysis on the handset.

"Listen, Loopy." They all called her that: Loopy like *looped,* crazy, off the charts; what the hell, she got results. "What we got maybe ain't what you're looking for."

"No! What I want is the facts."

"Good, 'cause here they are: There are four sets of fingerprints on this handset. We compared them like you asked to prints from Peter Adkins and Dave Strauss."

"And?" She hated dramatic pauses.

"Nothin'."

"So? Who'd you get?"

"Three prints matched other prints found around the Café Luxembourg, and all those prints matched people who worked there. Except one set that didn't match nothin'."

"One set of fingerprints on the phone from someone who doesn't work at the café?"

"Check."

"Someone who isn't Peter Adkins or Dave Strauss? You sure about that?"

"We checked against every set of fingerprints we found in the apartment on Water Street, Loopy, and nothin' matched up."

"Yo."

"You tellin' me. Seems like you got a party crasher."

Lupe put down the phone and thought it through. She'd have to double-check the alibis of those three people who worked at the café—but let's just say, she told herself, let's just say they all checked out and who she was really looking for was someone else. Someone who was still in Brooklyn. Someone who either took Lisa upstate and then returned for some reason, or someone who didn't take Lisa but who had called Marie Rothka just for the fun of it. A prank call? An accomplice? But Marie Rothka had recognized the groom's voice. . . .

Lupe felt her radar jump: turned on and active. If Peter Adkins had Lisa upstate, and someone else had called Marie from Dumbo at seven a.m., then maybe what they were looking for were two people, not one. That face Strauss saw last night in the window of Seventy-seven, thought he saw but wasn't sure . . . maybe Adkins didn't write that letter; maybe that face wrote it on Adkins's pad.

More facts. She wanted more hard data to get this straight. She picked up the phone to assail the FedEx voice-mail system one more time, and to her amazement got through to a real live human voice.

"Yes, Detective Ramos, I'm sorry I missed your calls before; I've been working on this." He spoke quickly in English but with a strong Indian accent.

"Glad you've been busy, Mr. Song." *Yeah, right.*

"Singh. Sanjay Singh. I've been through the entire system. It took a while but I finally managed to contact everyone on that route this morning."

"Shoot."

"Detective Ramos, I am sorry to say there is no electronic tracking of a letter or package or anything at all going to the name or address you gave me. Nothing at all. Yes, I admit, sometimes a missive eludes our system, but, my dear lady, in this case I can attest that no one at all picked up or delivered that package because I have personally spoken to everyone who might have. Detective Ramos, I have nothing to offer you. I am sorry."

She almost hated to stop his train before it crashed, just to find out how fast he could talk, but it came as a relief when he put on his own brakes.

"Thank you, Mr. Singh."

"Detective Ramos, please, I am happy to help."

She hung up the phone, plucked two paper clips from their holder, joined them, and pulled.

They were looking for *two* men, not one. One was Peter Adkins, who had Lisa upstate. The other was someone else, *the face,* who had stayed behind and watched, made the call and hand-delivered that letter himself. What she didn't know yet was which one was the real groom.

Dave Strauss's radar was working—if he had thought it was a waste of time to fly up to Gardiner, he would have said so—and her radar was working, too. It was brilliant of him to be moments from landing in Gardiner, New York. And it was brilliant of her to have stayed behind in Brooklyn. Whether or not Peter Adkins was the groom was something they'd figure out later. There was no time to be fair in how they divvied up the spoils; if they were lucky, if they could both succeed, they'd end the day with one living girl between them and a bad guy apiece.

Her phone rang again—suddenly she was the most popular girl in the squad room—but this time it was a call from inside the case. Officer Sullivan, the only dwarf on the NYPD, or any PD as far as she knew, was reporting in from Water Street.

"Boss, we got a situation down here. Susan Bailey-Strauss wants to get inside the building, won't take no for an answer. How do we handle her?"

Lupe wasn't sure. "Hold her there; we're on our way."

She shot up from her chair, letting it roll across the floor behind her as she hurried to the squad room door. Quick down the hall with a stop in the conference room to address the task force with the latest developments. Her new instructions were for Zeb Johnson to handle the situation with Susan Bailey-Strauss; for half the group to stay here and cover Dave and Bruno upstate; and the other half to go with her and deploy on foot, quietly, to prowl the waterfront. They would carry walkie-talkies, keep them turned to the lowest volume, and stay alert for anything or anyone suspicious. She didn't know who they were looking for exactly, but her gut told her the face was there, somewhere, lurking.

Lupe figured that Peter Adkins's abduction of Lisa had either piqued the real groom's interest today and brought him to the scene to get his kicks; or that Peter Adkins was the real groom and this guy was some true-crime lunatic who belonged in an asylum; or they were partners with a bigger plan.

One thing was for sure: The case had split in two. There was what, or who, she needed to find here in Brooklyn. And there was Dave's pursuit of Lisa, and Peter Adkins, upstate.

Lupe walked at a fast clip along the glossy linoleum

on her way to the staircase down and out of the precinct, uncapping her lipstick with one hand and speed-dialing her cell with the other. Bruno's number was still out of range, but this time Dave's wasn't and he answered quickly.

"Yo, it's me; you still in the air?"

"Landing," Dave told her.

"Good." The lipstick went on smooth, thick and pink. "Lemme get you up to speed."

Chapter 23

"The local cops've been in and out," Ramos said in the rapid clip Dave was getting used to. He could just barely make out her words under the roar of the helicopter. "Adkins's car's parked at the house and they found traces of yellow paint and—" She stopped herself.

"And?"

"No one was at the house when they got there, Dave. But there was some blood on one of the beds. It looks like he had her tied up."

Dave's stomach turned as the color red spilled through his mind, oozing through mental byways he preferred not to visit. If he didn't find her, he thought, if he didn't find her in time . . .

"Doesn't mean—"

"Yup, I know what it means and what it doesn't mean. Someone's meeting us when we land?"

"Officer Bob Andrews, I was told."

"Good."

"Dave, before you go, I've got a coupla things to run by you."

"Shoot."

"We found the handset from the café."

Dave sat forward, his seat belt cinching his hips. Outside, a horizon of pale blue sky blended with green countryside.

"Where?"

"In the playground by your building. In the sandbox."

So close to his home, Dave thought, *so close*. "But the call was made at seven in the morning; the whole area was already searched; it doesn't make sense."

"It makes sense if Adkins has Lisa upstate and someone else made the call in Brooklyn. Get this: Adkins's prints were not on the phone, but someone else's were, someone Forensics can't identify. Listen to me, Dave: Unless Adkins wore gloves, it wasn't him. And another thing: FedEx never delivered any letter to your apartment this morning."

The helicopter began its descent over Gardiner.

"Someone else," Dave said.

"That's what I'm thinking." She paused, then added, "The face."

"The face," Dave echoed, remembering the ghostly visage that had pulled away from the window before he was certain he'd really seen it. A pale, humorless, watching face.

"He was in the apartment, Strauss. *He* wrote the letter. Borrowed Adkins's pad."

"The roof hatch," Dave said, his mind's eye following the face, or the groom, or whoever he was, onto the connected rooftops of Water Street, watching him snake through the darkness above while, below, their attention was glued to the front door. "Why the *hell* didn't we station someone on the roof?"

"We can beat our idiot selves up later, Strauss. I got

one more thing for you to chew over." She must have walked outside, because suddenly Dave heard city traffic noises. "Marie Rothka remembered something the groom said to her a coupla times on the phone: 'The apple doesn't fall far from the tree.'"

"A cliché," Dave murmured. Easy to remember and also to forget. "It has to mean something. But if Adkins *isn't* the groom—"

"Know what I'm thinking, Dave?"

He realized it suddenly: cider mills, fresh donuts, apple picking. "It's leaf-peeping season up here."

"That's right. We don't know who's who, so we'd better follow any lead that might work in both places."

"I'll ask the locals about the apple trade," Dave said. "Looks like we're about to land."

"Stay in touch, baby."

Dave was about to hang up when he hesitated. "How's Susan doing?"

"She's doing," was all Ramos said.

The pilot gradually circled them toward a clearing below. As they descended, what from above had been an abstract mosaic of colors and shapes began to congeal into fields, trees bursting with autumn hues, clusters of houses and long, snaking roads. The helicopter rattled to a landing in a whir of propellers and finally made purchase with the ground in what appeared to be an abandoned field. Long, dry grass whipped and swayed dramatically in the artificial wind. Bruno got out first, followed by Dave, and together they pushed through the still-churning air to the two cops who were waiting for them, standing near a squad car.

"I'll be here," the pilot told them.

Dave turned, saluted his thanks and then approached

the waiting police. The older officer stepped forward first, hoisting his belt above a hanging gut.

"Officer Bob Andrews, Gardiner Police," he introduced himself.

"Detective Dave Strauss." He offered a hand and they shook. The chunky high school ring Andrews wore dug into Dave's skin. He pretended not to notice.

"This is Detective Alexei Bruno," Dave said.

Andrews shook Bruno's hand, which took the greeting with an outsize squeeze; Dave imagined with some satisfaction that Bruno's big grip would override the hard metal bite of the ring. Andrews didn't flinch. From behind them, a throat deliberately cleared.

"Oh, right," Andrews said, stepping aside. "This here is Officer Rufus Braithwaite."

Braithwaite was slight and pale, with bright orange hair. He reminded Dave of Opie from *The Andy Griffith Show* he'd watched on TV as a kid. Braithwaite nodded in greeting but didn't speak.

The detectives piled into the back of the dark blue patrol car. Andrews automatically took the wheel and Braithwaite sat in the passenger seat, arms folded, lips set together in silence. Dave sensed a tension between his local hosts but couldn't decipher it and didn't particularly want to; it was an annoyance, considering the reason for their visit. Andrews turned on the siren and the patrol car pulled out of the field, racing into the silence of a country road. Now and then, a car swished past them in the opposite direction.

Strauss spoke first. "We understand you've been to the house."

"Yes, sir, went right over there after I caught the call," Andrews answered. "The Stutley place's been rented out a while now, tenants coming and going.

Now this current tenant, name of David Strauss, no one seems to know him."

From the backseat, Dave watched a smile flicker across Braithwaite's face. Andrews, however, didn't seem to catch the connection between the Stutley tenant's name and that of the man sitting in the backseat of the patrol car. Dave glanced at Bruno, who winked.

"Red car full of garbage, old candy wrappers and some such," Andrews listed what he had found at the scene. "Traces of yellow paint, blood. This Strauss fellow is not what you'd call a model tenant."

One corner of Braithwaite's mouth edged back up and he pushed it back down. Andrews meanwhile kept on talking, his rounded nose flexing as he spoke, eyes on the road. As they drove, Dave counted five apple orchards. Five orchards in just under four miles.

"How many orchards do you figure you've got in the area?" Dave asked the front seat.

"A whole lot," Andrews answered. "Big business, this time of year. Cider, donuts, pumpkins, pies, you name it." His collar was too tight, rippling the back of his neck. Beside him, Braithwaite nodded but held his silence.

"Do they all have stands on the side of the road? Or are some just orchards, tucked farther back?"

"I'd say most if not all have retail close enough to the road," Andrews answered with the bravado of someone pitching his town to a skeptic, as if Dave were there to buy real estate. "The orchard business brings revenue to the area. They want you city folk to know they're there—the bigger the better. Am I right, Rufus?"

Braithwaite raised his eyebrows, didn't smile, and nodded once. "Yep." He shifted his gaze between Dave and Bruno. Dave waited a moment, but the man said nothing more. Andrews turned the steering wheel right, then left. They slowed down on the long, unpaved entry to the Stutley house.

As they drove along the dirt road that sliced through well-established woods, Dave felt his pulse escalate. Lisa had been here, not too long ago, on this very road.

The large white house appeared in a clearing at the end of the drive. A cadre of police and neighbors were entering the woods in groups, calling out Lisa's name.

Andrews stopped the squad car well behind a red car parked near the house. Dave was sure he had seen that red car before, but in the quick redux of déjà vu the sense of recognition blurred with the present. He was sure and he wasn't sure; he would have to examine the murky recollection later.

Techs had already been over the car, so Dave and Bruno were free to inspect it. Strands of long blond hair had been found in the trunk, and there were visible traces of yellow paint on the driver's gas pedal and on the rubber floor mat. The lab would have to verify that the hair was Lisa's and the paint matched the crime scene in Brooklyn, proving that the abduction had taken place in front of the factory, but they had already established that Peter Adkins's fingerprints were all over the car and that it was registered in his name. The sloppy trail of evidence and the revelation that they were probably dealing with two men, not one, brought Dave back to the nagging suspicion that Adkins wasn't the groom. The more he thought about it, the more he hoped it was true; whereas the groom had always been elusive, Peter Adkins now seemed eminently decodable—and catchable. And if Dave could find Adkins, chances were he'd find Lisa, too.

Dave and Bruno entered the house behind Andrews, who took long strides with a heavy step. Braithwaite hung back, coming in silently after them, holding open the door, which squealed on rusty hinges. They walked directly into a spacious living room filled with furniture Dave guessed had once been nice but now looked forlorn. The windows were open and there was a long gash in one of the screens, revealing a slice of the chilly late afternoon. Andrews stood in the living room, nodding, saying, "So this is it."

It was Braithwaite who headed directly for the stairs. Evidence had been found in a bedroom and it was the silent subordinate who knew where it was. Dave got it: Andrews had passed the call on to Braithwaite, figuring it would pan out to nothing, and now he wanted in on the action. Dave wondered if Andrews had enough seniority over Braithwaite to merit the younger man's passivity or if something else was at play here. He began to worry that Andrews's arrogance and Braithwaite's silence could slow down the hunt.

Braithwaite led the three men down a long hallway, past seven doors—bedrooms, closets, a bathroom—to what appeared to be the master bedroom. It was large, with a dusty antique dresser and a four-poster bed whose blankets and sheets were rumpled. A forensics tech worked quietly at the foot of the bed where Lisa's socks lay collapsed on the floor. Dave recognized them: white with a band of silver glitter. He could see those socks on her feet, and the frayed hem of her bell-bottom jeans. He saw their kitchen floor at home and realized he was remembering yesterday morning, though it felt like years ago.

His eyes moved up from the floor and along the

bed. The details of ropes and blood hit Dave viscerally
now that he was seeing them in person; the ropes had
tied Lisa, and the blood presumably was hers. He
forced his eyes to stay open; he would see and feel
whatever the room could tell him, regardless of how
badly it pained him. He scanned the bed, inch by inch.
The wall behind it: yellow-and-red floral paper, possibly concealing blood spatter that the techs would pick
up if it was there. Lisa had been here, in this room, on
this bed, today. He could smell traces of Susan's perfume; Lisa must have borrowed some again. He had
never thought to ask either of them what it was called.

Bruno left the room and Dave could hear him walking down the hall, going in and out of other rooms.
Dave's eyes continued to negotiate this one. Red-and-
yellow-plaid curtains framed an eight-pane window of
old, wavy glass; the view was of the lawn leading into
the woods. An oval hooked rug seemed to have been
displaced and floated crooked toward the center of the
room. A bare bulb swung from a cord hanging from
the ceiling. Dave then noticed that on top of the
dresser there was a mostly full bottle of soda, and next
to it a half-filled glass. The soda in the glass was still
carbonated: Peter and Lisa had not been gone long.

Chapter 24

Wednesday, 5:15 p.m.

Officer Zeb Johnson appeared at Susan's side in the crowd of reporters and onlookers outside Seventy-seven Water Street and immediately took charge of a situation that had quickly gotten out of hand. Susan had not realized how much resistance and curiosity her desire to see that third-floor apartment would cause.

"Detective Ramos told me to escort Mrs. Strauss upstairs," he said. "Move aside, please, Officer Sullivan."

Johnson was three times the size of the cop who had been shouting at Susan that she would not be allowed inside the scene of an investigation under any circumstances, and spoke with a tone of authority free of the kind of condescension the dwarf probably faced all the time. Johnson then smiled brightly enough to melt even the belligerence of Officer Sullivan.

Sullivan heaved a long breath and stepped aside.

As soon as they were in the quiet of the front hallway, Susan turned to Johnson. In the dim light of the narrow hall, he looked even larger than he had out on the street.

"Thank you, Officer," she said. "I just wanted to—"

He lifted an extended finger to his lips, shook his head and turned down the hall. She followed. When they reached the stairwell, he asked her to wait. He took his cell phone out of his pants pocket and fingered the blue-glowing rubber buttons, then seemed to change his mind. He slipped his phone back into his pocket and hunched toward her.

"Tell you what," he whispered close to her ear. "I'll take you up and you won't touch anything. I mean *anything*. You'll stand in the middle of the place and you'll look around, see what you want; then we'll go."

His decision to bring her inside had been an improvisation, Susan realized, and now he was trying to figure out how to cover himself and help her at the same time. She wondered why he was willing to risk it, but wasn't about to ask.

"Okay," she whispered back.

Susan followed Officer Johnson up to the third-floor landing, where another officer was positioned outside one of the apartments, guarding the door. Johnson nodded briskly to the officer, whose eyes flicked on Susan as, stomach churning, she walked into the apartment the detectives had been so interested in.

She immediately saw why.

The room was nearly bare of furniture but its walls were papered with images. Images of her. And Lisa. Especially Lisa. Even Dave. Scanning the dizzying montage, her eyes landed on an old photo-booth strip of Susan's and Peter's teenage faces pressed together, expressions shifting in each shot; but there were only three frames here and she remembered four. The Family Dollar Store had just installed the booth and each vertical strip cost five dollars. Susan had paid but Peter kept the pictures, which had irritated her a little at the time, though she'd said nothing.

Technicians seemed to hover everywhere, but when Susan focused her mind on them she realized there were only three, a man and two women, matter-of-factly collecting some kind of physical data from this place where clearly Peter Adkins had lain in wait.

Well, he had never been shy, she thought, and almost laughed; and then the prick of humor blossomed into tears. She remembered loving that boy, so pleased all those times she had left her home to find him standing outside waiting for her. She had thought it meant that he cared. *This,* she remembered thinking as a girl just about Lisa's age, *this is love.*

And now he had Lisa. She was with him. And it wasn't love, nor had it ever been love. It had been obsession.

Susan closed her eyes and visualized Lisa alive. Alive. *Alive.*

Suddenly she recalled Peter the first time she was with him after she had learned she was pregnant. It was late January and she was just four weeks along.

She contemplated how to tell him but nothing came to mind. They were sitting in the backseat of his mother's car—she had gone into a store to run an errand—and Susan thought it might be a good idea to tell him here, when his mother would soon return, preventing him from making a big scene. On the last errand his mother had bought apples to make a pie, and Peter pulled one from the bag at his feet. He polished the bright red Macintosh apple on his sleeve and took a big bite of it. He didn't offer Susan an apple, or even a bite of his, and that instant of selfishness was the moment she decided she did not want him anymore. She had sensed something inchoate lurking within herself, something averse to the idea of spending her life with this exciting, demanding boy-man, but that apple bite was the crystallization of her brand-new decision. That crisp snap of sweet apple misting the air between them.

"I love apples," he said, staring past the car's front seat and through the windshield. He loved apples, and she would never marry him. She ran away from home that very afternoon. That morning of errand running with his mother was the last normal time they spent together before her lies and his anger laid down a minefield they could never cross.

Susan thought of Marie's recollection, *the apple doesn't fall far from the tree.* Apparently the groom had said so many odd things in his phone calls to her that had blended together over the months. Was Marie's memory of that statement what had made Susan think of Peter's apple now? Could it possibly be true that Peter was the groom? Susan had trouble believing it; and yet, what if he had remembered that errand-running morning as a last, missed chance and in his sick mind pieced it together with the chestnut about progeny?

The apple doesn't fall far from the tree.

Now when she pictured him taking that first bite of the shiny apple there was no crisp biting sound, no sweet mist in the air; there was just the airlessness of this apartment with its obsession walls and the awful smell of something rotting.

She glanced toward an open door that led into another room where presumably she would find a bedroom or a kitchen. Was that where the terrible smell was coming from? She didn't want to see anything else; but she had come all this way, and for what? She had come for the truth. She would look in the room, she decided; but after just two steps forward Officer Johnson cleared his throat. She looked at him, at the invisible tether that seemed to emanate from his kind eyes: *Keep still; don't touch; only look.* She had promised to behave and so she would. She stopped in place, like a little girl caught in freeze-tag.

She supposed she was lucky he had brought her up here at all.

She supposed she was lucky that the other people here seemed willing to ignore her.

She supposed she was lucky to know what Dave knew: to know this.

But what exactly was this?

Her gaze landed on an eight-by-ten glossy print of Lisa taped midway up the wall: She had been caught in a thoughtful moment, up close, revealing the slight forehead crease when she was deciding something. Her rainbow-striped fleece scarf fluffed up past her chin; the photo had to have been taken as far back as last winter, since it hadn't gotten cold enough yet this year for scarves.

Taped neatly beside that photo was one of Susan and Dave, taken from behind, two minuscule figures walking hand in hand on a summer evening in the direction of home. Susan remembered that night: She was wearing an orange-and-pink sundress and they were just leaving the factory where Dave had helped her unpack a large shipment of unsweetened chocolate from Denmark, five-pound slabs. Lisa was out at a friend's and they had gone home to cook dinner, but instead had made love and ordered in. Looking at the clandestine

glimpse of that innocent moment, Susan felt a rush of
love for Dave; love, and confidence that he would find
within himself the capacity to forgive her.

Below and above were photos of Lisa, Dave and
Susan, alone or together in varying combinations. The
photos were all different sizes; some were black-and-
white and some were color. Some of the subjects had
been cut out and placed on a different background.
Others were layered together on the wall like a collage. Susan felt a terrible mourning at the visual ca-
cophony in which random moments of their lives had
been spliced together and sliced apart.

How long had he been watching them?

Then her eyes landed on the newspaper article
about Dave, with Susan pictured along with her
teenage sister, Lisa, the couple's new roommate. So
that was how Peter had found them. Below the article,
a chilling message had been written directly on the
wall: *I am slain in the spirit.*

So that was it; that was the meaning of the letter. It
was how the true evangelicals thought back home:
When you married, you absorbed each other's spirits
into your own; you lived together and you lived in service to the Lord.

Peter had once told her that he loved her almost as
much as he loved God and that he knew exactly what
he wanted from both of them. In her innocence she
had been so thrilled by the sentiment that she didn't
ask him what exactly it was that he wanted.

She felt the churning in her stomach again. The
smell in the apartment seemed to heighten. She
stopped breathing and held still. The room began to
spin. The sensation reminded her of something, and
then she realized what. When she was a little girl, she

used to stand in the middle of the old metal merry-go-round, ordering her mother to *push, push,* so she could relish the dizzy imbalance of the ride. How had she ever enjoyed that sickening blur? Then she understood that she had never liked the dizzying aspect of it but the sensation of power it gave her. She had prided herself on never falling off. She had held on stoically, pretending to be the center axis of the ride, and that image had kept her steady.

Like it or not, she was the center axis of this ride, too; she reminded herself of that. She would look at the rest of the photographs, every single one. There could be something here that no one else would recognize.

But before she could resume looking, before the dizziness fully subsided, she remembered something else. Something completely different and until now irrelevant.

The apple doesn't fall far from the tree.

A dozen chocolate apples, made from handcrafted hollow molds, undeliverable to the address on the invoice. The credit-card charge had been challenged by the bank; it wasn't the first loss Water Street Chocolates had incurred via the Web site. The expensive special order had been dismantled, each apple individually wrapped in cellophane and placed in the shop for sale. The failed address was a defunct farm or an orchard somewhere in upstate New York, if she remembered correctly.

"Where is Dave?" Susan asked Johnson.

He looked at her and seemed to consider whether or not to answer. But she knew he would; he had given her everything else she had asked him for so far.

"Gardiner," Johnson said. "Upstate New York. They flew in, should be there by now."

"Why are they going there?"

Johnson half smiled. "I've already gone out on a limb here."

Even without the details, Susan felt safe in assuming that something had led Dave to Gardiner. Something important. She wasn't sure if the delivery address for those chocolate apples had been in Gardiner, but it was ringing a loud bell in her memory. Maybe the *apple falling far from the tree* saying had been some kind of foreshadowing by the Groom—a clue—and maybe if she could find the invoice for those chocolate apples she could give Dave a location he didn't have. Maybe Lisa was there.

"I need to get to my office," she said. "Can you help me get through that crowd outside?"

He nodded, eyeing her. "Why?"

"Please trust me; it could be important."

She hurried out of the stinking apartment with Johnson right behind her, running down the steps until he urged her to slow down.

"Keep cool," he told her, "or they're going to chase you."

When they emerged from the building, Susan lowered her head and followed Johnson through the crowd. Reporters called to them and cameras snapped, but they didn't respond. They walked slowly now, moving in the direction of Susan's shop. With each step, she prayed as hard as when she was a little girl sending out elaborate wishes at bedtime. But now her desires were concrete and immediate: to find that invoice. It would either be in the "Invoices—Unfulfilled" file drawer or the overflowing "To File" basket on the shelf above her desk.

"Tell me what I can do," Officer Johnson asked her

as soon as they were inside her shop, making their way through the factory and to her office.

Susan flicked on the light, and the white rectangular room where she spent so many hours of her life popped into focus. Things were mostly in their places here, including the colorful slips of personal reminders tacked to the bottom corner of her corkboard: the name of a book she wanted to buy for Dave; tonight's tickets to the Brooklyn Academy of Music; the address of the restaurant where she was supposed to meet a friend for dinner later in the week; a two-day-old phone message from Carole.

"See that wire-mesh basket on the second shelf up?"

Johnson looked in the direction she was pointing.

"Start looking for an invoice for a dozen chocolate apples, dated late September, upstate New York. I don't remember the name of the town."

Johnson lifted down the basket and began sifting through papers by the handful.

"Better do it carefully," Susan said. "Look at every one."

Meanwhile she opened the top file drawer and took out the slender file that held invoices that had, for various reasons, gone unpaid. Some customers habitually paid late and responded to dunning on their own schedules: some always on the second month, or the third, or the fourth. After a quick search, she was satisfied that the invoice she wanted was not in the file cabinet, so she joined Officer Johnson at the desk, where he had made a pile of papers already seen. She grabbed a chunk and began to peel off one paper at a time: weekly payroll records, receipts, supplier confirmations, proof of the dull minutiae involved in running even the most creative of enterprises.

"Hold it." Johnson was staring at a white paper. "Check this out."

She scanned the paper quickly and there it was in black ink: one dozen chocolate apples in a decorative wicker basket, cellophane wrapped with a frosted green bow, undeliverable to the address on the order—an intersection of two numbered routes in Gardiner, New York. No name or phone number had been included in the order—she no longer accepted special orders without them—but there had been a request for a special note: *The apple doesn't fall far from the tree.*

Susan picked up the office phone and speed-dialed Dave's cell. She didn't know how far their network reached, and in the lull after she dialed she could almost hear that dreaded canned recording telling her the call could not be completed.

"Ring!" Susan chanted into the phone. "Ring!"

Chapter 25

Dave's cell phone started ringing—he saw from caller ID that it was Susan—just at the moment Officer Braithwaite took a step into the bedroom and said, "Excuse me, Detective Strauss?"

"One second," Dave told the officer as he answered the call.

Susan spoke quickly but clearly, telling Dave about a basket of chocolate apples, specially ordered online, that had been undeliverable to an address in Gardiner a few weeks ago.

"Whoever placed the order asked for a special message on the card," Susan said. " 'The apple doesn't fall far from the tree.' "

The apple doesn't fall far from the tree. There it was again.

"You said the intersection of routes Forty-four and Fifty-five?" Dave asked her. "Nothing more specific?"

"That's all I've got," Susan said. "Do you have any idea where that is?"

"I'm going to find out." With Braithwaite standing

there, Dave kept his voice low; and as if in response
to his quiet control, the volume of Susan's voice rose
suddenly.

"I'm sick with worry, Dave! I'm so sorry about
everything. It's all my fault, all of this. *Please* tell me
you're going to find her!"

His eyes settled on the messy bed with its streak of
blood. He looked at Lisa's peeled-off socks, crumpled
on the floor. "Yes, I'm going to find her," he said. "I
will. I promise." But even as he said it, he knew this
promise could turn out to be unkeepable.

"Dave . . . ?"

"Sweetie," he said softly. "I've got to go now."

Braithwaite had stood patiently by, pretending not
to listen.

"Officer," Dave asked him, hooking his phone back
onto his belt loop. "Do you know the intersection of
routes Forty-four and Fifty-five?"

His pale, freckled face lit up. "As a matter of fact, I
do. That's what I wanted to tell you just now. There's
an apple orchard tucked back off that intersection, and
since you were asking before about out-of-the-way orchards, well, I thought I ought to mention it."

"What orchard?" Dave snapped. He had asked
about apple orchards *fifteen minutes* ago.

"That would be Childress Farms." Braithwaite
sounded confused, possibly even hurt, by the new,
hard tone in Dave's voice. "It's one of our smaller orchards and it's a ways off the road. It's the only thing
there besides a gas station that's been out of business
for years now."

"How far do these woods go?"

"About two miles in, I'd say."

"If you walked through, where's the closest orchard?"

"Childress Farms." Braithwaite's voice had fallen nearly to a whisper.

Dave stepped briskly past Braithwaite on his way out the door. "Let's go."

In the yard, Dave told Bruno where he was going. Bruno stayed behind to search the woods while Dave, with Braithwaite, hurried into the squad car and drove off the Stutley property.

"Faster," Dave ordered Braithwaite, who was driving too carefully along the dirt road. Everything this man did was heavy with caution, and it irritated Dave, but he needed the local cop for his knowledge of the area. In the side mirror, Dave watched Bruno diminish in size as he lit a cigarette and followed Bob Andrews into the woods to join the search party.

Braithwaite pressed harder on the gas. He said nothing, probably ashamed, and rightly so. What else was he withholding for just the moment Dave learned it another way?

The straight asphalt road along Route Forty-four sliced through cornfields on either side; fields of dried, wilting stalks whose bounty had long been picked or perished; fields beginning their seasonal decay. Death into life into death, Dave thought, suddenly aware of the tightening coil of his desperation. He knew they could be too late. The thought of actually losing Lisa exploded in his mind, and the browning fields beside the road seemed to evaporate into a haze. There was no God. He was certain now. And thinking of it this way surprised him, because he had never entertained the possibility that there was. It was Susan; she had entered him, changed him. Love had muddled and confused the clear thinking of his mind—but he would take it any day over the unanswerable questions that troubled him. He would even trick himself into belief, if that was what Susan required for their marriage to survive the staggering blows of today. He would blind himself willingly, refusing to see human life as biological accident or dried-out fields as scientific inevitabilities, cycles of life, but rather as mysterious blessings: *The Lord giveth and the Lord taketh away.*

He was human, after all, and just as vulnerable to hopelessness as the next guy. He could almost see himself tomorrow—having failed Lisa, having failed Becky, having failed Lolita—walking the edges of these very fields in tattered clothes, proclaiming the justice of the Lord's will. Slain in the spirit.

In spite of himself, he would become the personification of what he most reviled; wouldn't that be the ultimate punishment for a nonbeliever? To become another Elvis-Jesus rocking the world. By his side would be three teenage spirits with long floating hair, girls no one saw but himself, angels.

"I know He took my baby away because He has a plan for her," the mother wept against Dave's chest outside an East Brooklyn housing project after her six-year-old daughter had been brutally raped and murdered by her neighbor's boyfriend. Dave kept quiet, letting her take comfort from his silence as he despised her passive stupidity, because no child deserved that, and the boyfriend was a perverted creep who didn't deserve to live, and brutality like that had no plan, only accident.

The open fields of America invited unreasonable hope and unreasonable desperation. He saw it now. Faith was necessary, if false.

On the left, the field gave way to forest. It was the same woods that harbored the Stutley house on the other side. Miles of woods in which, Dave believed, Lisa was now being led to an orchard of some significance to either the groom or Peter Adkins or both. Or maybe she had already arrived.

They approached the intersection of routes Forty-four and Fifty-five. Just as Braithwaite had said, there was nothing there but an abandoned gas station.

"Here we are," Braithwaite said, turning right onto a dirt road posted with a faded wooden sign announcing CHILDRESS FARMS.

Dave turned back to look at the dense forest on the opposite side of the road that marked the edge of Stutley's land. It didn't make sense that Adkins would risk taking Lisa across an open road; but this was the location of the Internet order and there was nothing else here. Obviously, the order had been placed for a reason.

"It's just a bit up this way," Braithwaite said.

A long wooden fence snaked beside the road. After a couple minutes the orchard appeared. There was a small, weathered white house, a big red barn and, beyond that, hundreds of apple trees. Bushels of apples were haphazardly arranged in front of a makeshift farm stand with a sign asking that five dollars per bushel be left in the coffee can.

"Who comes here?" Dave asked. "It's so far off the main road."

"Locals, mostly," Braithwaite answered, pulling up in front of the house. "John Childress is likely home. Hardly leaves the place since his wife died. Old man's determined to die on his own land."

They got out of the car and started up the stone walk to the house. Dave let Braithwaite press the bell. As they waited, Dave glanced behind him at the bushels upon bushels of unsold apples. The orchards seemed to spread endlessly behind the house, a web of gnarled branches laced together, dotted red.

Inside the house, he heard footsteps approach the door. He wished he had brought his gun, but Braithwaite had his, snapped onto his belt holster next to a pair of handcuffs. Dave wondered if the man was swift enough to actually use the gun . . . because if Lisa was inside this house and if Adkins had one, they would have to act quickly.

The door creaked open and there stood a skinny old man who reminded Dave of one of the apple trees in the orchard. From the sleeves of his undershirt, gnarly arms protruded like branches that were a little too long for his body. His blue jeans were worn and baggy, beneath which the legs assumedly matched the arms: strong, bark-skinned limbs. He had a head of moppy white hair and sharp green eyes. He hadn't shaved in at least two days.

"Yello?" he said, gauzy behind his screen door.

Dave had expected Officer Braithwaite to speak first, since this was his jurisdiction, but he just stood there.

"Detective Dave Strauss." He showed his gold shield. "Are you John Childress?"

The old man nodded. He opened the door, stepped onto the porch and keenly eyed Dave's identification. Clearly Braithwaite didn't feel it necessary to produce his own, since he was in the uniform of the local police.

"Not from around here." Childress's voice was gruff but not unwelcoming.

"New York City," Dave said. "Brooklyn."

Half of Childress's mouth crooked up and froze in place. "Well, well, well. What can I do ye fer?"

Dave wasn't sure if the hick locution, the *ye fer,* was genuine or for the city slicker's amusement. He decided to ignore it. "We're looking for a girl," he began, "who was abducted from Brooklyn last night."

The ridicule dropped off Childress's face. He began to listen carefully as Dave explained what was necessary to convince him they needed earnest answers, and quickly.

"Haven't seen a girl." Childress rubbed his whiskered cheek; Dave noticed a cluster of blackish lumps on his skin beneath the growth. "The Stutley house, you say?"

"That's right."

"Don't know the current tenant. Last ones were all right, used to come by for apples regular. Told them to take what they wanted, didn't care if they paid."

He was chatting now; lonely. Dave forced patience upon himself, knowing that often it was during the idlest parts of conversation that something essential flared out.

"My wife, she loved chocolates, all kinds. Eight years ago, before she passed, I would have told you"—he snapped his fingers—"'talk to Althea! She spends my money like there's no tomorrow.' Chocolate apples." He shook his head wistfully, and Dave knew this man spent his days in yearning for a long-departed wife.

"So I guess you yourself didn't order any chocolate apples from New York," Dave said. "I guess that's not something you would do."

Childress smiled. A front tooth was broken off at a jagged angle. "No, sir, that's not something I would do."

"What about one of your workers?"

"Let 'em all go a few years back. Couldn't afford

'em; didn't need 'em. This place has been paid off a generation, my kids are gone, no one wants the place anymore, and me . . ." He didn't finish the sentence.

Dave nodded and looked at Braithwaite, whose eyes were fixed on Childress. What was he seeing? Thinking? Why wouldn't he speak?

"We'd like to take a look around the orchards, Mr. Childress," Dave said. "And also the house, if you don't mind."

Childress didn't pause to consider it; he just swung open the screen door and stepped aside to let them in.

Dave went in and Braithwaite followed. Childress let the screen door bang shut behind them. The living room was worse than the Stutley house, where old furniture had soaked in years of dust; that was mere neglect. Childress had embalmed the place with plastic wrap, evidently seeking to stop time. Every stick of furniture and every surface was clumsily swathed to preserve Althea's arrangements of doilies and knick-knacks. The book she had presumably been in the middle of reading sat on a side table, bookmark posted between the pages; Dave couldn't see the title beneath the thick skin of dust that had settled over the plastic. The only things not covered were the pictures that hung on the walls: a painting of a barn and scattered chickens, with a woman bent over a butter churn; a wizened photograph of Childress Farms a century ago; and a family portrait taken against the kind of blue-sky background used by most department store photographers. In the picture, John Childress had short brown hair, tan skin and looked about forty; his plump wife had dyed-black hair in a shag haircut and a cheerful smile; and with them were two boys, both blond and toothy with moss-green eyes and forced smiles. On the bigger one's right cheekbone was a bright red slash that looked as if it had been recently stitched.

Dave stared at the image of the blond-haired boy with the bright scar beneath one eye.

"Yep," Childress said, following Dave's gaze, "Theo was a wild one. Got that scar riding his bike full-tilt down a dirt hill. Fell flat on his face. He was a thrill seeker, that kid. Nearly wore my strap out on his behind. Had to tie him down more than a few times to keep him still."

Beads of sweat gathered on Dave's face so quickly they trickled down his temples. He wanted to *run,* to take action, but first he had to understand. Was it possible? Could he be standing in the childhood home of the groom? Was that blond boy with the angry scar on his cheekbone the scar-faced blond man Ramos and Bruno had sought on Water Street on Monday? *Someone* had ordered chocolate apples sent to this location, and requested the special note with the delivery, and whispered those same words on the phone to Marie Rothka. *Theo Childress.* Did the groom now have a name?

With his perfectly wrong timing, Braithwaite chose that moment to speak. "She made the best apple strudel, your wife."

Childress lit up. "Yes, indeed, she did!"

"She sliced the apples real thin and they melted right in your mouth. Not too much sugar and no cinnamon at all."

"That's where you're wrong, sonny boy. She used a sprinkle of cinnamon. Just a sprinkle."

Childress positioned himself in front of Braithwaite now and leaned forward to get a close look at him.

Braithwaite looked solidly back, nodding; two men seeing each other with decades peeled off.

"Randall Braithwaite!"

"It's Rufus, sir."

"Rufus Braithwaite! Used to play around the orchard with Theo!"

"Mostly Andy."

Childress pulled back his head and nodded slowly. "That's right, it was you and Andy. Had a tetherball set up out back, if I recall."

As the two men spoke, Dave moved away from them and stood in front of the gaping door. The screen mesh had come away from the door frame at one side where the edge had frayed. He could see the massive treetops of the forest from here, but not the road.

"Yep," Braithwaite said.

"Andy wasn't too interested in the orchard. It was Theo I always thought'd be the one to stay."

"Where are they now?" Braithwaite asked.

"Andy got it in the first Gulf War."

Dave turned around. Braithwaite's already pale skin had blanched even more at that news.

"Theo's some kind of computer consultant, works overseas. Said trees weren't enough of a challenge." Childress shrugged his bony shoulders. "They always challenged me."

"Didn't Theo plant a few apple trees of his own, way back when?"

"A few trees? I gave that boy his own orchard across the road! I kept it going after he left home, but when Althea died, there was no point."

"I remember now," Braithwaite said. "A dozen apple trees planted in a semicircle in a clearing across the road."

"The apple doesn't fall far from the tree," Childress said bitterly. "Well, that old chestnut's rotten to the core, isn't it?"

"What did you say?" Dave asked.

Childress looked at Dave; he seemed a bit surprised to realize that the New York City detective was still in the room. "Sometimes I think it was my grandpa coined that old cliché. He started this orchard in 1871, taken over by my father, then by myself, and when I had two sons, well, it was a given one of them would stay on. The apples stayed on the orchard, stayed by the tree." He shook his head. "No more. When I'm gone, it's over."

"Can you show me the orchard?" Dave asked.

Childress reared backward. "Just step out that door! It's all around you!"

"No," Dave said. "The small one. Theo's orchard."

Chapter 26

Wednesday, 6:06 p.m.

Pebbles and sticks bore into the soles of Lisa's bare feet as she was hustled through the woods, a riot of autumn leaves quickly absorbing them into hidden territory. Walking behind her, he pressed the gun firmly into her back, just to the right of her spine, nudging her forward. She understood that he might pull the trigger at any time and realized that there was one thing she wanted from him before he did whatever he was going to do. No, two things. She wanted to know if he was really her birth father. And she wanted to know if he was the man Dave had lost last year, the one who had kidnapped that girl Becky. Lisa wanted to know if she carried the genes of a killer, because if she did, if he *was* that man, then she didn't know how she would be able to live with herself. If he was that man, and if this was the day she was going to die, knowing she was tainted might help her go more easily.

"Where are you taking me?"

"To a special place."

Special. What could be special to a man like him? Even if he wasn't Becky's kidnapper, he was the opposite of everything Lisa had wished for in a father. *Special*—it was a word he should not have been allowed to use.

Her foot caught on something sharp.

"Ouch!"

She stopped abruptly and bent down to assess her bleeding left foot. He was slicing her open bit by bit: first the accidental cut to her inner arm when he was knifing off the ropes on the bed, and now this. She sat all the way down and as her body met the ground she felt as if something heavy within her kept falling. Falling and falling through her body, past her body, beyond caring. Not that she didn't care; she *cared*. It was just that . . . she didn't know how to think of it . . . but obviously the day had not gone quite as planned, as *he* had planned. She was beginning to get the feeling that he wasn't really sure what he wanted from her, exactly. She decided to take a chance.

"Why don't you get it over with?" Sitting cross-legged on the stony ground, she looked up at him and waited.

He stared down at her, the gun tight in his hand. He looked stricken with confusion, as if he wasn't sure what she meant.

"I don't think you really want to kill me," she said, knowing it was a risk; also knowing that risk was all she really had to work with. "You just want to get to know me, like you said before, and that's a pretty *normal* thing to want." She stressed *normal* to throw a lifeline into the chaos of his mind, thinking maybe, *maybe* it made sense to give him the benefit of the doubt even though he didn't deserve it.

His forehead tensed and his blue eyes began to cloud in such a strong reaction of bafflement it frightened her.

"You don't believe me, do you?" His voice was small and soft, creepy. "That I'm your father."

"I . . . I don't know what to believe."

"Susan told me she had an abortion, but now I know the truth. When I look at you, I see my *flesh.*"

The way he said *flesh,* savoring it, made her want to vomit.

"What I don't understand . . ." She faltered, then regained herself; she had to face him now if she was going to have any chance at all. "What I don't understand is why you kidnapped me."

He hesitated, as if *kidnapped* didn't fully agree with his own perceptions.

"It's my turn," he finally said. "And she was wrong to lie."

"Is that what you told yourself when you came up with this plan?"

"It's what he told me."

"Who?"

"Him."

Oh, Jesus—*Jesus.* Was that it? "But that's an *idea,*" she said, "and I'm a *person.* Can't you see that?"

Shaking his head, he seemed to struggle with something. "He planned it all out for me. He said he was my brother. He told me it would be best for everyone, and I deserved my turn."

Right at that moment, the sun tipped out of the sky, the trees darkened, the air chilled.

"Turn for what?"

He stared at her, and in the pause Lisa remembered something Susan had once told her about her high

school boyfriend: that he was handsome and super-
cool—her word had been *magnetic*—and that his only
brother had drowned a year before they'd started dating. Now it was obvious Susan had been talking about
Lisa's very own father, that this was the guy, but *magnetic* was not the word she'd use for him.

"And isn't your brother *dead?*" Lisa asked a second
question before he'd answered her first.

A storm gathered in his face as he leaned aggres-
sively toward her. But before he could say or do anything, a car door slammed in the near distance.

"Get up!" His hand tightened around the gun, his
knuckles turning white. "Right now! Get moving!"

Her body automatically obeyed; she sprang up,
stepping forward onto her injured foot. They continued deeper into the woods, swallowed by trees that
seemed to multiply, growing denser and more ablaze
with color. She smelled bark and damp earth and without making sense it became the smell of this man's
rage and confusion.

As they walked, her eyes slid to his profile. He had
an unassuming face, plain, really—*not* handsome, at
least not anymore—and Lisa wondered what Susan
had seen in him. She figured he was about thirty-one
or -two, just a little older than Susan, yet he looked
middle-aged in a way she was not. He was a loner and
a stone skipper, and she recalled now that the first
time she'd seen him, standing at the edge of the water
in the Empire-Fulton Ferry State Park, he had seemed
as bland and innocuous as anyone else, just some guy
who couldn't get his stones to skip without sinking.
She wished he hadn't done it this way, that instead he
had just come up and introduced himself. She could
almost see the two of them sitting together on the park

bench, talking. His turn would have been a better turn, a real turn, if he had just gone about it without all the drama. He glanced over and found her looking at him and he kind of smiled at her. She found herself thinking he had a nice smile. She had a strange sensation, a desire to know him, yet she knew it would never be possible.

They began to emerge from the densest part of the woods. The trees thinned and pale light trickled through. After another fifty feet or so they stepped out of the woods and into a large, lopsided clearing. It looked like some kind of orchard, with a semicircle of trees heavy with fruit. Apples. They were all over the ground, some perfect, some rotting. Somewhere beyond the orchard, Lisa heard the vague buzz of traffic.

They walked across an open expanse to the opposite side of the orchard, where the trees were planted evenly, about twenty feet apart. Lisa's eyes swept the heavy branches dripping with apples, then the partly green, partly burnt canvas of earth speckled with fallen fruit. The orchard was abandoned, that was obvious, or else all these perfectly good apples would have been gathered and sold.

Her eyes stopped on a hole between two of the trees. It was at least five feet long and narrow. Just about her size. Next to it was a mound of dirt spiked with a shovel. Nearby, between another two trees, was a swell of earth about the same size and shape as the hole, but filled in and sparsely overgrown with grass.

"He didn't tell me about this!" he said.

The gun was still at her back, but she felt it pull slightly away, as if he were distracted. She got the feeling he was as surprised as she was to be confronted by the two graves: one old, the other freshly dug.

"This is wrong! This was not the plan! He didn't say anything about this!"

Lisa didn't know how to think of him or how to think of this moment, except that his agitation seemed genuine. She wished she had asked him his real name because she saw now that it might have been useful. She had to calm him down, and had to start somewhere.

"How long has God been talking to you?" As soon as she'd said it, she realized she might have found a subtler way to ask.

"What?" His voice was shrill, his face bright red. "You think I actually talk to God?"

"You said—"

"This is *wrong*," he said again. Poking her with the gun, he moved her over to the open grave and stared down into it. It was a good yard deep. "He never said anything about *this*."

"Please don't," she begged. "Please, please, please don't!"

"This is *wrong*," he said again.

"Yes," she whispered, "it's wrong; it's very wrong."

Her fear seemed to distress him even more than the orchard and the new grave. He looked at her with his blue eyes and his flushed face and his dimpled chin just like her own.

"If I let go of you, you're going to run away."

It was a statement, not a question. If she hadn't been so scared, she would have said, *Duh.* Of course she would run away; it was all she had in mind, nothing else. If not for the gun . . .

And just as she thought it, he looked down at the gun in his hand. "Here," he said, and handed it to her.

She had never held a gun before. The metal was

smooth and warm from his hand, and it was heavy. It felt strangely delicious to have the gun, because the gun was the power, and now she could do it: run away, or even shoot him.

Then he dug into his pocket and her heart nearly exploded, thinking he had something else, another gun or the knife from before, and they would have to fight. She couldn't fight; she didn't know how and she didn't want to, but if she had to, she would; she would. . . . But between his fingers was a little piece of paper, which he gave to her.

It was a tiny photograph, a one-inch square. It looked like it had been cut from one of those four-frame photo strips you got at the mall. Only this was older, the colors were faded, and it showed Susan when she was a teenager, and she was kissing a boy. And the boy was him—and he *was* handsome. Their heads were tilted so their faces fit and their lips were pressed together and their eyes were closed.

He walked to the nearest tree and sat down at its base, lowering his face between his knees and wrapping his arms around his bent legs. She stared at the photograph, knowing it was time to make her move, but she couldn't. She was frozen. So it was true: He was her father. She felt a tinge of pity for him; he was so ridiculous and so cruel.

He lifted his head. "I love you," he said into the empty space in front of his tree.

"What?" Lisa couldn't believe she had heard him right.

"I love you."

This was nothing like any kind of love Lisa had ever known or imagined. So he loved her. So this was love.

For one whole night and one whole day, he had terrorized her.

And now he had given her a gun, and he had given her this photograph as proof.

Soon it would be completely dark. She had to make a decision.

She thought of Meg from *A Wrinkle in Time* and Joni from her mother fantasies and Susan from her real life. She thought of how much her three heroines had inspired her and knew she couldn't let any of them down.

She pointed the gun at him. "Tell me about your brother."

"Only if you make me a promise."

A *promise?* Was he kidding? After all he'd put her through, why should she promise him anything?

"No," she said. *She* had the gun now.

He closed his eyes, laid his head back against the tree trunk and seemed to think something over. Then he began to speak, slowly and carefully, keeping his eyes closed.

"Sometimes I can see how wrong this has been. But I don't have any real control over my mind. That's the problem, Lisa. That's why I need you to help me."

She just stared at him; she had no idea what he was talking about.

"You're right; my brother died. Robbie drowned." He opened his eyes and stared at the space in front of him, like he was watching a movie. "I helped him drown."

"You mean . . . you killed him?"

"I never meant to. When it was over I was horrified. I need you to believe that, Lisa. And I need you to do something for me."

"Stop asking me for things!" Her voice was sharper than she'd intended; sharp but true. "You have no right to ask me for anything."

He nodded as if he agreed with her, but his words said otherwise. "You were taken from me before I even knew you existed. When I found out about you, I knew he had come back, through you, to find me."

"You mean your brother, Robbie?"

This was too much. So her father had killed a boy who would have been her uncle? And now he thought *she* was this uncle? That he was somehow *in* her?

"I need his forgiveness, Lisa. If he forgives me, I'll be saved. It's the only way. He's a part of you; I can *feel* it. Will you forgive me?"

His face was red and sweaty and she hated him; she hated him for doing this to her and she hated him for not being a father she could have loved. Because she wanted to love him—she *wanted* to—but he had made that impossible.

"Why should I?" She steadied the gun in his direction, just in case.

He shook his head slowly from side to side, as if there were no way she would ever understand, which was probably true.

"I want some answers," she said in the demanding tone her father, Bill, used when he was unhappy with something she'd done. "Why did you kill your brother?"

He closed his eyes again. "My wife helped me understand something about my mind, that I can't control my illness alone. Even the medications don't really work anymore. And to be honest with you, when I look at the world, sometimes I think I'm the only one who's sane."

The more he spoke, the more her fear of him drained away. Something inside his mind was making him do things even he didn't understand. Or maybe, Lisa thought, someone outside himself was giving him ideas.

"Tell me about *him*," Lisa said.

"I loved my brother—"

"No, the other *him*. The one who called himself your brother and came up with this stupid plan. Did somebody put you up to this?"

"I don't talk to God, if that's what you think. That's what Robbie thought, but he was wrong. Maybe *he* does. I wouldn't be surprised."

Something then occurred to Lisa, and she looked around the clearing, trying to see into the dense surrounding forest. Nothing was visible except tree trunks creating a variegated darkness in which anyone could hide at this time of day.

"Who is he?"

He sighed deeply. "He was my patient." His voice sounded thin and vacant, like the last moment of a bubble before it popped. "Theo grew up here. He said this place was special to him and he would share it with me. He said it was my turn to have what was due me. He said if I found you, I'd be saved, and it would be over."

"Your patient?" Like he was a doctor. Like that could be possible.

"I was his therapist." He laughed bitterly, and Lisa believed that, crazy as it sounded, he was telling the truth. "He convinced me to stop my medication so I could *feel*. He drew me a map, showed me how to get here, loaned me the house he rents near his family home."

She glanced at the filled-in mound, the other grave. "What for?"

"He said he tried to find you for me, but he made a mistake. He said it was something I'd have to do myself if I wanted it done right. He told me that my only chance of being saved was to find you, and that when I got here with you, I would know what to do—"

"Lunatic," Lisa spit.

"I thought we'd keep on going, maybe to Canada—"

Lisa thought of the terrible day Becky Rothka disappeared on her way home from their school; how they were the same age and looked a lot alike.

"Did he kidnap a girl named Becky?" she asked. "Did he think she was *me?*"

"I don't know how much of what he says is real."

So why do you listen to him? she wanted to shout, but instead asked, "Is he here now?"

"It wasn't the plan," he said, following Lisa's anxious gaze as it traced the periphery of the woods, "but maybe. Someone dug that grave."

He began to weep and lifted his face in her direction, like he was the victim, like she had somehow cosmically hurt him and now she owed him something.

"*Please* help me," he cried. "You could shoot me; it could be over. *Please.*"

She had never seen eyes that desperate before. A million thoughts and feelings rained through her body all at once in big, waxy slabs that couldn't penetrate. She felt heavy and incompetent; deaf and dumb; dizzy. She did not know what to do.

So this was her father.

And she was his daughter.

He was begging her to kill him.

And in a way she really wanted to. She *hated* him. He had proven he was a dangerous man.

She straightened her arm and it shook, she was holding the gun so tightly. The trigger under her finger felt stiff; to pull it would take tremendous effort. But she was strong; she could do it. She wanted to do it, but then again she didn't.

She heard crunching sounds in the woods.

If that psycho Theo was here, she thought, and if he was about to join them in the clearing, he would kill her anyway—just like he had killed Becky last year—so she might as well do it. She could find out if revenge was sweet or rancid. She could do this forbidden thing—she could kill her own father—and immediately be freed of the act's burdens.

"How many bullets in this gun?" Her voice was a rough whisper, but he heard her loud and clear.

"Six."

Enough for both of them—her father *and* Theo.

But *shoot* someone? It was *wrong*.

She had to decide. Someone was coming. Any moment, it would be too late.

Chapter 27

Dave followed Officer Braithwaite and John Childress into the woods. As soon as they pierced the overgrowth, Dave saw a scant, foot-beaten dirt path. Childress, in front, used his bare arms to push aside the brush; Braithwaite cringed at each backswipe of branches, but persevered. The deeper they went into the forest, the dimmer and quieter it became. Day was petering out, fading to twilight. Dave felt a chill at the back of his neck.

And then he heard it: a voice looping over the treetops, seeming to cause a shiver in the orange-and-red haze of leaves. It was a high, strong voice that seemed to sail at top velocity. A frightened yet determined voice. It was *Lisa*.

"Christ Almighty," Childress sputtered.

Dave broke into a run behind Braithwaite, who was racing now, the fabric of his uniform undulating over swiftly moving muscle. Sweat streamed down Dave's face. The voice soared above them. As he pushed deeper into the woods, he listened for its source. Was it getting louder or weaker? He couldn't tell, with the sound of his own heaving breath pounding in his ears.

He sprinted past Braithwaite, ignoring the high, thorny bramble that slapped against his skin. Childress moved at a good clip for an old man but Dave passed him too, his feet pounding the old path as he cut through the overgrowth with slashing arms.

The voice was getting closer now, or he was getting closer to the voice.

And then—it stopped.

Now the only things Dave heard were the labor of his own breathing and the crunching of his feet over the leaf-covered earth.

Until a single gunshot cracked the relative silence.

Dave's body kept running while his mind stopped on that moment, on the blast that echoed and echoed and echoed throughout him. He ran into the ominous silence of Lisa's stopped voice. In the air was the smell of smoke, something burning.

He was getting closer, sprinting toward what looked like a clearing just ahead.

He raced along the final stretch of path, noticing apples on the ground, nested in leaves and moss to the side and also, increasingly, underfoot. He kicked one aside. Then he entered a grass clearing covered with apples in various states of decay. Apples and apple trees.

Lisa stood in the middle of the clearing, pale and shaking, holding a gun.

Seeing her, a river of raw, agonizing joy rushed through Dave. She was *alive*. She was *safe*. He had found her. But he hated that she held a gun in her young hands, and his next thought was to fear for her safety in a new, different way.

Braithwaite and Childress ran into the clearing

behind Dave. Braithwaite gaped, apparently stunned by the physical reality of an actual girl. Childress hinged over at the waist, hands propped on his knees, struggling for breath.

Dave's eyes followed the direction of Lisa's gun. There, across the clearing—amidst the crayon scribble of autumn colors, the greens and browns and reds and oranges and golds and yellows—sat Peter Adkins, leaning against a tree. There was a deep gash in the bark a yard above his head, where the gun's backlash must have redirected Lisa's inexperienced shot. From that, Dave could see what was happening here: Lisa had shot at Adkins and he had let her. She was preparing to shoot again.

"Lisa!" Dave called. "Don't do it!"

She seemed terrified and frozen, stuck in her determination to finish what she had started, as if she had made a momentous decision and could not now turn back.

"Lisa, honey, please listen to me." Dave calibrated his tone to ease out the alarm he felt at the thought of Lisa shooting her birth father. It was possible the law might forgive her, in light of what she'd been through, but she would never forgive herself. He took a step toward her. "Sweetheart, listen to me, please. It's over now. *Over.*"

With the gun still trained on Adkins, Lisa looked at Dave. There she was—their Lisa—and yet she almost looked like a different girl. Her blond hair was wild around a paper-white face. Her bloodshot green eyes considered him with a lack of mercy of which he would not have thought her capable. In that moment, he felt astounded by his love for this girl and frightened by the vulnerability he felt on her behalf.

She gritted her teeth and shook her head. Tears filled her eyes. "I thought you were going to be *him*," she said, lowering the gun. She began to shake uncontrollably.

Dave ran to her. She let her body buckle into his and he held her, hearing the swish and crunch of the gun falling from her hand onto the leafy ground at their feet.

Braithwaite meanwhile hurried over and hand-cuffed Peter Adkins, who submitted without a fight. He lay on the ground like a trussed pig, weeping, and Dave actually felt a stab of remorse for this awful, tormented man. Yet at the same time he hated him as he had never hated anyone else—except the groom.

Dave lowered his mouth to Lisa's ear and whispered, "Who is *him?*"

"Some guy who put him up to all this," Lisa cried.

The Groom, Dave thought: *Theo Childress.* What if it *had* been Childress who had taken her? The near miss of that possibility sent a chill through Dave's exhausted mind.

"Are you okay?" he whispered.

"I don't know." She nodded and shook her head and nodded. "I guess so."

"I love you," he whispered. "And Susan loves you. We love you *so* much, Lisa."

"Just how many fathers do I have?" she asked in the tiniest of voices.

"A bunch, I guess," he answered.

As they drifted into a warm, safe silence in each other's arms, his mind began to process the possibilities. All it would take to prove that Theo Childress was the groom would be to match his fingerprints to those found on the phone handset from the Café Luxembourg, the letter Susan had received that morning, and the letter Marie Rothka had received last October. In the most basic way, his fingerprints and any DNA traces would make the connection between the two crimes and definitively identify him. But there was more to understand and more to do; the world would not be safe until they caught him.

"Small," the groom had said in his call to Marie that morning, "but not as good."

How had Theo Childress known that Lisa was a spirited girl? How had he known anything about her other than the bare-bones facts in that one article nearly a year ago and the news bulletins today? How, Dave wondered, had the groom known enough about Lisa to torment both Marie and Dave? And how did Peter Adkins fit into any of this?

Because Theo Childress and Peter Adkins had known each other, Dave thought in a flash of understanding. They had researched, discussed and planned this together.

Dave lowered Lisa to the ground, where he could cradle her better on his lap, and wondered how she had survived this ordeal. Had her lack of goodness been her strength? Not that she wasn't *good*—she was wonderful—but she wasn't anyone's perfect little girl. Tears pooled in Dave's eyes as he felt her skin against his own and smelled in her hair the scent he had recognized back at the Stutley house.

Lisa's breath slowed. Dave couldn't see her face but he kept still so he wouldn't wake her if she had fallen asleep. His eyes now wandered the apple-strewn clearing.

A hole had been freshly dug in the ground between two trees, with a small mountain of dark brown earth piled next to it. A shovel poked out of the mound. Next to it, on the other side of the dirt pile, was what appeared to be a filled-in and grown-over grave. By the confused expression on John Childress's face, it looked as if he were seeing this graveyard for the first time.

Dave had a feeling he had finally found Becky Rothka. He also realized he could be wrong; the grave would have to be opened and its contents analyzed. It was almost comforting to think of it in scientific terms. But then he recalled Marie Rothka's face just that morning, lined with a year's worth of anguish, and any small comfort shattered. He thought of the groom whispering into Marie Rothka's telephone ear, "The apple doesn't fall far from the tree," as if she might have divined something from that, and the memory rising in Marie's mind just in time to save Lisa, in a cruel twist that would also deny her any more hope of Becky's return.

There was a rustle in the trees, and Bruno, Andrews and some of the searchers rushed into the clearing. They stopped, taking in the scene. After some confusion, Bruno and Andrews helped Braithwaite lift Adkins, handcuffed, off the ground, forcing him to his feet so he could walk himself out of the orchard. Dave knew that Adkins would face federal kidnapping charges and possibly also accessory to murder, depending on how far back his association with Theo Childress went.

As Adkins was walked past, Dave said, "Wait a minute."

Bruno and Andrews, with Adkins between them, stopped. Bruno's forehead gleamed with sweat and he was breathing heavily. His large hand held Adkins's arm in a vise grip that looked profoundly satisfying to Dave.

Dave looked up into the face of the first man Susan had loved; the man who had fathered Lisa; the man who had sought to destroy their family.

"Why?" Dave asked him.

"I believe in redemption," Adkins said with such earnest confidence Dave pitied him. "I have to. Otherwise I'd go . . ."

He didn't finish but Dave knew the rest: *crazy.*

Dave watched Adkins being led from the clearing. He was not a large man, and whatever charisma had once drawn Susan to him was gone. All he had left was that inner stalk of confidence, that hope of redemption. He looked meek, Dave thought, insubstantial and pathetic.

As if he could read Dave's mind, Adkins turned around to deliver a final, desperate blow:

"Don't think this day is over."

Dave instantly knew what he meant. It fit like a puzzle piece into Lupe Ramos's hunch about her suspicious character from Monday and the face floating in the window last night. He *had* been real. He had been watching from the apartment at Seventy-seven, where he later wrote the letter on Adkins's pad. He had escaped over the connected rooftops and somehow gotten into the Café Luxembourg to steal their phone in a flourish of misdirection, then put on his FedEx cap and entered Dave's building—and stayed there. Theo Childress, the man with the scar on his right cheekbone just under his eye—the groom—was still in Brooklyn . . . and he wasn't finished.

And then Dave recalled his first thought that morning when Marie had phoned him with news of the groom's call: *It would only have been more perfect if he had taken Susan, instead.*

Chapter 28

Susan parted ways with Officer Johnson in the lobby of her building, where he got busy sharing the good news of Lisa's rescue with everyone and anyone who was there: the police who had been guarding the building's front door, Alan the doorman and a few of Susan's neighbors. They knew only the basics—that Lisa had been recovered, mostly unharmed—from a brief call the Gardiner police had made to the sergeant at the Eight-four.

Susan had left an effusive message on Dave's voice mail and was waiting to hear back from him. To Lisa she had written, *Dear Lisa, my daughter, my sister, my truest love. I'm sorrier than you can know. This should never have happened to you. I understand that it's my fault, that a single huge act of dishonesty turned into the terror of last night and today and, bottom line, you were made to face it alone. I was a coward when it mattered most, and it was you who paid the price for my cowardice. And for Peter, too—forgive me for him—though believe it or not, he was once someone who seemed worth loving. Life is a strange, strange animal—badly behaved and unpredictable. We make mistakes.* Immediately after sending that long-winded e-mail, she had edited herself by quickly thumbing into her BlackBerry another one: *Five acorns. Remind me to explain what that means.*

A swarm of reporters flowed into the lobby. Johnson deftly put them off.

"Detective Ramos will make a statement to the press in about twenty minutes, right outside," Johnson said, "so just hold tight."

Susan stood in front of the elevator, on her way up to the loft; she and her parents were flying to Gardiner in an hour and she needed to pack an overnight bag. She held a shiny white cardboard candy box, tied with a frosted orange ribbon, which she had loaded with Lisa's favorite chocolates: dark-chocolate squares filled with freshly shaved coconut; milk-chocolate caramel pillows; uneven latticed circles of white chocolate and crushed almonds; white-, dark- and milk-chocolate hearts. As she waited, she closed her eyes, relishing the momentary darkness and blocking out the voices in the lobby. Since she'd heard the news that Lisa was safe, a throbbing headache had unleashed itself inside her skull. It was as if all the dread she had managed to hold back throughout the day were now rip-roaring through her mind. All the things that might have happened. The pain and fear Lisa may have suffered. The loss of her. The loss of Dave. The absolute ending of her life as she knew it and the unbearable guilt and loneliness to follow. It all came rushing at her now, mixed with a kind of relief and happiness so intoxicating she could hardly believe it was real.

The elevator doors dinged open and she stepped inside. She had always found it bizarre, standing in this mirrored cube with dozens of copies of herself, but now the company, if hallucinatory, cheered her despite her pounding head. Balancing the candy box in one hand, she pressed the button for the fifth floor. The doors closed and she felt a slight jolt as the elevator started upward. With her free hand she dug into her purse to get her apartment keys ready in advance, as was her usual habit.

She breathed deeply in and fully out, feeling more grateful than she had ever been for anything in her entire life. She couldn't wait to see Lisa. Expectation of seeing and touching her daughter—her *daughter*— filled her like helium gas. Lisa was safe. The nightmare was over.

The elevator slowed at the third floor, dinging as the doors parted. It was not unusual for the elevator to make extra stops on the way down, but on the way up it rarely happened. The doors sat open for a minute, but no one came. Then, just as the doors were closing, a FedEx deliveryman ran into the elevator. He must have made a delivery on this floor, had another one on a floor above and pressed the up button in advance to save time.

She smiled and said, "A lot of deliveries today?" just as she noticed he wasn't carrying a package.

The doors shut behind him. He did not push a floor button. The elevator began upward to Susan's fifth-floor loft.

She then noticed the fleshy scar on his right cheek-bone, just beneath his eye. His eyes were a musty green. The way he looked at her, directly, sent an electric shock through her body.

She realized he wasn't wearing a uniform. He had
on regular street clothes—khaki pants, a black T-shirt
and a jean jacket—and up close the FedEx cap looked
dirty.

She thought of the FedEx letter that had arrived
mysteriously outside her door that morning. That hor-
rendous letter. Her eyes frantically searched for the
red emergency button at the top of the panel. Dropping the box of chocolates, she lunged for the red button, learning in an instant that urgency and fear
together were like fire racing through your body to
your brain; that every fraction of every moment felt
like an hour; that it was impossible to move fast
enough through a fog of panic.

The red button was so close, just inches from her
finger, when he popped open a small switchblade and
jammed it into the edge of the inverted-arrows button
that held the doors closed, simultaneously jamming
shut the doors and shorting out the elevator. The lights
blacked; then a harsh fluorescent emergency light
filled the mirrored cube. The elevator ground to a halt
somewhere, Susan thought, between floors four and
five.

"Who are you?" Her fear was so strong, it choked
her voice to a whisper. She backed into the far corner
of the elevator. Behind her, she frantically positioned
the points of four keys between her fingers, creating a
spiky weapon, as she had once been taught in a childhood self-defense class. "What do you want?"

He came at her slowly, as if he had all the time in
the world, his eyes boring into hers with a look of almost inspiration. She understood at once that this was
the man the police had mistaken for Peter. Up close,
she saw that he resembled Peter in only the most basic

ways: height, weight, and hair color. This man's body was more tightly wound than Peter's had ever been, and he was older, with a sinewy neck and a broader, squarer jaw. His hands were also squarish and strong: one hand reaching out to grab her, the other holding another, larger knife that in the mirrors multiplied to dozens of gleaming sharp edges closing in like a collection of jagged teeth.

"He's a smart guy, your husband," he said in a voice that sounded hollow, dead in a way she had never heard a voice sound before. "Think he figured this out yet?"

"Figured what out?"

"Don't act like you don't know," he sneered. "He thinks he's smarter than me. He thinks he can catch me, but he can't. And even if he did, there wouldn't be any satisfaction in it—not now."

He took another slow step forward, clutching the knife. And she knew: He was the groom. She watched him approach her with the helpless terror of a slow-motion nightmare. Her parents were just half a floor above her and the police were just four flights below—and here she was, sandwiched between them, alone with a monster.

"What makes you think he was trying to catch you?" She tried to flatten the tremble from her voice, but it was impossible.

His sneer broadened into a full-blown smile, revealing teeth that were crooked and yellowed. "I left so many clues along the way and none of you saw them."

He was insane. She had no idea how to reach someone whose thinking was so skewed, but she had to try; there had to be some way into his mind.

"We were stupid," she said. "You're right."

He nodded slowly. "You're learning. That's good. Your old boyfriend was an easy student too, especially when I took away his fancy pills."

He was just inches from her now.

Her mind whirred in desperation to understand. Peter had had Lisa with him and was in custody now. Despite his lair at Seventy-seven Water Street, where he had been watching them—stalking them—for months . . . he wasn't the groom.

Yet the groom—this man—had somehow been an accomplice to Peter today. Or Peter had been made an accomplice to him.

Susan's fingers tightened around her splayed keys.

Peter had had one agenda. And this man had another.

He wasn't after Lisa. He was after Dave; Dave's heart: Susan. What he wanted was to hurt *her*.

She gripped her keys and prepared to swing them forward, at his face, into his eyes. She needed him just a few inches closer.

His left hand fell on her shoulder, fingers gripping into her flesh. He smiled again, enjoying this.

He was close enough. *Now.*

"I can see those keys behind your back," he said coolly, almost laughing. "Did you really think that would work?"

The mirrors.

She brought them forward anyway, aimed at his muddy green eyes and the dripping tear of that pink scar.

His left hand pressed her down with a physical strength she had never before experienced, completely overpowering her and buckling her knees. In the mirrors she watched dozens of his right hand sweeping dozens of glinting silver knives through the air, while his face registered an intensity of almost sexual fervor.

From above, part of Susan's mind heard an unlatching sound, while from below she watched frames of her life scroll by on an inner screen. Scenes she hadn't known were still lodged in her memory now gleamed like pearls on a strand, each one complete and perfect. Curled on the couch, under a blanket, clutching her favorite doll with its plastic face and sealed-shut eyes. Popping into the air at the high end of a seesaw. The blunt tip of her pencil stopping at the end bell of an important sixth-grade English test, half the questions unanswered. The impossibly soft feel of Peter's lips as his tongue slid into her mouth the very first time. Lisa's tiny newborn face, screwed into agitation after the shock of birth. Dave opening a shopping bag and putting his favorite coffee grounds on the top shelf of the freezer door when they were dating. A hangnail on Dave's thumb as he flipped channels and her desire to reach over and pull it off. A stranger in brown ankle boots and a long black skirt triggering a sensation that there was something Susan needed to remember but couldn't. Lisa's mouth pulling away from a slice of pizza, trailing a long ribbon of cheese. And yesterday: the unfinished line of yellow paint. This speeding filament of Susan's life passed through her mind with the relentlessness of a runaway train. And she knew: It was over.

But before the thought could crystallize, an explosion blasted into the elevator from above.

The knife fell, his right arm swung down and his left hand released her suddenly. He flailed backward, crashing to the elevator floor. Blood quickly soaked his blond head and dripped into the collar of his denim jacket as his lifeless eyes stagnated: dead green pools.

Susan froze, petrified; she was still gripping her keys and only now felt the pain of their metal edges cutting into her fingers.

Then, in the mirror directly across from her, she saw a series of familiar, identical faces. Framed in a repetition of the elevator's open escape hatch was Detective Lupe Ramos—or many of her. Copies of one small, pink-nailed hand held many reflections of a black gun.

Susan looked up, away from the mirrors, reducing the kaleidoscopic Lupe Ramos to just one woman leaning out of the gloom of the elevator shaft into the diamond brightness of the mirrored cube. Her face glittered with perspiration. Her cherry-pink lipstick was perfect.

"I'd say, 'Sorry I'm late,'" Lupe said, "but baby, it looks like I made it just in time."

Chapter 29

Dave had forgotten how dark darkness could be. In the city, there was always an ambient glow from somewhere else. But here, in the woods in deep night, the moon was blocked by trees and nothing shone. Shapes swallowed the darkness and darkened further still. There was no reflection, or resonance of reflection, anywhere.

Soon the Gardiner police produced a set of klieg lights that illuminated the small orchard with harsh intensity. Generator motors could be heard buzzing nearby. But Dave took no comfort in the familiarity of artificial light and noise. The seeing he had to do now was inward, and for that he craved a solitude he wouldn't find for many hours. In the meantime, he waited and watched as a body was exhumed from the older, overgrown grave.

He had heard the news from home: the groom had been there all along. He had gone after Susan. *Susan.* Dave's mind still couldn't land on the reality of the groom getting so close to his wife. The horror of what might have happened . . . and he hadn't been there to help her.

Another piece of news was a name that had turned up on Peter Adkins's roster of patients: Theo Childress.

Images floated through Dave's unprocessed memory of that day. The innocent face of a boy framed on his parents' wall, green eyes narrowed in a partial smile, slashed cheekbone. And the gnarled white figure of John Childress standing over a gap in the earth that was his legacy, thinking about his own lost children; thinking about his eldest son and lamenting the restiveness that had taken him so far, far away. How much had John Childress understood in that moment that Dave was just now figuring out?

Detectives at the Eight-four had already pieced some of it together. Starting two years ago, Theo Childress had sat in his therapist's office for twenty-three documented hours, talking. What had they talked about? Dave recalled an article he had once read about a case of reverse transference in which a doctor had fallen in love with his patient instead of the other way around, which was more usual. Love, Dave thought; what was love? Identification, certainly. Need. Habit. Imagination. Something must have triggered a longing in Peter's mind. A longing for Lisa, Dave supposed, combined with some basic instruction on how to abduct a child and a few tips on how to stalk her and where to hide her. Unmedicated, Peter's unique blend of schizophrenia and bipolar illness had provided fertile ground for Theo's evil seeds.

The first crime, against Becky, was to have been Theo's tour de force—possibly in a career of killing; other states were now revisiting unsolved murders, pulling evidence to compare with the new treasure trove of Theo's DNA—only he mistakenly victimized the wrong girl. The second crime, against Lisa, had been Peter's muddled replica of a mentor's master plan. Theo Childress had appeared in Dumbo to share in the pleasure and add the touches of detail—the call to Marie and the letter—that were his signature. It was what these people did. Together, they had left a trail of crumbs that would lead Dave hundreds of miles away, creating an opportunity for Theo to get Susan alone, denying Dave the chance to save her and catch him. Two birds with one stone. It had been a complex, brilliant, truly malevolent plan.

Dave felt the night air hard against his skin and pressed his hands into his pants pockets. He stood to the side of the clearing, thinking, as the local forensics team got to work. After a while Bruno came up next to him and slung a heavy arm over his shoulders. He felt he would sink, then stiffened himself and accepted the gesture.

"I'm going now," Bruno said.

Dave nodded. "Okay."

Bruno was on his way back to the city to begin the paperwork with Lupe Ramos; they were a strange but heroic team, and Dave had never seen better. While they sorted out the pieces in Brooklyn, Dave would stay in Gardiner overnight, here and also at the hospital with Lisa, who, for the time being, was sound asleep. Susan was on her way, shaken but determined to be there when Lisa woke up. After he left, tomorrow, officers Andrews and Braithwaite would work alongside Detective Jacob Goldman, who had caught the upstate pieces of the puzzle; it was now a matter of fitting them all together.

Goldman—a heavyset man, on the short side, with

bright red cheeks—walked up briskly to join Dave and Bruno.

"Call as soon as you get the dirty," Bruno said to Dave, meaning *the dirt,* meaning the forensics on the body and the gun.

"I'll talk to you later tonight." Dave patted Bruno on his massive leathered shoulder.

Bruno enclosed Dave in a bear hug, giving him the full aromatic experience, then released him. "I never doubted you, my friend."

"Thanks," Dave answered, keeping it simple.

"Chinzup."

Dave lifted his chin to indicate he understood and appreciated Bruno's meaning. Then he watched as this surprising man crunched his way through the clearing and was absorbed into a sea of trees.

"He was an engineer back in Russia, apparently," Dave told Goldman.

"Well, I'm open-minded."

Dave believed Bruno really could have been an engineer in his homeland, making sturdy but flamboyant bridges and buildings that reached and sprawled. He was tempted to learn Russian just for the chance to hear Alexei Bruno speak in his native tongue, free of malapropisms and retro slang. Walking alongside Goldman to the patrol car—Braithwaite was giving him a ride back to the hospital—Dave realized this was his wish for himself: to slip into the perfect context, to be effortlessly defined without need of explanation or any chance of misunderstanding. He had always felt strangely unwelcome in a world that couldn't quite peg him. There was only one place he felt comfortable; he could hardly wait to see Susan, and to bring Lisa home.

"Catch those Yanks last Sunday?" Goldman asked Dave as he bent into the car's front passenger seat.

"Caught the end of it on the radio. Jeter had a good night."

"I'll say."

Dave noted Braithwaite's pinched smile as he revved the engine. Goldman slapped the top of the car as it drove off.

"Yanks or Mets?" Dave asked Rufus Braithwaite; this could be his first chance to break into the man's silence in a way unfreighted by significance. And it would be good, after the long night and day, just to talk. "Or is it movies, books, what?"

"Gardening books," Braithwaite said. "And gardening. My wife's the reader—mystery, romance, lit-ra-ture. Anything with a good story."

Dave liked the way he'd said *literature,* stressing the first syllable, breaking the word into parts.

"If gardening's your thing, you should take the Childress orchard off the old man's hands," Dave said, glancing out the window as the velvet darkness was given shape by a cluster of houses. They were nearing town. "I think he'd practically give it away now." He knew that suggesting this to Braithwaite was out of bounds, but obviously the guy wasn't cut out to be a cop; sometimes you just needed permission from someone, even a stranger, to change your life.

Braithwaite nodded crisply, once, and turned up the hospital's driveway. They pulled to a stop in front of the hospital's main entrance. The double doors swung open and a white-suited nurse walked casually out.

"There was an article about me in the newspaper." Dave felt as if a stopper were being pulled out of him. Sharing his guilt with Braithwaite was as bad as giving him advice, but all of a sudden Dave felt he had to talk—to anyone. He needed the relief of confession. Was that how Susan had felt making her confession to Lisa last night? "I think Theo Childress saw it and showed it to Peter Adkins, or vice versa. I think that was how they found out about Lisa. I think after that, Theo showed Peter how to become . . . someone else."

That single article had made Dave's sergeant so proud of himself at the time, turning a failed search for a lost girl into a public-relations coup for the department, using Dave as the face of a questing, but human, police force. Dave should have refused to do it; but he was human; he had mistrusted his own judgment that it was a bad idea and even succumbed to vanity. One subset of words and two self-satisfied photographs on a page crammed with print ads. It had nearly cost him everything that was valuable in his life.

"Seems to me," Braithwaite said, "if they're out there looking for you, they'll find you any which way they can."

"Well, thanks for the ride." Dave held out his hand. Braithwaite took it, and the two men shook.

Lisa was still asleep when Dave walked into her hospital room. A serenity had settled over her face; a face that in wakefulness was astounding in its flexibility of expression, but rarely peaceful.

Susan was perched on the edge of a chair, the upper half of her body leaning on the bed. Her short brown hair was mussed, and she wore a tan sweater over the red pants Dave had seen her in earlier that day. It felt like another century now. Susan looked smaller, deflated, but she did not appear traumatized or particularly weakened for having encountered the groom, and for this Dave loved her more than ever. She was defiantly *alive* and she was *here*. They had won.

Bill and Carole Bailey sat in upholstered armchairs by the far windows. Dave acknowledged them with a nod. Carole, who had been crying, nodded back. Bill slapped his knees and almost rose, but at his wife's sharp glance he thought better of it and remained seated.

Dave walked up behind Susan and opened his palm across the back of her neck. Her skin felt cool. Her right hand immediately crossed her body and reached up, her fingers weaving into his. After a moment she twisted to glance at him with bloodshot eyes before turning back to Lisa, her daughter. Seeing them together for the first time since he had possessed that knowledge, Dave could see how clearly alike they were. Both were strong, warm, determined and beautiful, though in different ways. Susan's physical beauty hadn't filtered directly to Lisa, who resembled a version of Peter; instead, the beauty had transmuted into something intangible, soaking her with charisma, which ultimately counted for more than a pretty face.

"It's going to be all right," Dave said, pulling his thumb gently along Susan's neck until it rested in the crook behind her ear.

Her back rose and fell with a deep breath and exhalation.

Together they watched Lisa sleep. Dave noticed now that Lisa was wearing a necklace, a chain with a small gold crucifix. He recognized it as the gift Susan had received at her first Communion when she was a child; she kept it in her jewelry box on her dresser and had shown it to him once. He wondered how Lisa would react when she woke up and found it there. But Lisa's faith, or even Susan's, was not his battle to wage. He vowed to keep quiet on the subject and accept whatever they wanted to believe, though in his mind he saw that crucifix flying across the room on a wave of sound that was Lisa's voice.

Susan turned again to look at him.

"Thank you, Dave," she whispered.

His mind raced. What was she thanking him for? He hadn't saved Lisa; he had simply found her while she was in the process of saving herself. But then Susan reached up to touch his face and he knew. Beneath her terror for Lisa, she had been as concerned about their marriage as he had been. Hours had passed since her confession to him, and whatever betrayal she may have committed had taken on a more intricate patina. He was beginning to understand that the lies she had told herself were more harmful than those she had told him. What they had together before, and what they had now, was real. Lisa was alive. Susan was safe. There was nothing to forgive; they had come close to losing each other, briefly, but had each other back.

They were whole and together, a family.

Peter Adkins was on his way to a psychiatric prison, where he belonged.

And the groom, finally, was dead.

Epilogue

An autumn chill had set in. Dave huddled with Susan and Lisa for warmth. The cemetery's green lawns were dusted with dry leaves that spiraled at the slightest wind as they watched Becky Rothka's mahogany coffin being lowered on ropes into the broken earth. Dave felt the steep descent of a long-delayed remorse. Remorse and guilt; it was plain wrong and unfair that Becky had suffered. And died. And been left in a stranger's earth, alone. In the past few days, he had discovered that grief came in waves. He had never met this girl, yet he felt he knew her; her absence in the world had left a terrible scar.

Lisa's life was his redemption. Rallying, she had eaten and rested and talked through every part of the story she could remember in a recovery Dave thought both swift and remarkable. Aside from cuts and scrapes, mostly from walking barefoot through the forest but also from an accidental slip of Peter Adkins's knife against her inner arm when he cut the ropes on the bed, her injuries were internal, emotional. She was having trouble accepting a series of ill-fitting facts: that Peter Adkins was her biological father; that he had kidnapped her but was not the groom; that he had killed once before, in drowning his brother, but had no apparent intention of killing her; that he was mentally ill with two serious, hereditary conditions; and that he had confusedly taken the advice of an even sicker man who had directed him to lead Lisa to the crude grave of another girl who had not been so lucky. If that was luck. The knot of contradictions was almost too much to unravel, but Dave was accustomed to the illogical byways of the criminal mind. It was not, however, something he wanted Lisa ever to get used to. She would be visiting with a child psychologist the next day so that each thread of the knot could be gently unfurled and examined. Next week she would return to school, at which point Susan planned to spend her first full day at her chocolaterie since Lisa disappeared. They would go back . . . well, not quite to normal but something much like it.

Across the lawn stood the Rothka family: Marie, Charles and Charlie. Charles was as gray as Marie was gaunt, both rigid with grief beside their daughter's grave. Charlie at twelve was a large, burgeoning boy; his ruddy cheeks and messy dark hair looked fresh from sport with a gaggle of friends, anything to keep his mind off what had become the spine of his family life for the past year. His sister was gone. His sister was dead. Now she was buried. Charlie Rothka kept his hands jammed in his pockets and stood a full yard from his parents, avoiding eye contact with anyone but Lisa, who had been open and warm with the Rothka family. Lisa seemed to understand what she meant to them, that her life was the long shadow of

Becky's death. When Lisa had hugged Charles, then Charlie, then Marie, Dave had watched as the bereaved mother ran her fingertips gently over Lisa's face. The face that so resembled Becky's.

Detectives Lupe Ramos and Alexei Bruno had also come to the service, along with Officer Zeb Johnson, but the trio kept a respectable distance. Dave knew the drill, having attended so many funerals of strangers he couldn't count them. You were the dark suit against the wall or by the tree. You showed deference to the pain and helplessness of the family; unless spoken to, you held your silence.

About a dozen other people were there—friends, family and neighbors of the Rothkas, Dave assumed. They knew now that Becky had been killed within twenty-four hours of her capture. If they had found and buried her then, hundreds of people, swollen with fresh anguish, would have come to see her off. Dave's mind was still processing the autopsy report he had read late yesterday, with details he had sought for a whole year now pressing at his consciousness. Each of Becky's fingertips had been vertically sliced. That would account for the blood found with the green necklace beads in the Bronx Dumpster near where the letter was mailed; it also accounted for her inability to write the letter herself, which was the usual tack of a kidnapper hoping to convince you his prey was still alive. Later, she had been raped and strangled, probably simultaneously. The terror that poor girl had suffered was appalling, yet it wasn't the worst Dave had ever seen; he had worked on equally deranged and vicious crimes against people just as innocent as Becky Rothka. Becky. So now they had some answers, and her family had remains to properly bury. It was going to have to be good enough—but it was not enough.

There were some things forensics would never decipher: how and why and in exactly what ways the minds of two men with dangerous yearnings had come together. Peter Adkins's appointment book could tell them only that the two had first met before either girl's abduction. Who had spoken first about the girls? There were reasons therapist and patient were supposed to keep a professional distance from each other; too many psychic doors were open to safely approach the corridors of friendship. And yet everyone knew it happened. A first step was taken, then another, and before you knew it you were someplace you never meant to go.

What had Theo Childress said to Peter to make him think that he might actually be able to possess his lost daughter? And what had Peter said to fuel Theo's dangerous imagination? The thing was, they were two different men with two different minds and ultimately two different plans. Theo clearly envisioned and desired a darkness unthinkable to most everyone else on earth, probably even Peter Adkins.

What exactly Theo had wanted, they might never know. His demented journey had already gained at least two markers in cold cases that had been pried open and reexamined in the past few days: a girl in New Jersey three years ago, and eight months earlier a girl in Pennsylvania. He was starting to look like a bona fide serial killer; one more for the books. As for Peter, Dave would get his crack at interviewing him in a couple of days, once the psychiatrists had him stabilized. He looked forward to it, but what he really wanted was what he would never have: a chance to question the groom, face-to-face, and ask him *why* . . . the inevitable, unanswerable question that would always burn in Dave's chest.

Dave imagined himself in a drab interrogation room, questioning Theo Childress. But instead of two voices interacting there would be only one—his. He didn't really believe the groom would have ever talked, not to him. He could see a superimposition of two faces—the pale boy from the photograph and the scar-faced man who had gotten so close to Susan— staring him down with nothing but reticent mockery in his eyes. Now, standing beside Susan, mere inches between them, Dave sensed the loss of balance that had become so familiar in the last few days: the driving purpose mixed with helplessness; the ascendance of love overlaid by a memory of desolation as he had heard the news that his nemesis had trapped his beloved wife in an elevator.

Susan pulled him in close to her body. He felt her warmth and smelled the elusive scent of chocolate that seemed always to hover around her, mingled with her sweet perfume. And in a reaction disproportionate to her gesture, he felt an urge to weep, but contained it for fear of alarming her.

These two Octobers had stripped the skin off his life, and he felt weary to the core; weary yet strangely renewed. In one cold night and one long day, he had been made naked before death, a man unclothed and alone with only what he held in his hand, in his life, in his heart. Susan and Lisa, now more than ever, meant everything to him. Susan had explained that, in planning her confessions, she had been paving the way for a new baby. He would be a father! His imagination conjured the unfathomable beauty of life—how tender

it must feel to hold your newborn baby in your arms—
along with all the hazards he knew too well. What if
he failed to protect his own child? Panic swelled at the
thought that he might not be up to the task of father-
hood, once it became real; and then he looked at Lisa.
Lisa. He already *had* a child, flesh and blood, standing beside him. There was no question that he would
attempt to father this very particular girl, and that it
would be the hardest and best challenge he had faced.
He would watch every strand of her progress carefully; listen without judgment to each word she said;
be an eager audience to her songs; love and protect
her in every possible way; and if she was ever assigned to read *Lolita* or decided to tackle it on her
own, he would read it with her—they would discuss
every scene late into the night, if necessary, but most
of all he would urge her to interpret the story fear-
lessly and on her own terms. That was the key to what
he could give Lisa: the courage to reject prepackaged
answers, to question and to constantly seek.

Susan loved the way Dave looked in the dark blue
cashmere coat she had bought him last Christmas.
With the polished black shoes he almost never wore,
he looked a little like a businessman. But he wasn't.
He was a husband and a cop and soon, she hoped, a
father. He was so many things and none of them simple. She felt she knew him now. He had allowed himself to travel the depths of despair for her, but not only
for her; he had also journeyed for Lisa and for Becky
and probably for dozens of people Susan had never
heard of. He was an anomaly of hopefulness and cyn-
icism, determination and accommodation, loneliness
and devotion. She had come to adore him more, prob-

ably, than any other person she had ever known; except, of course, for Lisa.

Terrifying as the last few days had been and mournful as this hour was—across the gulf of Becky's grave, where stood Marie, her heart now a rattling gourd of lost hope—Susan felt within herself a slow trickle of returning life. Somehow, their family had endured a double threat intact. It had been like a roll of the dice, Becky perishing and Lisa surviving, and Susan would never forget how close she had come to *being* Marie. How Marie *was* Marie. She was resolved to return the friendship this kind woman had extended during the worst moments of the ordeal. She would never, she decided, abandon Marie, who at this moment looked as if she might dry up in a cloud of dust and blow away.

It was over. Becky was buried. Lisa was safe. Peter was getting the help he needed. Susan's secret was out. And Dave was coming to terms with all kinds of truths. She wanted nothing more than to forget the memory of that horrible face trying to reach her in the elevator. Couldn't Dave try to forget, too? Couldn't he just . . . stop? Stop worrying, stop thinking, stop being a cop . . . there, she had dared to think it. Her business made enough money to support them all. He could retire early from the police force; learn piano so he could accompany Lisa's songs, which he had once said sounded interesting to him; or just stay home and be a full-time dad for a while. She didn't care so long as she had him in her life.

But Susan knew that Dave didn't live his own life easily, that his was a quest and he would probably never quit the police until he could no longer chase the bad guys. He would never stop hunting for all the grooms in the universe, because there had to be more of them; just as he would never allow faith alone to guide him, because it didn't explain everything. She couldn't really fathom why he felt so responsible for solving society's ills, or for that matter why he needed to understand so much about the human condition. You were born, you lived and you died, and it seemed to her that it was dangerous not to believe in something along the way. But she wouldn't push her renewed faith on Dave because she knew that for their marriage to endure they would have to revive their old truce, their agreement to disagree. And she wouldn't ask Lisa to wear the cross she had removed so quickly upon finding it around her neck when she woke up at the hospital. It didn't matter. What *did* matter was the love, acceptance and forgiveness mother and daughter had established over the past few days. They had talked over *everything*. Susan had allowed Lisa to face her head-on, denying her not a grain of truth as the old party line was abandoned and their girlhoods were rewoven into the same fabric.

And then, finally, Susan saw her birthday puzzle complete. A lost memory had emerged at the center of the blue background she and Lisa had worked their way through together, at the card table between the windows that faced the river, when they needed a break from talking. Lisa had had an old photograph of the two of them digitized and printed on a blank puzzle: five-year-old Lisa in her Spiderman costume stood grinning on Susan's shoulders, with Lisa's little arms stretched out for balance, a gesture the picture had translated into something that looked more like flight. They had been laughing and both had been about to topple over, but what the camera had caught was their unbridled glee.

Susan squeezed Dave closer by pressing their linked arms tighter to her body. She realized for the first time that his familiar musky smell reminded her of the dried autumn leaves that swirled at their feet. A single leaf dropped into the grave, landing on Becky's coffin. Susan saw that Lisa had also noticed the leaf and wondered what her beloved daughter was thinking.

Over the summer, Lisa and Glory had attended an outdoor concert at Lincoln Center. A soprano stood on the stage, singing an aria from a Rimsky-Korsakov opera Lisa had never heard before but instantly fell in love with. Her voice reminded Lisa of butterscotch, rich butterscotch seeping over cold vanilla ice cream. She could taste the soprano's voice on her tongue. That voice came back to her now, as she shivered by the grave of this girl whom, for long hours locked in the dark trunk, she had believed she herself could become—and she felt herself whirl into the crisp autumn air on the wings of the gorgeous aria. Becky had already forgiven death for taking her, Lisa decided; and Lisa would try to forgive life for giving her such a crappy father. Here she was, flesh and blood occupying space on this earth, a biological accident, really; in her case, a biological minefield, but she didn't feel insane yet, and if she was lucky she might not have inherited a drop of her birth father's crazy juice. She was trying not to dwell on the possibilities lurking in her blood. What would be the point? Why complicate things now when she was home—safe, sane and free?

But just as she challenged herself not to worry about her own destiny, her mind began to tick. Well, she thought, maybe she *couldn't* stop herself from thinking, and maybe she *shouldn't*. Maybe it was just

a sorry fact of the human condition to explore the unknown. Sometimes Lisa thought people were like
ants, busily tackling urgent questions and mammoth
projects, cursed with the intelligence to make too
much out of the simple fact of being alive. So they
built supertall buildings, and invented seventy-nine
flavors of ice cream, and mastered languages, and
made up stories, and craved music, and trusted their
bodies to steel tubes that catapulted them at warp
speed through the skies. People just loved looking at
clouds from the wrong side. If they were dumb as
ants, Lisa figured, they would probably all be much
happier. But they weren't ants, and happiness was a
magic trick that caught you by surprise. Like Susan
being her birth mother, Dave turning out to be a pretty
cool guy, and the flood of e-mails Susan had sent her
while she was gone. They were love letters, really, and
if she never got another love letter in her life, at least
she would have these.

There were three things in her coat pocket today:
lip balm, a quarter and the picture of her birth parents
kissing. She ran her finger back and forth along the
rough paper edge of the tiny photograph, thinking
how, in a strange way she could never explain, this
was proof of her existence. She hadn't told anyone
about the photo; it was *hers,* and she knew if she said
anything it would end up as evidence. They had
enough evidence; she was back home, Becky was
buried and Peter—her birth father's name, *Peter*—
was locked up tight. In some ways it was all over, but
in other ways it was just beginning. There was a lot to
understand. For one thing, why had she needed to find
her birth parents in the first place? Discovering that
Susan was her mother had been confusing but ulti-

mately good news. She knew now that discovering Peter was bound to be a disaster any way it might have happened, and she also knew that if he hadn't found her first, she would have gone looking. The impulse to know him was right up there with trusting a total stranger: big mistake. Maybe if she hadn't been so determined to locate her biological parents, then Susan wouldn't have blurted out the truth, and Lisa wouldn't have stormed alone into the night or painted that yellow line or been easy prey for Peter. He had been watching her, skipping stones, and seized an opportunity. What if time had passed, he had never had his chance, and then he'd been hit by a car? Or what if his brain had exploded, fast-forwarding from part crazy to all crazy and landing him in an institution sooner instead of later, keeping him far from temptation? Or what if, for any reason at all, he had just changed his mind? Unlikely, Lisa supposed, her eyes settling on a dried leaf with crinkled edges that had landed gently on Becky's coffin.

Becky, Lisa thought, *I bet we could have been friends.*

SEVEN MINUTES TO NOON

KATE PEPPER

In a comfortable Brooklyn neighborhood, Alice Halpern waits for her best friend, Lauren, at the local playground. But when Lauren doesn't show up, and then fails to pick her son up from school, Alice watches her own life turn into a nightmare.

As the police desperately search for Lauren, who is nearly nine months pregnant, Alice, herself pregnant with twins, realizes she's being followed and has the creeping fear that she'll be next. As the investigation intensifies, Alice is shocked to see her familiar world turned upside down by the list of suspects. And as two new lives grow within her, she must fight to save them, her family—and herself.

0-451-21579-6

"A new force to be reckoned with in...suspense."
—Donna Anders

"Strikes terror into a
lazy summer day."
—DONNA ANDERS,
Author of *Night Stalker*

FIVE
DAYS
IN
SUMMER

"Mesmerizing....Your heart will be pounding long after
you've turned the final page."—LISA GARDNER,
New York Times Bestselling Author of *The Killing Hour*

KATE PEPPER

0-451-41140-4